Katy Hayes was born in 1965. A former theatre director, she now lives with her husband and two sons in Dublin.

By Katy Hayes

SHORT STORIES
Opening Nights

NOVELS
Curtains
Gossip

curtains

KATY HAYES

PHOENIX

A PHOENIX PAPERBACK

First published in Great Britain by Phoenix House in 1997
This paperback edition published in 1998 by Phoenix,
an imprint of Orion Books Ltd,
Orion House, 5 Upper St Martin's Lane,
London WC2H 9EA

Reissued 2001

A CIP catalogue record for this book is
available from the British Library.

Printed and bound in Great Britain by
Clays Ltd, St Ives plc

For
Tony Roche

Acknowledgements

I would like to thank my editor at Phoenix House, Alison Walsh, for her expert help with and enthusiasm for the work. Also, my agent Giles Gordon for advice and comments and my friend David Marcus for his help. As always, my thanks are due to my family, who provide endless support and encouragement. Also, thanks to Bernard and Mary Loughlin of the Tyrone Guthrie Centre at Annaghmakerrig, where some of this work was done. And finally, a big thank you to my husband, to whom this work is dedicated.

january 1997

the beginning of the end

It was getting dark, and Arlene was sitting in her office, staring blankly at the wall. Occasionally she stretched out her hand to the glass and glugged back a mouthful of whiskey. Occasionally she gnawed at her fingernails, bitten to the quick. From time to time, she lit a cigarette and puffed on it as though her life depended on every gasp, tipping the ash onto the floor. But mostly her mind was empty, thoroughly empty, as blank as a sheet of typing paper. She didn't even feel the whiskey take hold of her. She felt a delicious nothing.

She hadn't been in her office in a week, and there were piles of everything everywhere. Post in a pile unopened and unanswered. The waste paper basket overflowing like a melting ice-cream – at least that was what it looked like when she wasn't bothering to focus her eyes. It was funny, that. One always thought that focussing was an instinctive thing to do, until one ceased to be interested in the wide world, and then one realised what a shagging effort it was.

She had spent the week in bed. Had eaten nothing. Had thought about nothing. In fact, she had been a non-person for a week. It was amazing, she had thought that she was such a

1

crucial cog in the machine of life, but now she discovered that she wasn't. She had been absent, and life went on, oblivious. There was no evidence that life missed her presence one little bit. There was no indication that life gave a shit about her.

She started to sniff. Not sniff as in whingeing; sniff as in reaction to bad smell. She got up and wandered round the room to the tea stand and the bin, until finally she realised that it was herself who smelled. She sniffed her armpit. Yes, that confirmed it. A *major* whiff.

She needed a shower. She decided to go home and have a shower. Get clean. Cleanliness is next to ... eh, something. Yes, that was the solution. Stop this wallowing in dirt and self-pity. Get a grip. Get a *life*. She tried to put on her confident face, but it didn't really work. She looked like a loser wearing a sneer.

She stood up, and her legs went from under her.

'Oh fuck fuck fuck fuck fuck,' she half laughed, half mumbled.

Sitting in a heap on the floor, she considered herself. She was thirty-six, and had always felt young until now, when she suddenly felt ancient. She felt like Oisín, that she had for the first time put her feet on terra firma, after a lifetime spent in Tír na n-Óg, the land of the forever young, and the ageing process, which had been artificially stalled, now galloped through her system, rioted in her veins, *partyed* in her joints.

The phone rang. The machine answered it. Oh mighty machine. Is it any wonder that half the country is unemployed? Arlene summoned her ears and listened.

'Hi, this is Shannon Mercier calling for Arlene Morrissey at 11 AM New York time on Wednesday eight –'

2

It had that hollow far-away sound that long-distance calls have.

'– Yeah, well, I'm from the New York—Ireland Friendship Committee. Hi! Yeah, well, we're planning a festival, right, of Irish arts in New York for March, right, and we were wondering if you could supply us with seven performances of *Over the Moon*? The Isobel Coole play? We've booked the theatre from March seventeenth to twenty-third?'

Americans, so organised!

'Eh, maybe phone me back? My number is area code 212, then 78 40533. Thank you for your attention.'

That was a good one. Arlene started to laugh out loud. Great peals of uncontrollable laughter. Somebody wanted her to *supply* them with some performances of *Over the Moon*. And she didn't have to pitch for it? It had just dropped in her lap. Unbelievable! This would have really got her juices flowing a while back. Now? Well, now, she was in the mood for more whiskey. She struggled to her feet and poured herself another generous dollop. She clinked the glass against the bottle.

'Cheers, my friend,' she said.

'Clink,' returned the bottle.

Before she got the whiskey to her lips, a blinding migraine struck.

january 1996

synchronicity

Arlene Morrissey sat on her chair, drumming her fake nails against her fake walnut desk, and looking out her window at the street below, where cars dawdled bumper to bumper along the greasy rainy streets. Winter evening was recently descended, rendering the paltry neon of Baggot Street modestly splendid. A few shiny lights: a brave green Carlsberg; a saucy kebab sign. Las Vegas it wasn't. This was perhaps a good thing. How would you feel if you were sitting in a Dublin office and Las Vegas was outside the window? You'd feel pretty weird. You'd be *worried*.

Arlene's mind was hell bent on wandering.

Things were a bit slow at the moment, so she was catching up on some correspondence that had languished, in some cases for many months, in her tray. She had a lot to catch up on, lots of CVs from actors to peruse and reply to; a pile of turgid scripts to read and respond to; letters from various people; application forms for grants and awards; the lawsuit against the lighting company that had failed to deliver an entire rig for one of her promotions and left her giving everybody back their money (Ouch!). The lawsuit against Sefton

Collins for being drunk on stage and falling off it when his contract forbade him to take a drink during its term. How do you sue a beat-up guy whose wife has just kicked him out for being a bum? (Uggh!) Even thinking about that gave her phantom indigestion.

She made herself a cup of coffee and the phone rang. In between projects, when there was nothing too urgent on and she had no temp, she left it to the machine to answer the phone in order to avoid direct contact with sixteen-year-old budding Meryl Streeps. The young ones were all fans of Meryl Streep. Arlene couldn't see why, this was the nineties, after all. A generation babysat by video recorders. No message was left. Arlene hated that. People phoning and not leaving messages (Grrrr!). Maybe she should have picked it up. Then the caller would have *had* to talk to her. Who could it have been? Maybe it was –

Arlene was all set for another little mental wander, a stroll round the parks of the inner brain, but she dragged her thoughts back to the piles on her desk, threatening herself with doing the accounts (not them!) if she didn't knuckle down to the correspondence. She picked up the sheaf of papers pertaining to the lawsuit against the lighting company, deciding that this might be fun to deal with. It was a fat file, which meant that her lawyer was probably making a fortune on it (Hmmn!).

Ten minutes later, there was a gentle knock on the door and a startlingly dark head popped around it.

'Hello, are you Ar*lee*n Morrissey?'

'Yup, that's me, but its pronounced Ar-lay-nah. Not Ar*lee*n.'

'Sorry. Hi. I'm Isobel Coole. Do you know who I am?'

This line was saved from the outer reaches of arrogance by

5

a certain tentativeness in the question, a modest inclination of the head, a seemingly sincere desire to know the answer.

Arlene put down her pen and studied this visitor, who had now made her way past the door and to the desk.

In front of her stood Isobel Coole. Tall, slim, straight blue-black hair that looked like it had been ironed, and wide grey eyes that drooped, sad and empty. Vaguely vampiric. Pale skin that looked best at night. A bit of sun would do her no harm. A little twirl in Torremolinos. Arlene had seen her on the Pat Kenny talk show, and thought her a bit of a vision. She suspected that this was the kind of woman who spent vast sums of money in lingerie shops. You could tell by looking at her that her cashmere sweater was not pulled over a Dunnes Stores bra.

'Of course I know who you are, I can't open the newspaper without looking at your mug. Please come in and sit down. This is gas. I was thinking about you just a little while ago.'

'But I've never met you.'

Arlene made to reply, but Isobel gushed on.

'I did phone you about five minutes ago, from the call box down on the street, but there was no answer, just a machine.'

'Oh yes,' said Arlene, 'the phone did ring, but there was no –'

'I do hate talking to machines. I feel they lack empathy. I find it hard to explain myself when nobody's listening. So I decided to come in and leave this off,' she said breathlessly, waving a brown envelope. 'Why were you thinking of me?'

Arlene's comment seemed to have belatedly landed in this tornado woman's brain. It was as though she had rehearsed all she was going to say and blurted it all out in case she'd forget it.

Arlene waited for a moment, to make sure that Isobel's

whirlwind had subsided. 'Well, on my desk, I have an application form for the Lunar Theatre Jubilee Award. And what I need is a brand new script from a first-time playwright, and I thought of you, and if that brown envelope is what I think it is, I'm in luck.'

'Wow! That's incredible. You thought of *me*? You *like* my books?'

'Well, no, I haven't actually read them, but I will.'

'Oh.' Isobel's face dropped.

'I've read all about you in the papers, though, and I was idly wondering if you'd like to turn your hand to a play?' said Arlene brightly, paying no attention to Isobel's disappointed face. One never got anything done in life if one paid too much attention to people's disappointed faces.

'Wow! That's really weird. I've come in to see you today because I've just written a play, and I wanted to show it to you and see what you thought. I spoke to several people and they all recommended that I try you. This is *amazing*! We were both in each other's heads!'

'Synchronicity,' said Arlene.

She noted that Isobel had a way of speaking in exclamations. A slightly hyper quality. On the verge. That could get wearisome.

'I did meet you once, at the prizegiving party for the Longfoot Award which you won, about a year ago, in the RDS. Your book looked great. Great cover. *Candid* it was called, I bought it, look, it's on the shelf over there. Sorry I haven't read it yet.'

'Oh, that's all right,' said Isobel, aware that she might have looked a bit disappointed.

'But it's very hard to find time. You're looking at somebody

7

who doesn't have time to do the laundry. I throw out dirty clothes, and buy new ones.'

'I can't get over the coincidence!' said Isobel.

'And you've just won something else recently, haven't you?'

'Yes, the Carleton prize.' A slight preen. Nothing more.

'That's right. I saw all about it in the papers. What was the name of that book?'

'*In a Corner.*'

'You're a natural prizewinner.'

This was true. Isobel had always been a winner. When she was a kid she'd won forty quid on Ben Nevis in his first run in the Grand National. Ben Nevis was an outsider at 40/1. She was lucky.

As a tot she had developed great skill and achieved great success in the egg and spoon race. An astutely placed piece of chewing gum did the trick, holding the volatile egg to the shuddering spoon, and she just popped the gum back into her mouth when she crossed the finishing line. She was lucky, but she was also skilled. Success. Isobel craved success.

'So, naturally, I thought of you with this Lunar Theatre gig. It's very lucrative, you know, £5,000 for the writer and a contribution of £25,000 to the overall production budget. If we got that, we'd be half-way there.'

'How much would you need altogether?' asked Isobel.

'It depends on the script. Some shows are more expensive than others. What's your play called?'

Isobel took the bulky script from the envelope, and handed it over. Arlene looked at the cover, then at the last page, she sniffed it cryptically, and then flicked through it to get a feel for it.

'*Over the Moon*. Not a bad title,' said Arlene. 'Look, I'll peek at this tonight or tomorrow and phone you in the next couple of days. But right now, it's almost four-thirty. How about you let me buy you a drink?'

Arlene switched off the lights and locked the office. She was delighted to escape from work. Her brain was not in form today. She led Isobel outside into the dark and wet street, and then into the pub next door.

Cunningham's was a fine establishment that knew how to treat its regular customers. Arlene liked that. She liked being a client of this place. It gave her a nice anonymous place to belong.

It had recently been done up. Arlene had recommended the design team. Angles Design. A company that did a lot of work for Arlene on shows. They had made a right few bob out of this gig. Arlene would remind them of this, when the time came, as the time would undoubtedly come.

The management was delighted with what Angles had come up with. The theme was the Twenties. Glass pictures of skinny women with no boobs and long beads, smoke wafting from cigarettes held in jewelled holders between long fingers. Icons of cynical women from a cynical age. They had a lot to be cynical about, then.

Arlene felt cosy and proprietorial about both pub and decor. She loved to have a slice of the action.

She led Isobel to a corner where they settled themselves under one of the glass pictures.

'What do you think of these?' asked Arlene, gesturing above her head to the chilly ladies.

'Oh, yes, they're OK,' said Isobel. 'Very stiff, very brittle. Very cold.' She shivered.

Sheila, the regular bar-lady, came over to them. It wasn't too crowded, so she served them at their table. Arlene paid for the two drinks.

'It's well for some who can knock off at twenty to five,' said Sheila.

'Sheila, this is my new friend, Isobel Coole. She's a writer.'

'Howya. You're welcome,' said Sheila and smiled. 'You do know that you've fallen into very bad company,' she added as she went off about her business.

'Bad company,' said Isobel. 'I like the sound of that.'

'So, what made you decide to write a play?' Arlene changed the subject.

'Well, novel writing is a very lonely pursuit. There's nobody to have a pint with.'

'I suppose there isn't, really.'

'And, at the risk of sounding like a pretentious eejit, I think that the theatre is the real seat of the intellect. Aeschylus, Shakespeare, Chekhov, Beckett – real brains. For an art form to be truly intellectual, nobody must be interested in it.'

'Yes, you do sound like an eejit. You never said anything as dumb as that in any of the interviews I read.'

'Well, I wouldn't say anything as dumb as that to a reporter. So, why do you work in the theatre?'

'For the money.'

'So you make a lot of it?'

'I jest, kid. The theatre isn't a business, it's a black hole into which one pours cash.'

10

Arlene had become increasingly cynical about the business of theatre.

'I do, however, make money out of my casting agency, and I mount the occasional fashion show, or promotional spectacular.'

'Oh,' said Isobel.

'Why do I work in the theatre? The truth is, I don't know, kid. It's a question I keep asking myself. I suppose I hope to make a killing on some big hit that'll tour the world, but even though I have had several hits, I haven't quite made the killing yet.'

Isobel bristled at being addressed as 'kid'. Arlene, always perceptive, noticed it.

'Sorry about the kid thing. I call everybody kid. Even the cleaning lady, who is pushing seventy, I particularly call her kid. It makes her feel young.'

'Oh, I don't mind, I didn't notice,' said Isobel, blushing.

Arlene could read her thoughts.

'Have you a lover?' she said, sensing that Isobel was off balance, and taking advantage of the opportunity to ask a nosy question. Arlene liked putting people on edge. Liked playing games.

A lover? Isobel thought that this was odd. A very personal question from a very scant acquaintance. 'No, as it so happens, I don't.' This was not true. She was, in fact, living with a man. Conor was his name.

'Just as I guessed,' said Arlene.

'Why are you interested?' asked Isobel.

'Life's rich pageant. I'm interested in people dynamics. You are a specimen of Irish womanhood, a "hip chick", I might

11

say. I am a sort of barroom anthropologist. I study the form. I see how people behave.'

'That's interesting,' said Isobel. 'You like watching other people live their lives, 'cos it saves you from living your own?'

That's a bit fresh, thought Arlene. 'What gave you that idea?'

'Just a hunch,' and Isobel smiled broadly.

Arlene smiled back. She liked this. Isobel was her kind of gal. Unafraid.

'So tell me more about your people-watching. I'm fascinated,' said Isobel.

Arlene wasn't entirely sure whether she was being taken for a ride or not. 'Perhaps that is why I like the theatre,' she said, 'it makes for a nice hot-house in which to study the carry-on of the species.' She kept an eye on Isobel to see if she was being laughed at. 'Also,' she continued, 'I'm nosy. Very nosy. Some people call it gossip, I call it information.'

Arlene loved information. She loved to know things. She stacked up information in her brain in little piles, fact neatly placed on top of relevant fact. And she never disclosed any of it. She was miserly about her information. She could keep a secret very well. Secrets never escaped from her hoard.

'My profession thrives on information. Whenever I don't know something, I always know somebody who knows something.'

'Well, what made you think I was single?'

'It is now six-thirty and you are drinking your third pint. These are not the actions of a woman or man who has a juicy pair of arms to go home to, so you're either single or sick of him.'

'Well, how about you?' asked Isobel.

12

'Nah,' said Arlene, a little sloshed now. 'I obviously don't have a juicy pair of arms to go home to, because if I had, I certainly wouldn't be sitting here talking shite with you.'

She decided she wanted to investigate Isobel some more.

'C'mon, it's seven o'clock, dinnertime for any civilised person – let me take you out to dinner.' And without waiting for a reply, Arlene picked up both their coats and dragged Isobel to her feet.

Isobel laughed, and willingly put on her coat. They knew that they were going to be friends.

Arlene noticed that Isobel didn't eat, she just chased a few curried broadbeans round her plate for a while. Isobel didn't mind that Arlene left her script behind in the restaurant, a fact that they discovered when they were in the nightclub at two o'clock in the morning, and had to go running back to the restaurant in search of it. Arlene didn't mind that Isobel couldn't hold her drink and had to be carried to a taxi. Arlene just slung Isobel over her shoulder in a fireman's lift. She was very strong. When she was a kid she'd done weight training. And Isobel was as light as a handbag. Arlene took the sleeping beauty home with her because, try as she might, she couldn't manage to prise Isobel's latitudes and longitudes from her muzzy brain. Arlene had a spare sofa, to which she consigned the snoring Isobel.

Isobel Coole.

Not so cool when she's lying there snoring and stinking of drink with a little rivulet of spittle coming out of her mouth and dribbling down her exquisite chin. No. Not so cool.

the director

'The first thing that I ought to tell you about Marcus Harmony,' said Arlene to Isobel, 'is that he's bisexual. I tell you this, not as a piece of information or a crumb of idle gossip, but as an illustration of the fact that he is a great man for keeping his options open. Hence his "maybe" answer to my offer. He is also an exceedingly good director, I wouldn't be after him otherwise, obviously. He likes the script, has a few changes to suggest, which he wants to talk through with you. You discuss your ideas with him and get the measure of him and then we'll see if we have a good vibe, and if so, we're sucking diesel.'

'I'm very nervous, Arlene. What if he thinks I'm an eejit?'

'Stop being a wimp. You're obviously not an eejit. And so what if you are an eejit? Lots of the best people nowadays are eejits.' Arlene laughed at her own joke. Isobel didn't.

'Haven't you got an editor at your publishing company?' said Arlene.

'Yes, I do, but I'm used to him, and he's used to me. We were a bit bumpy at first, but he figured out how to handle me and we settled down.'

'Jaysus. You're obviously spoiled out of your brains. Now stop being silly. Marcus is a fine boy. If you don't like him, we'll find someone else. It's all very straightforward. Just don't be too defensive. Remember, he'll be nervous too.'

It was a chilly February morning. Arlene and Isobel were sitting in the office, shivering because the heating had gone on the blink. They were waiting for Marcus Harmony to arrive. The first major meeting of the project. Arlene felt a rush of excitement. She loved the early buzz of getting the show on the road. It was like sex. It was *better* than sex. Well, it was better than good sex; perhaps not quite as good as brilliant sex. She had a very positive feeling about this project. The karma seemed just right. It was going to be something really special. She smiled at Isobel, whose fluttery nerves were both irritating and endearing.

There was a knock on the door. Isobel immediately blushed. Arlene noticed this. It bothered her a little. Isobel had a habit of blushing. She would be sitting there, looking as composed as a cat, and suddenly, at a slight embarrassment, a very slight embarrassment, her lovely pale skin would turn red. It was a flaw. A very annoying flaw. It made Isobel look vulnerable. Arlene didn't like that at all.

Marcus came in. Arlene looked at him approvingly. He looked OK today. Usually he looked like his clothes had been borrowed from his sister and thrown on with a pitchfork. She had often seen him in an ensemble consisting of a pair of old trousers only barely hanging onto his arse and an ancient semi-unravelled jumper; his trainers tied with string. But he made an effort for a first meeting. In fact, today he was a touch over the top. The Ray Bans with the silver frames were a bit unnecessary. The black jacket was good, though, and so was the silver briefcase. Class. Marcus had class. Even in his unravelling jumper, Marcus had class. Arlene reckoned he and Isobel would get along fine. They were the same age, thirty-one. Both fancied themselves as intellectuals. They could talk about Kafka and shite.

' "In sooth I know not why I am so late," ' said Marcus.

'You're not late, Marcus, you're early. And your Shakespeare wearies me.'

Isobel stood up and proffered her hand shyly. 'Hi,' she said.

He took her hand and gave it a good tight squeeze. He liked to pack as much into a handshake a possible.

'So, kiddies, you need no introduction to each other. I will take you down to Cunningham's and stay with you for five minutes, just to make sure that there is no fighting and then I will let you get on with your meeting, since that is what I will be paying you to do.'

Arlene led them both into the bar next door. 'So what's the poison?' she asked.

'I'll have a diet Coke. You know I don't drink when I'm working, Arlene,' said Marcus.

This was true. He never drank when in a meeting, or during a rehearsal period. He made up for it after opening night though.

'I'll have a coffee,' said Isobel.

Isobel was looking lovely, as usual. She was all wrapped up against the cold. She had the look of someone who would feel the cold quite intensely, in the way that she would feel everything quite intensely.

Arlene's mobile phone rang – she went off to a corner to

answer it, leaving the other two to get down to business.

Arlene spent most of her time on the phone. She had two phones in her office, a car phone, a mobile, a phone in her bathroom shaped like a fish, and one in her living room in the shape of a piano. The piano phone was a present from a composer she had worked with. It played a series of simple tunes, and occasionally scales. Its repertoire included Beethoven's Fifth, 'Twinkle Twinkle, Little Star', and the music from the shower scene in *Psycho*. She had answering machines on the phones at home and in the office, giving detailed accounts of her movements: 'Arlene is not here right now, you will get her on her mobile at 08' etc, and then a cute little tune. Arlene Morrissey was nothing if not available.

'First off,' said Marcus, 'I love the play. I think it's great, and I think you've real talent as a writer. Well, I s'pose that's obvious because of your books.'

'Oh, you liked my books?'

'Well, no, I haven't actually read them yet, but I've read all about them and you. I have been so *so* busy for the past couple of years, I've hardly had time to read anything that isn't directly concerned with research for a show. Your books will count as research for *Over the Moon*.'

'Oh,' said Isobel, a little crestfallen, a soupçon dismayed, a tad cheesed-off.

'I don't have any free time at all. To read or write. I used to write poetry,' he said, 'but I find I don't even have time to write a couplet now.'

'Have you ever written a play?'

'Nah. My gift is the realisation of other people's dreams.'

'That's a beautiful thing to say.' Isobel Coole took off her hat and scarf and began to thaw.

Marcus was very capable with people. As a director, he needed to be able to win trust quickly. He had his strategies: his little secret flatteries; his gentle bullyings; his charming coercions.

'So, now, the play. There's no point in me telling you that you're a genius and how much I love it. One doesn't call a dentist to admire one's teeth. Problems. Let's get down to them.'

'Oh, please, do tell me how much you love it. I do really need to hear that.'

'OK, OK. Well, I just adore the central character. She's such an enthralling mixture of innocence and sensuality. Nuala. I feel that Nuala represents her generation, *our* generation. She's a boom baby, with a loud voice. Well, not really loud in the decibel sense, quiet in fact, but the effect of it is megaphonic. She's crucial to things. The play will either achieve its potential or not on the strength of that performance. And, it is heart-breakingly sad. There won't be a dry eye in the house by the end of it, I swear to you. The theatre is the one place where true psychological violence can be wreaked on an audience. I assure you, your first play will be a triumph.'

Isobel sighed, and smiled a little. 'That is so kind,' she said, and smiled a little more.

home sweet home

Arlene was reasonably satisfied that Marcus and Isobel would get on fine. Marcus was a very easy person to work with. He was popular with everybody. Everybody loved him. This was a good thing, because he was the sort of person who needed everybody to love him. He couldn't bear anybody to have a bad impression of him. Even total strangers. He was full of kindness to all. Kicked over the crutches of cripples in an attempt to bestow coins in their begging bowls.

Arlene had shagged him once. He was the sort of person that it was impossible not to shag. His need to love the world often led him to make love to the world. He had a strong, low-key charisma. In another time he night have become a member of a religious order. The sort of monk who was having it away with everybody. Spreading love like jam. A Rasputin type. However, despite his gentleness and his beseeching eyes, he had very rough stubble at the end of the day, and Arlene had emerged from the encounter with a pretty nasty beard rash on her chin. The encounter had oddly made them very fond of each other.

She strolled down the length of Baggot Street as far as

the Grand Canal bridge, and instead of turning immediately towards her apartment, she went for a dawdle along its banks. Not a big enthusiast for the great outdoors, she managed nonetheless to love the canal. This was how she liked nature, in straight lines and performing a useful function. Civilised. Emerging up, as though from a crack in the city.

She liked the fact that she could walk to work. Her apartment was the entire top floor of a Georgian house overlooking the canal. It was a pleasant and spacious place, with one bedroom, a small junk room, a very large living room, and a little kitchen and bathroom. It was decorated in greys and pale pinks. Expensive stress colours. She had bought it seven years ago, in 1989. It had been a bargain.

Part of the reason it was such a bargain was because there were two mad people living downstairs. The developer, from whom Arlene had bought the apartment, had purchased the entire building, but had overlooked the fact that the people downstairs had security of tenure. They were an ancient couple, with very grand accents, obviously reared to better things than a mere floor of an old house. Mr and Miss Cartwright were their names. Brother and sister. Arlene suspected them of indulging in a forbidden passion and producing sinister issue – cats, thousands of them.

There was always a strange smell of decay and cat piss as Arlene passed their door. They called the cats the Tickles family. There was an ancient tabby, Lady Tickles and her fancy man, Sir Tickles. And lots of little Tickles. The Cartwrights were unpredictable in their behaviour, sometimes greeting Arlene warmly, sometimes not.

Arlene suspected that the developer had intended to either

intimidate the old pair out of the place, or do them in in some way, but he'd undergone a conversion at the end of the eighties, and become a Born-Again Christian, so he'd had to abandon his plan. Anyway, you had to go to London to be a proper yuppie. We weren't the right raw material here. Too much religion. Not enough dress designers.

Arlene didn't worry about the pair downstairs and their empire of cats. They were just another detail in the pageant, a turnip in life's great stew.

She let herself into her apartment and automatically threw an eye at the answering machine. It blinked a 2 at her. She pressed Play.

'Hello Arlene. Surprise, surprise . . .'

Arlene couldn't mistake that voice.

'. . . I'm going to be in Dublin for a few days next month, the eleventh to the fifteenth of March, and I got your number from directory enquiries. I hope you don't mind me calling, but I'd very much like to see you. I'll be staying at the Shelbourne. Please call. Beep!'

Arlene sighed, and stared at the machine as though the speaker were inside it. Her heart started to race, and she got that shiver of repulsion down her spine. Dick Whelan. Could it really be him?

The next message: 'Arlene, it just occurred to me that I never said who I was, and you may have forgotten my voice. It's Richard Power, or Dick Whelan as I used to be in the old days. Please call. Beep!'

Dick. She hadn't heard from him in ten years. What could he be doing here? she asked herself, but then she started to get a migraine. She suffered from hereditary migraine. It was a big thing in her family, mind-numbing headaches. Her two brothers got them frequently, but they now lived in California, where they've found a cure for everything. They got hypnosis. They were hypnotised into thinking that they didn't have migraine when they did. Arlene was sure this wasn't healthy.

She turned out the light and lay on the sofa. She tried to think of pleasant things. Her mobile rang.

'Hello.' At this stage, there was a laser show going on in her head.

'Hi. Arlene, Marcus here. Yes, I think things will be fine. Isobel is cool.'

'You had a good chat?'

'Best.'

'And you think that the script problems are curable?'

'Yeah. Remember, she's a novelist. She doesn't know anything about stage-craft.'

'And that awful ending?'

'I'll get her into the rehearsal room, and really show her the problems. It'll be fine.'

'Great news, my friend. She's a nice thing, isn't she?'

'Smashing. So I suppose we'd better talk cash?'

'Not, now. I've a pain in my brain. Tomorrow.'

'Fine. I'm just going to take Isobel out for a bite to eat. She's lonely, I think.'

'Fine. I'm dying. Goodbye.'

Arlene lay back on the sofa trying to rid her brain of all thoughts.

Her home phone rang. The dinky one shaped like a piano. Jaysus. The phone would be the death of her. She let the answering machine answer it, that was its job after all, and crawled into her bedroom, into her bed, to sleep.

It was not a deep sleep. It was a fitful, rapid-eye-movement job. Full of dreams. She dreamed that she was keeping two elephants in the car park behind her building, and due to the combination of an unforeseen drought and her forgetting to give them water, one of the elephants, the more enterprising one, escaped. It hopped over her six-foot-high wall. Unheard of for an elephant, she knew, but this was no ordinary elephant. She went chasing around the streets of Dublin to get it back. Up and down various streets and squares, enlisting the help of taxi-drivers and policemen. The elephant crashed into the food department at Marks and Spencer's, pausing to nibble some ready-washed lettuce. Do elephants eat lettuce? After his snack, he went running amok in the Stephen's Green shopping centre, pursued up and down escalators by her. She woke some hours later, exhausted.

When she got up, she played the machine.

'Hello, Ms Morrissey, it's your well-wisher again. I saw you in town this morning; you crossed the road at South King Street without looking to left or right and you were almost knocked down by a navy-blue Volvo travelling north at speed. At lot on your mind? You'll have to watch that. Click!'

Not him again. What a weirdo! This was about his sixth or seventh call. The calls weren't exactly threatening, more unsettling. Arlene decided that she'd better tell the police. It was getting a bit beyond a joke.

She had considered changing her number, but it was necessary to her job that it be readily available. Also, Arlene did not like to be intimidated. She did not like to give in to pressure. She wondered who it was. It was obviously somebody who knew her, knew her job, her movements. This was all she needed. A lunatic following her around. Like she didn't know enough lunatics already.

She made herself a cup of coffee. So Richard Power would be in town. She was amazed that he had called her. Not many people remembered any more, but fifteen years previously, Arlene had been married to Richard Power. He was then known as Dick Whelan.

They had met when Arlene was a little scut of a stage hand, working for peanuts on a production of *Uncle Vanya* that Richard had a part in. She was twenty, he was thirty-five. It hadn't worked out. That was an understatement. It had been a romantic disaster of Titanic proportions. He had become very successful afterwards and had changed his name to Richard Power. Power was his mother's family name. Arlene changed her name back to Morrissey. Dick and Arlene Whelan were no more. They had disappeared in an explosive melt-down.

Arlene hadn't thought about him in a long time, but now the old skin-crawling feeling came back to her. She shivered. Food. She hadn't eaten since breakfast. She would order herself a pizza.

She rang Domino's pizza delivery and ordered a small pizza with pineapple and pepperoni. Cooking was not a big thing in her life anymore. She had used to be good at it.

There had been no communication between herself and Dick since the break-up. Just a big black wound which had festered for a while. A long while. Time passed, as it does. She read the odd article about him in the magazines, in which he never referred to the marriage in his past. A bachelor boy, they thought him. Arlene had always been curious as to why he didn't look for a divorce in Britain. Probably felt it would leave him in a position where he'd be expected to marry someone else. Maybe that was what he wanted now? A divorce. That was it. He was coming over here to ask her co-operation in a divorce.

Arlene reckoned that she would probably ring him up and meet him. She was sure she'd be able for him now. In fact, she would relish the power that her current success gave her. She wasn't the kid she used to be, and she would like him to know that. She would like to let him see how together she was. He was a good actor, and a major name. You'd never know when he might come in handy.

The buzzer sounded. Arlene looked into the black and white intercom and saw a be-helmeted person bearing a pizza. She pressed the buzzer. Nothing happened. Shit. It was on the blink again. The damn thing was constantly breaking down.

'I'll be right down,' she called into the phone. She ran down the three flights of stairs and opened the door.

'One small pepperoni and pineapple, an order of garlic bread and a tub of coleslaw. Is that right?' said the guy.

'Sure is,' said Arlene. 'I'm starving.' She signed his docket.

'Ms Morrissey,' said the guy, 'I'm sorry to bother you, but I wonder could I give you my CV?'

Under that helmet lurked an actor.

He handed her a CV. 'Brendan Coffey is the name.'

Arlene nodded. They were everywhere. She wouldn't be surprised if there was one *in* the pizza.

'I've seen you in a couple of things,' she said. 'If anything comes up, I'll bear you in mind.'

'I badly need a break. My girlfriend has just had a baby, and that's why I'm delivering pizzas.'

Sob stories. Arlene hated them.

'I sing too,' he said and he launched into a fairly harmonious rendition of 'There Ain't Nothing Like A Dame' there on her doorstep.

Arlene smiled stiffly at him. Her pizza was getting cold.

the award

Today was the day.

Arlene arrived into her office at eight AM. She was a firm believer in the early-bird theory, but considered it could have been more nicely phrased. Who the hell was interested in worms? She decided to get on the blower, and do her utmost to find out what the story was. She knew that Isobel had been shortlisted, but couldn't find out anything beyond that from her discreet enquiries with her many contacts.

It was time to end the discreet enquiry and commence full frontal. The ceremony was tonight, and the organisers wanted to keep everybody in suspense. They obviously thought they were the bleedin' Oscars. She was determined to know, because she didn't want Isobel to be disappointed publicly.

Arlene suspected that Isobel and Marcus might develop into an item. She wasn't sure, but she thought it was on the cards. This would be an excellent development, and a terrible one. Excellent in that they would then have very good lines of communication open. Terrible, in that they would be bound to have a row and blow the project sky-high. Arlene was keeping an eye on the situation. It was probably a bit premature to speculate.

Isobel did seem happier, though. The droop had gone from her eyes. A bounce had come into her walk. 'Working on this play with yourself and Marcus is how I imagine getting out of solitary confinement feels.'

Never a one for the understatement, was Isobel.

Arlene made a couple of calls and finally she got Miriam Coughlan – Bingo! Miriam Coughlan was an old school-friend whose husband was on the judging panel. Miriam was Arlene's age, thirty-five, but she had an almost-grown-up family. She had got pregnant when they were in sixth year in school, by her boyfriend, who was thirty to her seventeen. He was now her husband. Miriam had never been very bright at school, had been in the bottom stream. In fact, four girls from the bottom stream were up the pole by the time they sat their Leaving Cert. Proof positive to Arlene at the time that the thick would inherit the earth. But Miriam was a late developer, and they were great pals now.

Miriam owed her. This was a big mistake on Miriam's part. There was no such thing as a free favour. And for what did Miriam owe her? Arlene had got Miriam's mentally unstable brother a job with the lighting company that she was now suing – a ferrety-looking boy whom you would instinctively mistrust with small children. Miriam was convinced that her brother's life would be much improved by a job. As it happened, she was right. The job cured him. He really got into bulbs and plugs and became one of their brightest sparks. Transformed him. He got a girlfriend. A delightful girl from Mullingar. Cathy was her name. Blonde.

Arlene knew that Miriam was annoyed at being used to access her husband's work. She could hear the irritation in her voice. Miriam was determined to pretend that she didn't know what Arlene knew she damn well did know.

'You see, Miriam, I really need to know. Isobel is quite fragile. Yes, I know you wouldn't think it to see her on the telly, but in fact she is, and I want to protect her from any public disappointment. I'd just like her to be prepared for a let down. That's all you need to say to me. Do I need to prepare her?'

'I honestly don't know, Arlene. Mick and I are having a lot of rows at the moment, so he's not really speaking to me.'

'Well, in that case, Miriam, he's not going to mind if you tell me.'

'Arlene, you're putting me in a very awkward position.'

'Would you advise me to prepare her for a disappointment?'

There was silence for a moment.

'No, Arlene, I don't think that that would be necessary. Yes, for God's sake, she's won. By a unanimous vote. There was nothing to touch *Over the Moon*. There, I've said it. You're a mean hound.'

'Thanks Miriam. You're a right pal. I owe ya one. No, I owe ya two.'

'Promise me one thing. No telling anybody before tonight.'

'Promise and love you.'

Arlene turned to her computer and wrote up a press release.

She tried to phone Isobel to tell her, but without success. There was nobody in Isobel's flat. She tried Marcus's but there was only a machine there. Being unable to get someone on the phone really bugged her. She was dying to tell Isobel. To bestow the prize on Isobel. It was as though it was in her gift.

Later that afternoon, Isobel and Marcus strolled into her office, looking flushed – the three of them had arranged to go together to the awards ceremony.

'Where were you all day, Isobel? I've been calling and calling.'

Arlene tried unsuccessfully to keep the annoyance out of her voice.

'I was out, up the Dublin mountains with Marcus. He was explaining to me all about motivation.'

'I needed to get you. You're going to have to let me know where you are in future. I had some information.'

'Arlene,' said Marcus, 'you may have two phones in your office, a phone in your car, a mobile, and several kitsch phones in your apartment, as well as a bed phone I presume, and a waterproof job in the bath, but they are fuck-all use to you when the object of your incessant calling is up the shaggin' mountains.'

Marcus was getting smart now. Arlene didn't like that at all.

'Arlene, what's the information?' asked Isobel.

'Oh, find out for yourself,' she snapped.

'Hey, the Queen Bee is in a bit of a mood,' said Marcus affectionately. He stood behind Arlene's chair and started to rub her shoulders.

Arlene hated it when Marcus called her the Queen Bee. It made her feel like stinging him. She handed the press release to Isobel.

Isobel gasped. 'What!'

Marcus snatched the press release from her.

'Is this serious?' asked Isobel Coole. Red face and shining eyes.

'Yes,' said Arlene.

'How do you know? I thought nobody was going to be told 'till tonight,' said Marcus.

'I know everything,' said Arlene stiffly. 'There is very little that goes on in this town that I don't have a handle on.'

Tension hung in the air for a moment, like a big fat vulture. Isobel had no idea what the problem was, but Marcus did. He knew, from old, that Arlene was unreasonably obsessed with control. She needed to keep things in her own grip, and when she felt they were slipping she got nervous and displayed signs. Betrayed herself. Arlene liked telling people what to do. Like a head-mistress.

Isobel broke the moment by practically jumping on top of Arlene. She let out a loud un-ladylike bellow. 'Yaaaaaw! I don't believe it, I'm thrilled.'

'Congratulations, Isobel,' said Marcus, and then he added, 'and Arlene.'

'Of course, Arlene, thank you. It would never have happened without you,' said Isobel.

Arlene, mollified, took out the bottle of champagne she had put on ice earlier.

'We're moving, lads. This is a definite green light,' she said, just before the bottle went pop!

the star

Arlene had to admit that she was a tiny bit nervous meeting Dick on the evening of Tuesday the twelfth, in the bar of the Shelbourne Hotel. They had agreed to get together for a drink, and then perhaps have a bite, but first they would see how they got on.

She had been sitting in the lobby for less than two minutes when she spotted him going up to the porters' desk. Yes, he was unmistakable. He looked just like he did in the movies. She had watched him age on celluloid over the past ten years, a nice safe distance. He had been voted one of Britain's ten sexiest men in some magazine or other.

For her, now, he was the antithesis of sexy. The sight of him gave her shudders up and down her back. She stood up to meet him. He walked straight past her.

'Richard.'

He stopped and turned.

'Arlene?'

'Yeah.'

'My God, you've changed.'

This was very true. Richard did not recognise her. She had

changed an awful lot. Firstly, there was a change of hairstyle – it used to be long and girlish, now it was short and styled. Her clothes were completely different – chic suits and heels and stuff; she used to go round in baggy dungarees and little skirts. But probably the biggest change, and Arlene was very aware of it herself, was that she now had an attitude. She gave off an air of command, of authority.

'Arlene, I would never have recognised you.'

'Well, don't worry, I recognise you.'

They went into the bar.

'What's your poison?' asked Richard.

'Gin and tonic.'

'Some things don't change.' He went off to the bar. Poison. It was from him that she had picked up the term. To her surprise he came back with a G & T and something that looked suspiciously like a Club Orange.

'I'm on the really hard stuff now, Arlene. Drinking fizzy orange is really hard.'

'Oh?'

'Yeah. I've given up the jar. I'm in AA now.'

'How long?'

'Six months, and six days. I go to a great meeting. It's in Islington and very well dressed. They're great. Lots of theatre and film people. You'd be surprised who fetches up there. Anyway, enough about me. I can see things have changed a lot for you.'

'Yeah, well, where to start?'

'I suppose start with work.'

'Well, I've set up my own company, doing promotions and theatre productions. I am also a casting agent. I do a lot of the big films that come in here. I do all right, I'm not making a fortune, but I'm enjoying myself.' Arlene was annoyed at how insecure this sounded. Annoyed at how much vulnerability was signalled by her pride. Boast boast, brag brag.

She changed tack. 'Dublin still isn't entirely used to women businessmen, but it's coming round.'

'Oh you've turned into a feminist, have you? I wouldn't have thought that was your style.'

'Well, no, I haven't, but what would you know about my style?' Arlene wished that the aggressive note would go out of her voice. Shut up. Be *nice* to him.

'Sorry.'

'No. I'm not a feminist. Do I look like a feminist? How many feminists do you see going round with these kind of clothes and this kind of hairdo?'

'Indeed, not many.'

'No, never liked the word, it always had connotations of unemployment. The feminist is a bit low-down in the pecking order for my tastes, Dick.'

'Please call me Richard.'

'Sorry, Richard. The feminist was the prototype of the modern woman, an early evolutionary model, now discarded because of certain design flaws. Would never wash with the wives of powerful men. Lacked upward mobility.'

She could talk! She hadn't used to be able to talk.

'The concept of the independent woman,' continued Arlene, 'will have to be renamed, like they renamed "Windscale" "Sellafield" after the nuclear leaks, and they renamed "Long Kesh" "the Maze" after internment. Somebody needs to do a PR job on the "F" word before it can be repeated in polite society.'

'I see your point,' said Richard.

'I'm a modern woman in a modern world, doing very nicely, thank you. Have you become a feminist?'

'No.'

Richard was gifted at rubbing her up the wrong way. Nobody could do it quite like him. She had forgotten how thoroughly he could do it.

He took out a packet of cigarettes and offered her one. Silk Cut. The brand she used to smoke.

She shook her head. 'I gave up. Only losers smoke.'

'Thank you. I'm tackling one addiction at a time,' he said, unruffled, un-insultable.

Arlene felt rage rising. She shouldn't have come.

Her mobile rang.

'Excuse me.' She stuck her left finger into her left ear and balanced the phone against her right.

Richard noticed her long nails. She always used to bite them. It had driven him mad. It came to him in a flash – it had been like living with a mouse. The dark bedroom and suddenly the gnawing, scraping sound of her grazing on her fingernails, followed by a crunching sound as she chewed.

Suddenly she was twenty-two again. The noises she made at night disgusted him. She used to masturbate in her sleep. He would be lying there, insomniacal, and she would have dozed off and then quietly she'd start. It would get louder and louder, and she would always wake up before she came.

Arlene switched the phone to her other ear. 'No, Mick, I want you to take your time. Not a rush job, you understand?'

When they discussed it she said that it was a good sign that she woke up because it would be a bit sad if she slept through an orgasm. It was just an affliction she had. Some people talked in their sleep. She wanked. She had been a terribly sexy girl. Frighteningly sexy. He looked at her now. She had filled out a little, her breasts were larger, and lower. Her hips more rounded. But mostly, she didn't have that shining face any more. This new face was handsome, but the old one had shone. Her lips had got thinner, and her eyes sterner. More serious. More sad?

'Fine, brilliant, excellent, I'll pick 'em up then. I love you. You are God's gift to producers. I owe you a blow-job. 'Bye, 'bye.' Peep.

She turned back to Richard. 'That's my printers. They are angels. They stay in late and do everything, but sometimes, if I give them too tight a deadline, the work is a bit sloppy, register's off, you understand. Mick is the guy's name. They're a small outfit called Blob Printing. Terrible name, but it grows on you.'

Richard laughed. 'Did I hear you correctly, or did you say you owed him a blow-job?'

'Yeah. It's an ongoing joke. I keep telling Mick that I'll pay him in blow-jobs. But he always insists on cash. Even on a small order, a batch of six-by-eight flyers. That time the fee was only fifty quid so I was a bit worried. But he still went for the cash. I was nearly insulted.'

Arlene enjoyed this casual talk. It made her feel good about herself. Aggressive. Un-fuck-around-able. In charge.

'I'm sure you were.'

'He must have an obliging wife,' she said, and she blushed when she thought about it.

36

He blushed too.

There was a pause for a moment.

'Why are you in Dublin? Some big movie deal that I haven't heard about?' she asked.

'No, actually, I came to see you, Arlene.'

'What on earth for?'

'I need to see you, Arlene,' his eyes avoided hers.

She stared unflinchingly at him.

'I left part of me behind here, and I've come to see if I can get it.' His hand shook as he put his cigarette to his lips.

Suddenly Arlene thought that he might be in deep trouble. For the first time in this conversation, she stopped thinking about her own discomfort, and realised that there was something wrong with him.

'I've reached a crisis,' said Richard. 'It was partly the drinking, but it was other things as well. I talked it through with my psychiatrist and she advised me to come back here, and when I thought about coming home, I realised that I had to.'

Arlene blushed again. What was she doing blushing? She never blushed. Her mobile rang again.

'Excuse me.' Relieved, she turned away. Richard sighed loudly. The mobile wasn't going down very well.

'Hello?'

'Hi, Arlene, it's Isobel.'

Arlene could hear tears in Isobel's voice.

'Hi, pet.'

'Arlene, I need to see you. Are you free?'

'Not entirely.'

'Oh.'

'But I could be later. You can go to my place if you want, and I'll see you later. You know where to get the key?'

'No.'

'The Cartwrights downstairs. Just tell them who you are. They'll give it to you. His name is Jack and her name is Helen. The cats are all called Tickles. If you explain who you are, I'm sure they'll believe you and give you the key.'

'Arlene, you're a pal.'

'I sure am.' Click.

Arlene turned back to Richard. 'I'm very sorry.'

'Can't you turn that damn thing off?'

Temper temper. He hadn't lost that. He was losing it now.

'Yes, I suppose I'd better. That was Isobel Coole. A red-hot young talent. I'm producing her first play, called *Over the Moon.*'

Work. She would steer him back onto the subject of work. She liked talking about work.

'Oh. Is that what you're working on now?' he said. The moment of his emotion had passed.

'Not quite yet. It should be going on in September, then hopefully touring. Would you do me a favour? Would you read it and tell me what you think of it? You're so experienced, your views would be extremely valuable.'

Richard knew he was being flattered, but didn't mind. He liked flattery.

'It would be a great help, and I would appreciate it a lot.' Arlene pulled the script out of the bag and plopped it down in front of him. He picked it up gently in his hands and opened it gingerly.

'Glad to. I'll look at it while I'm resting over the next few days.'

Arlene knew she'd hook him if he liked the part, and she was sure he would. He seemed shook. Looked like he needed someone to tell him what to do. She'd nail him.

the writer

Arlene skipped out of the Shelbourne, relieved to have escaped from don't-call-me-Dick Richard. She walked briskly along Baggot Street to her local off-licence/deli to pick up some red wine and some fancy cheese. She had been buying there for six years and Martin Campbell knew her taste in wine, red only and Spanish usually. And he knew her taste in cheeses. More wide-ranging, but she favoured the mature ones, strong, sometimes reeking, occasionally oozing.

'Hello, Arlene. You've a great life, stocking up with the red wine and it only Tuesday.'

'Oh yes,' said Arlene. 'Hey diddle-dee-dee, the theatrical life is the one for me. We never do a day's work.'

'Well, you must be having a nice little party, that you're bringing this lovely snack home,' said Martin, as he guillotined her cheese. 'Your friend, the dark one, went by, towards your place. About an hour ago.'

Martin sure kept his eye out. Very little went past his window that didn't register.

'Yes,' said Arlene. 'Isobel Coole is at my place. What an addition to company that will be.'

'And yis haven't a man between you?'

Arlene was fond of Martin, but just as she was deciding that he was an almost reasonable human being, he always opened his big gob and put his foot in it. Martin had a way of saying the wrong thing. Always. He had once told her that he'd been to see one of the plays she'd produced, and left at the interval because his companion had dozed off. Told her this quite calmly. Didn't realise that he was causing offence. She had concluded a long time ago that he was missing a few departments upstairs. He was single, and the companion he was referring to wasn't the product of some sort of a steamy homosexual encounter as Arlene had first surmised; it was his aunt. Aunt Isa.

Arlene heard quite a lot about Aunt Isa. In fact, more than she absolutely required to know. Indeed, she was familiar with Aunt Isa's hysterectomy, her intestinal-tract infections, and was occasionally privy to information about Aunt Isa's bowel movements. No, it didn't seem that Martin was involved with homosexual lovers, or with women. He seemed to have no inclinations in any direction, except perhaps an unhealthy fascination with, and love of, cheeses. It might almost be described as a physical attraction. Martin Campbell was attracted to his mighty cheeses. He would pick up a chunky Camembert as tenderly as if it were his first-born. He occasionally turned up at work with a great big black eye. Arlene suspected that he went out at night, got drunk and picked fights. A sort of Jekyll and Hyde of the Dublin suburbs. Arlene was fascinated by Martin. He was quite a specimen.

'Goodbye dearie,' she said. This last morsel, a trifle tart.

*

Arlene trotted down the street. She was feeling quite cheerful. The oppression caused by Dick/Richard had lifted. She had a great life. So much independence. It was probably her most prized possession. The one thing she would never sacrifice. She went up the stairs, past the cat piss smell, to her flat, and opened the door with some trepidation.

There sat Isobel, in front of the fake gas fire, looking quite composed, but there were dark hollows around her eyes. Her face seemed to have collapsed, subsided, caved in, as a river bank appears after a storm.

'Hi, Arlene, I'm so, so sorry to disturb you. You're very good to let me come round.'

'Sure, kid. Don't worry. I'm glad to have the company. I've brought us some tasty treats. Lovely wine and some Swiss Emmenthal. Kills all known problems, dead.'

'There was a phone-call about an hour ago, just after I got here. I didn't pick it up, obviously, the machine took it, but I couldn't help hearing it. It sounded like a weirdo.'

'Oh, him again.'

'He's called before?'

'Yeah. He calls quite frequently.'

'And doesn't it bother you?'

'Yes and no. I'm beginning to get kind of used to his little voice.'

'Have you told the police?'

'No. I haven't got round to it yet. I suppose I don't really think that he's too dangerous. I reckon he'd have pounced on me by now if he was going to. He's just some loser with a sad brain who likes leaving messages on my machine. I think that it's somebody I know.'

'How so?'

'Well, he mentions my clothes, and what I've been doing that day, sometimes. And I just get this feeling.'

'Gosh, Arlene, you should call the police. This could be serious.'

Arlene pressed play and the machine whirred into life.

'Hello, Ms Morrissey. I saw you today in your red suit. I wasn't sure about it. I don't think that red is your colour. Click.'

'It's very weird,' said Isobel. 'You'd really better phone the police.'

'Yes, I've been meaning to. I will. So, tell me, chickie, what's the problem with you?' Arlene got a corkscrew and started opening the bottle of wine.

'God, you're probably going to think that I'm a pathetic fool. You're so tough, a dodgy phone-caller doesn't bother you.'

'I wish I was deep, instead of just macho.'

'Well, it's, you see – do you remember the first night that we met, I told you I was single? Well, that wasn't true. I've been living with a guy for the past three years. Conor is his name.'

'I know.'

'How do you know?'

'Well, I asked some questions about you and discovered that contrary to your own fiction, you were shacked up with a lad called Conor, who wrote copy for an advertising agency.'

'Oh,' said Isobel, a little taken aback. 'What else do you know about me? I hate people being nosy about my business.'

'Fuck-all. The information I look for is just common

knowledge. I don't hire private detectives. C'mon, don't take it so seriously.'

'All right.'

'Right so, well what's the problem with Conor?'

'Well, we're in trouble. He just doesn't treat me very well, and I find him very difficult to deal with. He doesn't bother to phone if he's going to be home late from work. He puts me down in front of people. He criticises everything I do.'

'He sounds like a cunt,' said Arlene, struggling with the corkscrew.

'And now I think he's seeing somebody behind my back.'

'You think?'

'I'm almost sure.'

'How are you almost sure?'

'I found a pair of ladies knickers in his pocket, that weren't mine.'

'Maybe he's a transvestite?'

'He's not.'

'Are you sure? Lots of people are transvestites nowadays.'

'No, he's definitely not a transvestite. He's right wing and intolerant. He won't even wear a cravat, for God's sake, in case somebody thinks he's a pouf.'

'They're the ones who can't be got out of women's clothes. The thrill is doubled if you're disgusted with yourself. Self-loathing adds to the frisson.'

'He's *not* a transvestite,' said Isobel, narked now.

'Sorry,' said Arlene, realising she'd taken her little joke too far.

'Believe me, that wouldn't bother me. He's seeing somebody else.'

44

Arlene finally opened the bottle of wine, and poured out two glasses.

'It sounds like a bit of a bad scene,' said Arlene.

'What should I do?' asked Isobel.

'Before I answer that, I have to ask are you seeing Marcus?'

'Don't be ridiculous. What made you think that?'

'Just a hunch.'

'Of course I'm not. What could possibly have given you that idea?'

Arlene felt a little foolish about her speculations. Her private concocted dramas.

'What should I do, Arlene?'

'Well, it seems pretty obvious.'

'Nothing seems obvious to me.'

'Leave him.'

'Just like that.'

'Yeah, he's obviously giving you the pip. Give him the boot.'

'But what about the three years we've spent together?'

'What about them? Isn't three years of your life enough to waste on a cunt like that, or would you rather waste five?'

Arlene reckoned that Isobel's collapsed face signified some trauma deeper than an imminent row with her boyfriend. But this would do for the moment. She sensed that her practical advice wasn't going down terribly well with the romantic Isobel.

'But Arlene, it's a very difficult thing to do.'

'What's difficult about it? You just write a note saying, "Dear Conor, you're a fool, I'm off to find somebody who has enough grey matter to appreciate my perfection. Please leave your key on the mantlepiece". And then you leave town for the weekend.'

'Appreciate my perfection. What a nice phrase.'

'I thought you'd like it.'

'But that's a very difficult thing to do.'

'Look, let's say we made a mistake and one of the actors that we've cast turns out to be unsuitable once we start rehearsing. Say, the part of Nuala in *Over the Moon*. Crucial part. Absolutely crucial.'

'Does that happen?'

'Occasionally. What do we do?'

'Well, I don't know.'

'Well, I do. We fire them and get somebody right. Sad, but simple. We pay them off and we give them the boot. They go to the bar, have a good old cry, contact their lawyers, bad-mouth me to everybody they meet, then they get a very fancy film offer which they would've had to turn down if they were still contractually obliged to me, and they're thrilled with their good fortune. Next time I meet them in the street, they wave at me and blow kisses, and everything is hunky-dory and everybody is as happy as a pig in shite. Six months later they're licking my ass because I've just been given the casting contract for something else, and they want a slice of that. You see. One has to do what one has to do for the greater good of the larger picture. If you cast somebody in a central role in the more crucial drama of your own life, and they turn out to be a cunt, then surely it's even more necessary that you give them the boot.'

'I can see the sense with *Over the Moon*, Nuala would have

to be correctly cast. It makes more sense about the play than it does about real life.'

'That merely proves that you are both a fool and a genius, Isobel. Here, have another glass of wine.'

Isobel started to feel a little better. Arlene's good humour was infectious.

'Can I sleep on the sofa again?'

'Of course, pet.'

There was a pause as Isobel struggled with something that she was ashamed of. 'I wish – I were beautiful,' she said.

Arlene laughed. The gazelle in front of her, with beautiful eyes and features, and hair that would tangle a heart. Something stopped her from telling Isobel that she *was* stunningly beautiful, though she knew that that was what Isobel wanted, no, needed, to hear.

'What?' was all she managed.

'You know, Charlotte Brontë would have swapped all her talent for the kind of looks that would make men fall in love with her.'

'How do you know? Were you talking to her?'

'It's in the books.'

'Well, then she was a fool,' said Arlene.

'I would give it all up,' said Isobel, 'if a man were to love me enough.'

'Ah, Jaysus, you're raving now. For an intelligent writer, you can be a right thick. Go to bed.'

'I'm thirty-one now. I've only a few years left in me.'

'What do you mean? You're in your prime.'

'I feel old,' said Isobel.

'All the more reason to dump this Conor bloke if he's not measuring up. Silly name, Conor.'

After they had both gone to bed, Arlene peeped through the cracks of the door into the living room to see if Isobel was asleep. Just as she thought, no, she wasn't; she was sitting up smoking a cigarette, occasionally dabbing her eyes with a hanky. She was wearing a dainty set of french underthings in a lemon yellow colour.

The sight of Isobel like this made her shiver. A slip of a girl in sexy underwear, dying for an opportunity to please. She looked a lot younger than thirty-one. Arlene had been right about the underwear. It's funny how you can tell that about people. Marcus? He wore high-cut-sporty-black-sexual-athlete-gent's briefs. You would guess this by his wiry body and tanned skin and his both macho and effeminate taste in dress.

Richard Power? Dick had always been a plain white cotton Y-fronts man. Ordinary underwear, like his mother used to buy him. It gave him a vital link with normality. Arlene reckoned this would not have fundamentally changed over the years since she'd been with him. Perhaps the cotton had become slightly more upmarket. She always did his laundry for him. It's funny how the little things remained so vivid. She used to enjoy ironing and folding his underwear. It had given her a thrill.

Arlene woke at eight-thirty with a slight hangover. Too many G & Ts and too much wine. She got some coffee and muesli together and tried to wrap her brain round her commitments

48

for the day. Her piano phone rang. It played 'The Entertainer', one of its repertoire. Da-da-da-da, da-da, da-da, de-de- Arlene always tried to catch it before it got to the second phrase.

It was Dick.

'Hello, Dick.'

'Arlene, do you mind not calling me Dick? I'm used to Richard now.'

'Sure, Richard, Sorry.'

'Sorry to phone so early, but I had to call. I love the script. I think it's very, very good.'

'Great! How good?'

'Good enough.'

'So you'll do it?'

'But you never asked me to do it. You just asked me what I thought,' he said teasingly.

'Did I not? Silly me.'

'We'll talk. Dinner tonight?'

'Nah, I'm tied up tonight. How about tomorrow?'

'Sure thing.'

Arlene went over to the sofa and found a note there. The sofa retained the dents of Isobel's body, and the cushion held the shape of her head. The note read: *I got up early and stole away. I am ashamed of myself, but you are an angel straight from heaven. Love, of the undying kind, Isobel.*

I-so-belle. Well-named was this Isobel, thought Arlene, as she picked up a few jet-black hairs from the cushion and wrapped them round her fingers before putting them in the bin.

the script

Arlene met Richard the next night in the Trocadero for dinner. He was dressed in a good suit. She had gone to some effort and put on a nice little cocktail dress. She noticed that various people recognised him. The waiter, a couple at another table. She had forgotten that. He was a big fish, particularly after the recent BBC drama serial, where he had played the priest. Nothing like the telly to turn you into a household name.

She smiled at him. She felt better about meeting him today. He liked the script. His potential usefulness blunted her instinctive rage.

They ordered their meal. He requested trout and she stopped herself from saying, 'a little fish for a big fish'.

'So, tell me what you think, Richard.'

'I love it. I think it's a wonderful portrait of a really fucked up man who simply cannot communicate. The character, Mark Delaney –'

He flicked through the script and found a speech.

'Look here:

```
Mark: I don't care if everybody else is out all night
and going off with their boyfriends for the weekend.
You're not everybody else, you're my daughter, and you
will be in here at eleven thirty. Just because all
your friends are complete sluts with no respect for
themselves or their bodies, not to mind their future
husbands. No man wants another man's leavings. You'll
thank me for this, when you're older.
```

I think that this is *so* interesting. He hides his possessiveness of his daughter behind a fairy story of religious scruples and morality. And the most interesting aspect of it, and this is where I think that Isobel Coole has real talent, is that despite the fact that he's a pathetic, miserable, self-centred power-freak, I had lots of sympathy for him.'

This was typical, thought Arlene. A Judas complex. Now fully reformed, Richard had discovered a newfound magnanimity, an ability to understand the corrupt and the fallen. A brand-new Christian is born. Hallelujah!

'He's a really typical kind of Irishman, from a very specific background. I feel like I know him. He's not a million miles away from my own father.'

Arlene had never met Richard's father. He had been dead before she arrived on the scene.

'I think the wife, Colleen, is beautifully drawn, you can see that she is a shadow of her former self – I love the flashback devices that show her and him courting in the Fifties and it's obvious that she's dying for it but he won't go near her. A youngfella from Loughrea in County Galway who does very well for himself professionally, half of it is pure blarney and blackguarding of course, but he does very well, nonetheless. Marries Colleen, his childhood sweetheart, who he hauls out of the bogs and into a fancy house in Foxrock and has Nuala.'

Richard was very enthusiastic. His sparkly energy was invigorating.

'It's great the way their religion creates such a firm bond when they are younger, and there's even a sense of the erotic charge of self-denial early on. There's a sense that their Christian devotions enhance their sex-life. It gives it an elemental eroticism. It's mind blowing.'

'Yes, I must say, I think the religious stuff is very good. It's almost like the external stimulation of pornography,' said Arlene.

Richard continued in a rush. 'The idea of setting it during the 1983 abortion referendum is brilliant, isn't it?'

Yes, it is interesting,' said Arlene.

'It really give the guy something to get worked up about, and people who feel strongly that abortion is wrong feel it *very* strongly. Also, Mark Delaney being fifty when the daughter is nineteen is great. Somehow, I believe, it's very important that he is still virile whilst he is being sexually possessive of his daughter.'

Arlene looked at her fifty-year-old ex-husband. Still virile, eh? I wouldn't doubt you.

'Well, you sound very turned-on by it, I have to say.'

'Well, I am. There is one problem. My agent will have a fit, because I know that you won't be able to afford to pay me my usual rate.'

'And what it your usual rate?' she asked with a coy smile.

'Arlene, I never discuss money, not even with you. I spent too much of my career talking about money when I was younger. I simply refuse to discuss it now. It's not just fees, but money generally, I refuse to discuss. I have an agent who does my contracts, and I have an accountant who tells me when to slow down on my Visa card. They are both very well paid for their services, I presume.'

'What do you mean, you presume.'

'I have no idea what they're paid, it's some sort of per-centage.'

'Richard, you surprise me. They could be robbing you as we sit here.'

'They're not, I have a lawyer who looks over their shoulders.'

Arlene didn't quite believe this financial story. Nobody could be that foolish. Nobody could have such a scant respect for money.

'Anyway, you get on to my agent and we'll see how it goes.'

Arlene knew he'd do it. Partly because he like the rôle and partly because he needed a stint in Ireland. He needed to come home. A thought struck her.

'Any lassie hovering in the background?'

'No. There've been a few, but none with enough patience to put up with me.'

'Oh.'

'How about you?'

'No, I've no lassie hovering either,' she said with a little grin.

'Arlene, I'm stuck.'

'What do you mean?'

'I'm just stuck in life. I needed to talk to you. I have reached a glass ceiling.'

'What do you want to talk about?'

'The past.'

'Why?'

'Because I'm stuck back there, and I can't go on.'

'Well, what can I say?'

'I'm afraid that I hurt you, that I wrecked you.'

'Do I look wrecked?'

'Admittedly, no you don't.'

'Well then?'

'But I need to *know* that you're not.'

'Oh, for God's sake, I'm obviously not wrecked,' snapped Arlene. She was annoyed by the turn that the conversation had taken. If Richard had come here to salve his conscience in some way that was all very well, but she didn't want to get involved in it. It had taken her a long time to put the lid on the past herself, and she wasn't going to allow him to take it off again. The past was a torture chamber. She had been different then.

There was silence for a moment. Arlene decided to steer him back to the script. Work. Yes, talking about work. That was easy.

'I meant to ask you, what do you think of the ending?'

'I'm not wild about it. It seems a little melodramatic. I'm not sure that he'd do *that*. Why do you ask?'

'Well, I'm not wild about it either, and neither is Marcus, so I just wondered what you thought.'

Later that night, in bed, Arlene thought about Richard. She wondered if she could afford him. It was dawning on her that his fee for this show would not be in pounds and shillings. It would be in an altogether different currency. He did seem changed, much more considerate now, a much gentler person. But she could still catch glimpses of the earlier Richard. The Dick Whelan-ness of him. People don't change *that* much. A wolf now wearing a lambswool jumper. He could play good for a while, he was an actor after all, but for how long?

She fell asleep. The grip she had on her brain relaxed, the past visited her, randomly, but in great detail. The lid opened, just a crack, but enough.

the past I

It was 1980. She was a kid in a maid's outfit, and he was a vision of sophistication. A black linen suit, and a loose-fitting white shirt, tied gypsy style, at the neck. It was a production of *Uncle Vanya* and he played Doctor Astrov. She was assistant stage-managing, and had to rearrange certain things as part of the action on stage, hence her costume.

She had sex with him in a toilet backstage during Act 2, and got her foot stuck in a mop-bucket. Though she was young, she wasn't thick, and she knew that it wasn't Dick Whelan, actor, having it away with Arlene Morrissey, stagehand. It was Doctor Astrov going against his higher nature, compromising his socialism and fucking a Russian peasant, mentally exercising the natural order of things, long gone, long past. Power. Playing with power.

He treated her as that servant plaything. He wiped himself in her apron after, and she, instinctively knowing the nature of the game, said, 'Thank you, sir'.

They started having it off every night, at the same time during Act 2. They didn't speak otherwise, didn't acknowledge one another. Arlene suspected that Dick was embarrassed that she was so young, and was afraid that people would think him a cradle-snatcher. She wore no knickers, which made it easier for him to fumble among her petticoats and find her. He guided her, like a partner in a dance, manoeuvring her this way and that, and almost as though she had been trained, she followed his unspoken instructions. They did it every way permissible in a cramped cubicle, but he never kissed her. His favourite sex was fellatio. She knew this because he smiled and stroked her hair when she did it and wrinkled up her little nose at the taste. Tenderness, ahh! Self-sacrifice is its own reward.

On the last night of *Uncle Vanya*, Arlene accompanied the cast and the rest of the crew to a last-night party in a restaurant near the Quays. She wondered if he would say anything to her, if this would be the end of it, if he would see her again. He didn't treat her any differently to anybody else in public. She flirted with one of the teccies to try and make him jealous. Fat chance. He wasn't the jealous kind. He hadn't the requisite vision.

At about four o'clock in the morning, after umpteen bottles of wine, as he was sliding to the floor, she made a strategic intervention, propped him up and steered him towards a taxi and home to her flat in Stoneybatter.

The taxi driver helped her carry him in.

'Yer boyfriend is half cut,' he said, as the two of them hauled him indoors and the pale gray light of morning established itself in the sky.

'Thanks,' said Arlene, as she followed him out to pay him and tip him for his help.

'It's none of my business,' said the taxi driver, 'but I've seen that lad a lot, and he's always going home with different birds. You're a nice girl. I'm just warning you.'

Strangers in the street warned her about Dick Whelan. Even the dogs in her cul-de-sac didn't like him, and barked at him incessantly.

She tumbled him into bed, and he momentarily regained consciousness.

'Thanks, Olga,' he said.

'Who's Olga?' she asked.

'You're Olga, a Russian peasant of my acquaintance, who likes getting a blast of me from time to time.'

'I'm Arlene,' she said and smiled.

'Arr-lay-nah, a good name for a Russian peasant,' he mumbled.

'A Russian queen who is going to rule over you,' she said sweetly, as she slipped nakedly in beside him.

That was how it began. Arlene thought it was so cool. She thought it the coolest thing on earth.

the gardaí

Arlene came home to find two Gardaí on her doorstep.

'Hello, can I help you?'

'Yes, we're looking for Arlene Morrissey.'

'That's me.'

'Well we want a word with you about a matter.'

'Oh, Guard, I'm so sorry, I've been meaning to pay that fine for ages but I just haven't got 'round to it yet, I'm terribly sorry, it's just that I've been so busy and –'

'What fine?' asked one of them.

'A parking fine, wasn't it? Perhaps?'

'I don't know anything about a parking fine,' the same man – the older one – said.

'Oh, well in that case, neither do I,' said Arlene.

'It's about these phone-calls you've been getting. I'm Garda Ryan and this is Detective Sergeant O'Hanlon,' said the younger guard.

'Oh, you know about them? You'd better come inside for a moment.'

The three of them climbed up the stairs to Arlene's flat. The Cartwrights sounded like they were having a row. Voices were raised, and though it wasn't possible to make out the words, the cacophony had the unmistakable rhythm of a row, the up-and-down aural sculpture of discord. The smell of cat piss on the second landing was worse than normal.

She promised the Gardaí tea and put on the kettle. No matter what the weather was like, and today was pretty chilly, Guards always looked like they had too many clothes on. Sergeant O'Hanlon was about sixty and quite tall. Garda Ryan was less than Arlene's own height. He seemed all of five foot four. Must've joined the force after they'd dropped the ban on runts.

'So, tell me what you know?' said Arlene.

'Well, very little at this stage,' said Sergeant O'Hanlon, 'just what your friend Ms Coole told us.'

'Isobel was on to you?'

'Yes, she phoned us in Pearse Street yesterday morning, and said that you were too busy to deal with it, and had asked her to report it on your behalf. Some unknown person or persons making persistent nuisance calls.'

'Oh, right, eh, okay. I'm just a little surprised.'

'But I thought you asked her to call us?'

'Well, actually, not in so many words, but it's great you're here.'

'Can I ask you first, Ma'am, that Ms Isobel Coole that called us, is that the writer?'

'Yes, as it happens, yes.'

'The writer who's written *Candid* and *In a Corner*?'

'You've read her books?'

'Well, no, I haven't actually, but my daughter, who's twenty-one, is mad about her, thinks that she's the greatest thing on earth. Rosa, that's my daughter – my wife called her Rosa because my wife's family were communists – just loves her books, and is dying for the next one. They make her laugh out loud. She comes into the kitchen to my wife and me and reads us out bits, and they truly are funny. But true as well. Funny-true. Do you like them?'

Shit! Arlene would have to get round to reading those shaggin' books.

'Yes. She's a wonderful writer.'

'Rosa heard I was coming here tonight and asked me,' here he took out dog-eared paperback copies of each of Isobel's novels, 'would I be able to get them signed?'

Arlene was stunned.

'I'm sorry,' said Sergeant O'Hanlon, 'I can deny her nothing, it's just that she has leukaemia.'

'Sure, sure, give them to me. I'll see to it.' Arlene had a feeling that she was being taken for a ride.

'Thank you Ms Morrissey. Thank you. Now, about this caller?'

Arlene put the dog-eared novels down on the table.

'Well, I think the first call came about six months ago. I didn't pay much attention. I can't remember exactly what he said. It was just a crank call. Then, just recently, they started up again. There've been about seven or eight in all, and about four have come in the last few weeks.'

'And what does the caller say?' asked Sergeant O'Hanlon.

'Well, in the first few, he said things like: "Hello, I'm really embarrassed ringing you like this, I'm really embarrassed ..." and then the caller would hang up, but lately he's taken to discussing my person and so on, reported sightings of me and things like that. The last one went something like, "I saw you today on Grafton Street in your red dress, and it didn't suit you," or something like that. Insinuating, rather than threatening. There's a weird, apologetic quality to them. They are odd.'

'Have you any suspicions as to whom it might be?' asked Garda Ryan.

'None really. I have to say that the voice sounds vaguely familiar, but I can't place it.'

'Have you any enemies, anyone who would want to do you down?'

'Look, I'm a producer. I have more enemies than friends. I get to do all the pleasant jobs, like firing people, and hitting them over the head until they obey their contracts. There are countless people out there who could have it in for me. I remember one actor I fired, his parting shot to me was: "when I finally lose my marbles, I suggest you get a big bolt on your back door, because Hannibal Lecter is *my* part".'

'This guy sounds like a prime suspect.'

'Nah, I doubt it. He's a little kitten really, he's just got a big imagination, and thinks he's a lion. Remember, this is the theatre. Drama is conflict and size *does* matter.'

Sergeant O'Hanlon liked this woman. She was brazen. And she wasn't taking the whole business too seriously. It occurred to him that she probably hadn't asked Isobel Coole to call the police at all. He went on, in any case. Might as well investigate it, since they were here.

'Nobody at all you could point the finger at?'

'Nobody and lots of people. Most of the people I know are

62

a bit odd. It could be any of them, or indeed, all of them could be ganging up on me.'

'Any old boyfriends that you broke up with a bit messy?' asked Sergeant O'Hanlon.

'No, not really. I've had loads and all the break-ups were a bit messy, but none were especially messy.'

'Nobody in particular?'

'Nobody really.'

'And he always leaves a message, never speaks directly to you?' asked Garda Ryan.

'Yes. He usually phones during the day and occasionally at night but always when I'm out. I suspect that the objective is to leave messages, rather than to talk directly to me. There have been a few silent phonecalls late at night; you know, I've answered and the person on the other end says nothing, but I actually suspect a friend of mine, Carmilla, of doing those. She has a bit of a drink problem, and makes mad phonecalls in the middle of the night when she's tanked. I think she was mentally destabilised by being called after a lesbian vampire. Carmilla. She also rings my mobile. The weirdo only ever rings my piano.'

'Your piano?'

'Yes, my phone here at home is shaped like a piano. Look.'

Garda Ryan and Sergeant O'Hanlon went over to inspect the phone. Sure enough, it was shaped like a grand piano. Its keyboard was a series of numbers from 0 to 9 and the back part came away and became a mouthpiece.

'Ms Morrissey, you seem to me to have been subjected to quiet a lot of what I can only describe as phone terrorism,' said Sergeant O'Hanlon.

'Look at that,' said Garda Ryan. The object of his attention was the blinking light on the answering machine.

'There's a message. Shit, I forgot to even look at it when I came in,' said Arlene. She pressed play. Obligingly, it was the weirdo.

'Hello Arlene, I see your actor husband has reappeared. That's nice for you. Richard. I hope you're happy, but I'd watch my back. Click.'

'That's what they're all like. Very observational. Very short. Hey. How does he know that I was married to Richard? Not a lot of people know that.'

'Married? You never said you had a husband,' said Sergeant O'Hanlon.

'You never asked. He's an ex-husband.'

'Could it be him? In our experience, nuisance calls and general harassment of women frequently come from husbands.'

'I don't think so. I know his voice so well, I'm sure I'd recognise it.'

'But if he's an actor, maybe he's a master of disguises,' said Garda Ryan.

Sergeant O'Hanlon stared at Garda Ryan with an expression of sorrow. It was hard to get through any joint interview without Garda Ryan making some sort of a display of complete foolishness.

'Can we take this tape back to Pearse Street? We'll play it for the psychiatrist and see what kind of profile we get. Any more messages, keep the tapes and pass them on to us. We'll see about whether to put a trace on your line or not,' said Sergeant O'Hanlon.

*

After the policemen left, Arlene picked up the two thumbed copies of Isobel's books from the coffee table. They were both neatly marked Rosa O'Hanlon on the inside cover. She opened *Candid*, the first novel. It was dedicated 'To Dad'. *In a Corner* was dedicated 'To Conor'. She decided to start on *Candid*. She made herself a cup of tea and settled down on the sofa.

She had read precisely two pages, when the doorbell sounded. She went to the intercom and there in the little black-and-white TV screen was Isobel. Not smiling, but not scowling. Inscrutable, for a change.

'I'll be down in a tick,' she said, suddenly glad of the company. Funny that, Arlene who loved solitude, eagerly running down the three flights of stairs to open the door. She would have to get the buzzer fixed. It was ridiculous that she had to run down three flights of stairs whenever anybody called to the door.

Isobel stood on the doorstep, along with three suitcases, several hat boxes, a hairdryer and a small coffee table. From her left hand dangled an ancient teddy bear and with her right she proffered a bottle of red wine.

'I left him,' she said. 'That was the best piece of advice I've ever received. Thank you,' and she kissed Arlene on the cheek.

Arlene stared at her in horror. 'This stuff!' she said, surveying the assorted luggage and junk. 'You're thinking of staying here?'

'Just for a couple of days. I didn't phone you to ask if I could because I literally had no choice. I simply had to fling myself on your mercy.'

'But I thought *you* were supposed to kick *him* out?'

'Well, it was his flat, I couldn't really.'

casting nuala

'So what do you think?' asked Arlene.

'Yeah, it's *quite* OK.'

This might have sounded a bit lukewarm, but coming from Corinne Cooper, it was high praise indeed. Arlene had never heard her admit that she liked anything. Corinne seemed to think that everything was rubbish. Arlene often ran into her on opening nights where Corinne said things like: 'I feel like I am in the stocks, without the diversion or challenge of the tomatoes.'

'I suppose that you're interested in me for Nuala?'

'Naturally.'

'Another juve. I'm twenty-five, I still get offered juvenile parts.'

'That's because you're so young looking, and you should be grateful.'

'I'm never grateful for a part,' said Corinne.

'I didn't mean for the part, I meant to God for your looks.'

'Sure. But this kid is nineteen, I've forgotten what it was like to be nineteen. Do they still like lollipops at that stage? Have they started to menstruate yet?'

'I'll get you some appropriate technical advisers.'

'I do like the scene where she's saying the nursery rhymes, kind of like a mantra.'

High praise indeed.

'I have Richard Power signed to play the father.'

'What! Richard Power? You're kidding.'

'No, I'm not.'

'How on earth did you get him?'

'I have ways. He loves the play and wants to work in Ireland as a bit of a rest from the entertainment superhighway.'

'It is quite good. I read some of it out to my husband in bed, and even he liked it.'

'And the part? Are you really tired of juves?'

'Maybe this'll be my last juve. My last and greatest. Go out with a bang, and next year declare that I'll only consider mature characters who have a substantial past.'

'Great, great. Marcus will be thrilled. He said that you were the only one for the part.'

This wasn't entirely true. Marcus did like Corinne's talent well enough, but it was Isobel that was pushing. She had seen Corinne in something in the Abbey and had fallen in love with her for the part of Nuala. Arlene could see why. Corinne was tall and slim just like Isobel, and she had long straight black hair. From a distance, you could take her for the writer. Isobel didn't realise how transparent she was being, wanting a version of herself cast in the lead role of her play, but Arlene did, and reckoned it was the way to go. The spectacle of rampant narcissism held an attraction for Arlene, a singular beauty.

But there was one big difference between Isobel and

Corinne. Isobel's eyes stared at you with honesty. But Corinne's eyes, they had the quality of glass marbles, those instruments of barter and competition. They looked all right from a distance. You couldn't properly see the meanness in them; you mistook it for hunger. But up close, her eyes were scary.

'How did you get Richard Power?' asked Corinne, impressed, the eyes narrowing slightly.

'He read the play and said it was the best thing he had read in ages, and that he absolutely must play the part, so his agent phoned me up and solicited it. I agreed, obviously. One doesn't look a gift box-office star in the mouth.'

Marcus sulked for a couple of days after Corinne accepted the part. It wasn't that he didn't want her, he thought she would indeed be very good, but he was unhappy that she hadn't been his idea. He didn't want to agree, at least not too quickly, at least not without some semblance of a fight. That way, he could use the brownie points his reluctant acceptance had earned him as a tool for emotional blackmail when the next point of disagreement came up.

'Phew!' said Arlene to the wall, when Marcus finally acceded. 'He'll make me pay for that. There's no such thing as a free imposed casting.'

housekeeping

Arlene walked home along Baggot Street, happy enough with how things were going. She had two of the main parts cast, Mark Delaney (Richard Power) and Nuala Delaney (Corinne Cooper); she had three-quarters of her budget together, counting the Lunar Award and an Arts Council grant. Richard's being in the play guaranteed her the final quarter. His name opened doors. So she had little to worry about on that score. She just had to decide which one of her victims she'd target.

She turned down by the canal and allowed its leafiness to charm her. It was now late April, and the weather was beginning to improve. Even the ducks looked relieved as they quacked up and down. She took a detour up the canal to savour the air. She liked it best whilst the seasons were on the cusp of change.

She sat down on the bench beside the statue of Paddy Kavanagh.

'So how are you today, you big lanky culchie,' she said, and smiled at him. She was horrified to see that there was a dollop of birdshit dribbling down his forehead and into his eye. She pulled some tissues from her pockets and attempted to clear it up. She got most of it off, and then went over to the canal to soak the tissues in water for a final wash. She returned him to his normal dignity. He might only be a statue, but she was sure he didn't like being covered in birdshit. It was a bit of an occupational hazard for statues. Poor old Eros at Piccadilly. God of love and pigeon shit.

'Look at the ducks, Paddy,' she said, 'haven't they a great life?'

'What the fuck else do you think that I'm doing, sitting here immobilised? There's nothing else to look at other than the fuckin' ducks.' Communicating with this statue was one of Arlene's amusements. He was almost real to her. He nearly breathed.

There were little families of mallard chicks being closely guarded by their parents. The poor hen, thought Arlene, so dull in its brown feathers, while the cock caught the sunlight with its velvety blue head. How come these male mallards didn't run off, leaving deserted ducks to fend for themselves on social welfare? Just as she was thinking this, four cocks came floating down the river, happy as larry, looking for all the world as though they were off to the pub.

Arlene smiled at Paddy Kavanagh, and at his clean forehead and eye. The warm glow after this act of compassion filled her soul. She liked that. Kindness to statues.

She reached her building and went inside. She climbed the stairs with the spring of spring in her step.

'Hello, Arly!' sang out Isobel from the kitchen, before she appeared in the living room with her sleeves rolled up, wearing an apron. Arlene was convinced that Isobel got some sort of sexual kick out of wearing that awful blue 1950s-style apron. There could be no other reason for putting it on.

Isobel was still here. She had been here six weeks. She had graduated from the sofa into the little junk room, and her junk had been despatched to the attic. Arlene couldn't make up her mind whether she liked it or not. In theory, she didn't like it. Arlene Morrissey was always independent. But in practice it had its appeal. Isobel had appointed herself head chef and general house keeper 'to make up for my being in the way', and consequently, Arlene came home to magnificent meals every day. Also, Isobel had set up her computer in the junk room, so she disappeared after dinner to do some work, and generally, it was almost as though she wasn't there.

'How was your day at the office, dear?' asked Isobel. Irony in the eyebrows.

'Tiring, dear, tiring,' answered Arlene with a grin.

Tonight was Friday, and Isobel had cooked something particularly spectacular.

'A little aperitif?'

'Indeed, give us a large whiskey, with ice.'

'I got a bottle of wine,' said Isobel, 'and I was advised by your friend in the Deli. Martin? Is that his name? He seems to be very knowledgeable about your tastes.'

'I give him reports on the wines I buy. Consumer feedback! He's all right. A bit odd, but essentially OK.'

Arlene went over to the windows and threw them open one by one. They overlooked the canal, which looked beautiful in the evening sunshine. Isobel had taken to spring cleaning the apartment and she used a vast array of incredibly smelly polishes and sprays. She went to such trouble, and was so

71

obviously pleased with herself, that Arlene hadn't the heart to tell her how oppressive she found the 'bouquet lavender' or whatever it was called, so she stuck her head out the window, and breathed in the traffic fumes eagerly.

Isobel had even managed to get rid of the smell of cat piss from the hallway below. She had hired an industrial carpet shampooer and had hoovered the stairwell from top to bottom. Arlene kind of missed it now. Isobel was a demon when it came to smells. Even Arlene's slutty bathroom had been attacked with Jif and vigour. Her comforting hairs had been banished from plugholes; the bath gleamed with an almost venomous whiteness; her collection of bottles of shampoo with dregs in them had been thrown out.

'Arlene, why do you have six shampoo bottles with a quarter of an inch in each of them?'

'Waste not, want not,' she'd said lamely.

Into the garbage went the bottles.

Her tea towels were deemed a public health hazard and binned. The living room was hoovered to death, including all its innocent cobwebs.

'What about my eco-system?' protested Arlene. 'Those spiders eat the flies that come in in the summer when I open the windows.'

The furniture was moved, and the underneath of each piece was hoovered, the first time since Arlene had bought the carpet. Isobel had her beady eye on Arlene's bedroom, but here Arlene drew the line. She didn't mind the rest of the apartment becoming like a domestic theme park, an advertisement for Mr Sheen, but her own bedroom was going to remain like a dog basket. Whenever she left her bedroom door open, she could see Isobel looking through it with the slightly sulky expression that indicated how unhappy she was at not being allowed to get at it.

Isobel came back from the kitchen with two whiskies and a tray of ice. She had now changed the blue apron for a shorter pink one. Arlene stared at her. It had to be a kinky fascination with aprons, there was no doubt about it. If Isobel dressed as a perfect housewife, she might *become* a perfect housewife. Positive projections, or whatever it was called.

Arlene kicked off her high heels and put her feet up.

'Oh, by the way,' said Isobel, 'I think your weirdo called again today. I answered and he just sighed twice, and then hung up. I thought it was him.'

'Poor bugger. He's used to getting the machine, so he's probably deeply disappointed at having to talk to a human being.'

'I don't think your weirdo likes me being in the house. Those sighs sound very bitter.'

'Tough for him. And he's not *my* weirdo. How do you know that he isn't phoning every woman in the area?'

'It's amazing that somebody would do that. I've been trying to get inside that kind of person's head. I think I might explore the idea in my next novel. The idea of a person who is addicted to nuisance calls.'

Arlene stretched the length of the sofa, ignoring that remark. 'Thank God it's Friday. I'm going to take the weekend off, and get some real rest. How was your day?'

'Oh, fine,' said Isobel. 'I've been working away on the play and taking on board all of Marcus's suggestions. I think that it's really coming together now. Can I show you a piece?'

'Sure. I'd love to see it.'

'And you don't mind that it's Friday night and the weekend?'

'Not at all. Looking at your play is a pleasure, not work.'

'Now are you absolutely sure you don't mind because...'

'Ah, Jaysus, if you don't shut up I won't look at it.'

'Sorry,' smiled Isobel, and went out of the room.

Arlene glugged her whiskey. Aaaah!

Isobel returned, with a sheaf of papers.

'It's a new opening scene that I've written. I think that it's much better. I'll just go in and put on the sole.'

Isobel was a marvellous cook. And she cooked very healthy things. Poached fish with green beans. Free-range chicken cooked in white wine, accompanied by vine tomatoes. Never anything as vulgar as spuds. All low-calorie. She dropped the occasional hint that Arlene could lose a few pounds. She had thrown out the jar of bargain mayo from the fridge and now whenever mayonnaise was required, she hand-whisked it from scratch. She threw out all the tins which had been the staples of Arlene's diet – beans, mushy peas, soups. And she practically threw up when she found a tin of Irish stew lurking in the back of the press.

'You can't possibly eat *tinned* Irish stew?'

'I eat everything out of tins.'

'But it's full of E numbers and monosodium glutamate.'

'I happen to like monosodium glutamate. It's one of my favourite ingredients.'

Arlene hadn't seen a tin since.

One evening she had been so hungry after Isobel's poached asparagus that she went down to the chippy over the bridge to get a large single and a battered sausage with fried onions, just to tide her over. She hadn't the heart to tell Isobel what she was up to, but said that she was going for a walk. Isobel's cooking was lovely, but it was minimal.

She sat on Paddy's bench to devour her chips, licking the grease from her fingers with relish.

'Paddy, this woman is starving me. I can feel the weight falling off me.'

'You could do with losing a bit. I hate to see a person who is half woman, half duck.'

'Thanks *a lot*.'

On her way back, she saw a bunch of young people with purple hair who had recently taken to gathering in a secluded spot near the bridge to drink cider. How passé. Didn't these young people know that they were part of the E generation? Somebody should tell them.

Arlene took another glug from her whiskey and looked at the first page that Isobel had handed her.

Over The Moon
A new play by Isobel Coole
Copyright © Isobel Coole 1996

Act 1 Scene 1
The DELANEY household. Lights fade up on NUALA, clearing the table after tea. Her mother COLLEEN, and her father MARK sit at the table. Nuala is nineteen, her mother is forty-five and her father fifty. It is 1983. Nuala is dressed demurely in a long brown skirt and a grey sweater. She hums melodically as she puts things away. Mark regards her, admiringly.

Mark: Isn't it great for a father to be so bloody proud?

Colleen: More coffee?

Mark: So bloody proud. Yes, thanks, Mum.

Colleen: Yes.

Mark: First prize!

Nuala: Oh, Dad, stop going on about it.

Mark: I always said she was great. It's from my side she gets it, of course. My mother was famous in Sligo for singing. She was a soprano too. But never played an instrument.

Colleen: She's a great girl.

Mark: Aren't you glad I sent you to those piano lessons when you were a tot?

Colleen: (*Under her breath.*) T'was I sent her.

Mark: A great victory. The gold medal.

Nuala: I want to go to the pictures with Cathy tonight.

Colleen: Ask Dad.

Mark: Cream?

    Nuala hurries to get it.

Mark: The sugar. It's been put away.

    Nuala hurries to get it.

Mark: What's on at the pictures?

Nuala: *Rumble Fish*.

Mark: Never heard of it.

Nuala: It's American. It's got a general cert.

Mark: What's it about?

Nuala: It's a family drama.

Mark: More coffee.

          Colleen pours it.

Mark: All right love. But I want you tomorrow night
          for my fundraising meeting.

          He pats her on bottom.

Nuala: Sure thing, Daddy.

Mark: You are so talented, my pet. I am so proud
          of you.

          (You can hear the tears in his voice.)

*Nuala walks to the front of the stage. She slowly takes
off her clothes; first the grey sweater, then a white
blouse, to reveal a tiny sparkly boob-tube. Then she
takes off the brown wrap-around skirt to reveal a tiny
mini skirt and stockings held up by suspenders. She
turns her head upside-down and unties her hair from
its ponytail and backcombs it. She stands up straight
again, and her hair is wild. She applies dark red
lipstick.*

*She gets a pair of thigh-high boots from a plastic
bag stowed under a bush at the side of the stage. She
puts all her other clothes into the bag, puts it back
under the bush and walks to the front of the stage.
Here she is joined by CATHY who is dressed in a similar
fashion. A car can be heard in the distance. She sticks
out her thumb. Lights flash by her, and the car screeches
past.*

Nuala: Damn.

Cathy: Fucker! Your Mother sucks cocks in hell!!

Nuala: Sssh! He'll come back.

77

Nuala starts to hum under her breath. Cathy starts to fix her knicker elastic. Another car approaches. They stick out their thumbs. It screeches to a halt.

Nuala: Deadly!

Cathy: Leg it!

They run offstage left to get into it.

The two girls appear stage right, as though getting out of a car. They talk to offstage as though answering the driver who has given them the lift.

Cathy: No thanks. I'm meeting me fella and he's six-foot four.

Nuala: Thanks for the lift.

Cathy: Where would damsels like us be without knights in shinin' armour like you?

The car drives off. The two of them wave.

Cathy: Sap. Shit! I'm after ladderin' me tights!

There is a snap lighting change to EARLY EIGHTIES' disco lights. Music plays and the two girls start to dance, in an alarmingly aggressive manner, shaking their shoulders and displaying their sexuality and femininity. 'Love is a Battlefield' by Pat Benatar rings out.

'We are young, heartache to heartache,

we stand, no promises, no demands,

both of us lonely,

love is a battlefield.

oh, oh, oh, oh, oh.'

Hmmmn, thought Arlene. This was good. She liked it. More

78

immediate than the previous draft. It didn't have any pre-amble but immediately got down to business. More in your face. She sipped her whiskey.

'*À table*,' called Isobel from the kitchen. Then, 'So?' almost white. She was so nervous showing her work to anyone. It was amazing. This girl had so much talent, so much success, but was so insecure. As Isobel served up the fish, Arlene noted that her hand was a little shaky.

'It's great!' said Arlene.

'You like it?'

'Yes. It's super. It gets in there real fast, establishes Nuala as a Jekyll and Hyde kind of character from the off. It's intriguing and dramatic at once. It engages with the themes of the play much faster. Yup. Very good.'

'Oh, I'm so relieved,' said Isobel. 'Do you think Marcus'll like it?'

'Yup.'

Isobel beamed.

'White wine?' said Arlene. 'Why did you get white? I never drink white.'

'It's better with the fish, and it's better overall for you.'

'But I thought you said Martin advised you. He'd never recommend a white wine for me.'

'He said you'd like this one.'

Arlene sipped it. Hmmmmn. It was surprisingly nice. She smiled at Isobel and tucked into the fish.

'Have some green beans,' said Isobel.

'Delicious.' Isobel really could cook. She went to a lot of trouble and was a perfectionist.

'Isobel, can I ask you a question?'

'Sure.'

'Did you used to cook these gourmet meals every night for this Conor creature when you were living with him?'

'Yes. Well, I work from home, and I like to cook. I didn't do it for him. I did it to amuse myself,' she said defensively.

'Fool.'

'I said I did it to amuse myself.'

'I meant him.'

casting cathy

'She's dynamite,' said Marcus. 'And she's perfect for Cathy.'

'If she's such bloody dynamite, how come I haven't heard of her?'

''Cos she only came out of drama school a year ago.'

What Marcus really meant by 'dynamite' was that he'd taken a shine to some young thing just out of college and wanted to get to know her better. Arlene didn't mind this. He was good, and this was one of the ways he worked. Getting his cast to fall in some kind of love with him.

'Look, come with me tonight to Players, she's in a new play there about drugs or something. They improvised it themselves out in Ballymun on a community employment scheme and it's supposed to be quite good. If you don't like her, fine, I'll shut up about her.'

'Marcus. You know that I'm always wary of using somebody inexperienced. But, I'll take a look at her,' Arlene conceded. 'You remember your "find"? The schoolgirl from Bray who turned out to be a kleptomaniac and robbed every other member of the cast blind? She might have been useful as a props assistant, but she brought a lot of tension into the rehearsal room.'

'I know you're wary, but it's nice to give somebody their first break.'

Yes, Marcus, 'cos they're nice and grateful, thought Arlene.

'We were all young once, looking for our first break,' said Marcus. 'I'll never forget that you gave me mine.' Marcus looked into Arlene's eyes clearly and directly and then he smiled. She softened. He looked grateful, too.

'OK. Meet you in Doyle's at seven twenty. I'll bring Hedda.'

Marcus and Arlene had taken to calling Isobel Hedda, because of her tragic air, her cold Scandinavian hands, and her tendency to take everything seriously. Only behind her back though. Never to her face.

Arlene invited Isobel to come along with them. It would get her out of the house a bit. She tended to sit in her room a lot, didn't seem to have much interest in going out. Was strenuously redrafting the play; poking and prodding at it; being a perfectionist.

'Improvised?' said Isobel. 'What does that mean?'

'It means that the actors made the play up themselves, in workshops.'

'So there was no writer?'

'Exactly. The theatre has evolved to such an extent that the writer has become superfluous. We only have to do away with the actors, and we'll be laughing.'

'Oh.'

'And finally, we'll drive away the audience, and then we'll be able to stay at home and save ourselves a lot of bother.'

The play was called *Day Trippers*. It was a bizarre piece, incorporating slides and videos and dance as well as dialogue. Some of it was quite hallucinatory. Arlene wondered if they had improvised it *on* drugs.

Janice Murphy was Marcus's quarry's name. Marcus asked her to join them for a drink after the show. She was very hyper after her performance, and talked incessantly.

'Well done, Janice. A fine performance,' said Marcus.

'Did you like it?'

'Yes,' said Marcus.

'How much?'

'Well, how do you measure these things...?'

'I'm only kidding you,' said Janice.

Arlene looked at Janice. Youth. Blaring, unmistakable youth. It irritated her. It impressed her. 'What age are you?'

'Twenty,' said Janice. 'I finished at the Gaiety School last year.'

'And how's it goin'?' asked Arlene.

'OK enough. I did a Fairy Liquid commercial –'

'I've seen that!' interjected Isobel. 'That's the one where you're there with your Mum, and you both wash up after her dinner party, and then you give your boyfriend a massage on the sofa, and he goes on about how soft your hands are.

Meanwhile, Mum is upstairs giving Dad a massage, and he remarks on *her* hands.'

'That's the one,' said Janice.

'You're very good in it,' said Isobel, positively.

Arlene remembered the ad. Janice had been grand in it, but it was hardly a demanding rôle.

'I lived off the wages from that for four months, but I'm afraid I'm back working in a diner to keep the rent paid. But I suppose that's to be expected.'

Janice started to put the array of studs and earrings that she had obviously taken out for the show back in her ears.

'Where?' Arlene asked, brightening.

'Coopers in Rathmines,' said Janice. She put three rings into her eyebrow.

'They do kebabs, don't they?' Arlene was permanently starving these days.

'Yes, they do.'

'I've always wanted to know,' said Arlene, 'how do they make those big kebab things that go round and round on the spits?'

'Well, it's minced lamb, from the butchers down the road, and spices and herbs. The biggest ingredient is curry powder, and we pound it all together and build the big yokes up, and then they roast slowly, draining off all the fat. The reason the fat is so yellow is the curry powder.' Janice put a diamante stud into the side of her lip.

'Oh, that's very interesting.' Arlene had this odd way of being interested in everything. It was almost impossible to bore her.

Janice looked like some sort of alien creature now that she had finished putting on her bits and pieces. There was no part of her face that wasn't pierced. She went off to talk to her fellow cast members. They all had purple hair and bumble-bee-striped tights on.

'So what do you think?' asked Marcus.

'She's OK,' said Arlene. 'She's got those weird earrings and studs everywhere. Why would a person willingly stick sharp instruments in their face?'

'Arlene, I'm surprised at you being so conservative,' said Marcus. 'It's just a dress code.'

Arlene wasn't going to give in too easily.

'She must be out of her mind. She could burst a vein or puncture her optic nerve or something.'

'She was wonderful,' said Isobel. 'So young, so fresh, so vivacious!'

Arlene would let Marcus have Janice Murphy. But she wouldn't do it too readily or easily. She'd make him fight for it. Make him pay for it.

'I'm starving,' said Arlene. 'Can I have a toasted ham and cheese?' she said to the barman.

Isobel glanced at her and looked hurt.

'With mustard,' said Arlene, salivating enormously.

the real star

Arlene walked along the South Circular Road, and turned right into Hope Street, a quiet *cul de sac* with small red-brick cottages on either side. Her heels made a pleasant click on the pavement, a breeze darted playfully about her ears. Finally, at the beginning of June, summer had condescended to appear.

Arlene was on the trail. She and Marcus had reached a joint decision that Marcia Range was the only person to play Colleen, the mother, but unfortunately, Marcia was proving elusive. Arlene had called her several times, left messages for her, posted her the script, and had received no reply. She finally got in touch with Marcia's agent, Judy Corr, who suggested she call round in person, as Marcia was having a bad time at the moment.

Once she turned into Hope Street, Arlene's ears were assaulted by a very loud, but pristine recording of *La Bohème*, emanating from the open windows of a house further along. Accompanying the recorded 'Mimi' was a rather dodgy cracked soprano, which joined in in fits and starts. Arlene reckoned she was in for a time.

She knocked on the door. Nothing. She didn't think that she was being ignored, rather drowned out by the din inside. She manoeuvred her way with some difficulty past an extrovert rose bush and into the middle of a flower bed in front of the downstairs window. She peered into the gloom. There was nobody inside.

She climbed through the window and took a look around. Marcia had moved into this house about twelve months ago, but Arlene hadn't been in it before. It was so hard to keep up with old friends when they weren't immediately useful. The house looked small from the front, but became the Tardis when she got inside.

The door from the drawing room to the hall was open, so Arlene went through it. 'Mimi' seemed to be coming from somewhere at the back of the house. It was deafening. Arlene wondered how on earth the neighbours put up with it. She made her way along the gloomy passage, and found herself in a breakfast room. She went quietly through the kitchen at the far side of the breakfast room, still finding no sign of Marcia. The French doors out to the garden faced south-west, and were getting the full benefit of the afternoon sun. Arlene went through these, and there found her woman.

Marcia was sitting at a wrought-iron patio table, wearing a pair of Jackie O sunglasses and a long pink robe. She was looking wrought. Her long, flyaway, dyed-brown hair, was caught up in a theatrical looking turban. She had one of those bodies that – despite putting on a bit of weight at this stage – still gave the impression of leanness. Her skin had that lightly olive, Protestant quality to it, that you get in Ireland. On the table in front of her was an enormous ghettoblaster, blasting away. The song came to a close.

Marcia pressed the off switch. 'I would be dead without Puccini,' she said.

'I think your neighbours will be deaf with him.'

'They are all deaf. I live in a house numbered thirteen on a road full of deaf people. Do you want a drink?'

'Sure,' said Arlene.

'Scotch?'

'Sure.'

Marcia went into the kitchen. She didn't look in too bad shape. Her hair was set, her clothes orderly. She was such a drama queen. A declamatory female looking for a pedestal. The sort of woman who might fling herself on the coffin at funerals.

The garden seemed reasonably well tended. There was a recently stocked bird feeder hanging from a crook on a dividing wall, and an array of tits were having a munch. They were gas. They were performing this fascinating pageant, flying in a group of three up close to the feeder and landing on a rose bush nearby. There, they looked surreptitiously around, chatting innocently amongst themselves, as though they were minding their own business. Then, once convinced that no-one was looking at them they darted to the feeder, nabbed a peanut, and flew off at speed over the rooftops, laughing all the way. Cute, thought Arlene.

Marcia returned with a bottle and two glasses. She poured.

'I'm sorry I haven't returned your calls, but I've been having a bad time. I should never have moved into a house numbered thirteen.'

Arlene took a sip and shivered. The scotch was a bit rough. Marcia didn't seem to mind it.

'He's left me,' said Marcia.

'What?'

'He's left me. Ran off and shacked up with a twenty-two year-old in a bedsit in Fairview. Wants a kid. She's willing. I'm on the scrap heap.'

'But Marcia,' said Arlene, 'I thought the two of you didn't want kids?'

'No. We pretended we didn't want them. We just left it too late, 'cos we were so busy attending to our careers. We did try. I had two miscarriages, and that was that.'

'You never said.'

'No.'

'Oh.' Arlene didn't know what to say. She wasn't very good at dealing with this kind of thing. Miscarriages were so, so, so messy. They weren't her scene. Finally she thought of an aspect to the whole sorry story that she could comfortably interrogate Marcia about. 'Who is Miss Fairview?'

'I don't know. Some kid he met at a nightclub.'

'You mean he's been trawling nightclubs, at his age? That's sad.'

'He's only forty-two. Younger than I am.'

'But only by a couple of years. That hardly counts.'

'Three years,' fibbed Marcia. She was forty-eight.

'Never trust younger men.'

Marcia went to turn Mimi on again.

Arlene stopped her. 'Did you read the script I sent you?'

'No. I looked at the character description, and put, no flung, the script back in the envelope. Hold on, let me get it.'

She went inside for a moment and emerged with a brown envelope scrawled with Arlene's dramatic writing. She pulled out the script and read, in a flat, expressionless voice.

Colleen is a broken woman at forty-five. She feels her life has been pointless and arid. Her only daughter, Nuala, is a stranger to her. Her mind and body have felt the toll of her three subsequent miscarriages, and her related stays in hospital for depression. Her husband Mark is withdrawing from her and investing his energy and interest in other areas. Colleen Delaney is at a crossroads, and has to decide which road to take. Will she pull herself out of the hole she's in, or will she be sucked down deeper.

Arlene stared at Marcia, stunned. 'You're even more perfect for the part than I'd realised.'

'Arlene. I am so depressed at this moment in time, that what I need to play is Puss in Boots in a panto, not Medea in your new script by Isobel Coole.'

'Marcia. Please read it and consider it.'

'I confess, I have read some of it, and it is quite good, but terminally depressing. Not a play to cheer myself up with.'

'The team is good. They'll cheer you up. The emotional trawling of the play will be rewarding, if not cheering.'

'Hmmmn.'

'You'll be playing opposite Richard Power.'

'Richard Power? You're joking!'

'Guides' honour.'

'How have you got him?'

'Magic.'

'God. I remember. You used to be married to him, didn't you, when you were a young thing, and he used to be called Dick Lennon?'

'No, it was Dick Whelan he was called.'

'Jesus, yeah. That must be years ago now. We must be truly ancient.'

'Yes, Marcia, but keep that under your hat. Be a pet. Nobody remembers anymore.'

'I remember,' said Marcia. 'Have you guys kept up contact?'

'No,' said Arlene.

'It must be a bit odd, working with him now.'

'Not really,' said Arlene.

'How did you get him?'

'I just figured out a way.'

'Richard Power and Marcia Browne. My mother'll be thrilled. She's a huge fan of his. He's a big hit with the older women, you know. She can boast about it to all the neighbours.'

'Marcia Browne? But your name is Marcia Range,' said Arlene.

'No. That fucker who just walked out the door of this house, his name was Range. My name is Browne, and I'm reclaiming it.'

'But you can't. People won't know who you are. Your name is your trademark. Besides, Marcia Browne sounds terrible. It sounds like a cleaning lady. You told me that you decided to use his name in the first place because Marcia Browne was so awful.'

'I'm not giving him the satisfaction of still using his name.'

'How about an interim arrangement. Couldn't you at least call yourself Browne-Range, to get over the hump?'

the first day of rehearsal

August burst forth in sultry splendour. A hot, hot summer was melting into a parched and sticky fall, like a runny ice cream going down inside the sleeve of a jumper. Jaded leaves surrendered to gravity and drifted down, their corpses crunching underfoot. The baked red brick of the city suburbs groaned as temperatures fell through the night and even the ants, yes even the ants, commenced their annual retreat.

Over the Moon went into rehearsal on Monday 12 August, in a room at the top floor of an old shirt factory on North Great Strand Street. Marcia's high-toned response had been: 'I'm sorry, I can't possibly rehearse on the *North*side.'

Arlene had nosed out this building through her contacts in real estate. It was a beautiful space, bright, vast, airy. Lovely springy floor which was comfortable and safe to work on. There was air-conditioning there from the sweatshop days, ancient air-conditioning that groaned throughout the building like a malign ghost. It was also a good walk across town from her office, and she therefore wouldn't be bothered too much by irrelevancies. There would have to be a *serious* problem before anybody came whingeing to her about anything. But most importantly, it was *cheap*.

Arlene bustled into the room at ten o'clock sharp. She was an impeccable timekeeper. She looked around. It was the first time that she had seen Corinne and Isobel in the same room, and the effect was startling. They really were very alike. She wondered if anybody else noticed.

All the troops were assembled, except Ms Janice Murphy. Hmmmn!

'Good morning folks. Lovely to see you all looking so well, and where might I ask, is Ms Murphy?' asked Arlene, in her clipped, first-day-of-rehearsal, schoolmarmish, parish-priesty voice.

'It is only ten o'clock,' said Marcus.

'Yes,' said Arlene, 'and she should be here at ten o'clock.'

'She'll be here.'

'Mr Power,' said Arlene, 'has conveyed himself from London this morning, a matter of several hundred miles, and he has managed to be on time.'

The front door banged several floors below and rapid ascending footsteps were heard along with a chorus of, 'Fuck, fuck, fuck, bollocks, bollocks, fuck, fuck, fuck.' Arlene had had a bad feeling about Janice Murphy from the start. She should have trusted her instincts.

The door flew open and in burst Janice. Her hair was still wet. She wore a just-emerged-from-the-shower look, her hair hanging down her back in dripping rats' tails. She'd had time to put in all her ear-rings and nose-rings, though.

'I am so sorry. So *so* sorry. I got a truly terrible bus. It wheezed its way into town like as though it was on fifty a day, and then it sat down altogether in Rathgar, and we had to get off. They've renamed Dublin Bus CitySwift, a misnomer if ever there was one. I'm truly, truly, truly, madly, deeply sorry...'

'Shut up,' said Marcus in a kindly voice, 'and don't be late again.'

'Now we are all *finally* assembled,' said Arlene, 'let me perform some introductions. You all know me and Marcus, so let me present Ms Isobel Coole, our distinguished writer. Mr Richard Power, who will play Mark Delaney. Ms Marcia Browne-Range, who –'

'–Range-Browne,' interrupted Marcia.

'Range-Browne,' continued Arlene, 'who will play Colleen Delaney. Ms Corinne Cooper who is to play Nuala, and Ms Janice Murphy who is to play Cathy.'

'Hi, hello, hi, hi, hello,' chorused everyone, and hands were shook.

'And this is Candy Johnson, our stage manager, Neil O'Mahony our designer, Tiffany Roche our costume designer.'

'Hi, hi, hi, hi, hi.'

'So,' said Arlene, 'I have some parish announcements to make, and then we shall read through the entire play. I will then hand you over to the capable hands of Marcus, your pilot on the creative journey upon which we are about to embark. I will take myself off to my office, where you may contact me if you have any problems, which I hope is rarely, if not altogether never.'

Arlene smiled at the assembled troops. Her chickies. 'We start rehearsal today, obviously (little laugh). The rehearsal period will last over four weeks. We open on Wednesday the eighteenth of September in the Lunar Theatre, after four previews commencing Friday the thirteenth of September.'

'What!' said Marcia. 'We can't possibly start previewing on Friday the thirteenth!'

It was just as well Marcia was as good an actress as she was, because otherwise Arlene might find her quite tiresome. 'I have a terrible relationship with the number thirteen,' said Marcia.

'Well, that's the date I have scheduled, but I will note your worries and bear them in mind,' said Arlene dismissively. 'Cheques will be available in my office on Thursday afternoons, unless you come to me and make other arrangements, which some of you have already done. It is your own responsibility to pick them up, not Carmel's to deliver them. Oh, by the way, Carmel is the administrator I've taken on board for the show. You'll see her if you come to the office. Richard and Isobel, I want both of you next Saturday for PR. The monthly magazines always have to be done quite a bit in advance.'

Isobel lit up a cigarette. She was *so* stressed.

'I'm sorry, Isobel, you can't smoke in the rehearsal room,' said Marcus.

'Oh, I'm sorry,' said Isobel, 'but I'm very nervous about the first reading. Maybe I could sit on the windowsill and puff it out the window?' She went over to the window and flung it open recklessly. She had been showing signs of temperament for some weeks now. She threw a leg over the sill and balanced precariously on it, puffing the smoke outwards. But the wind was unfavourable, and blew it back in.

Arlene walked over to her and peeped out. There was a sheer drop of four floors below. 'Isobel, that looks very dangerous out there. Marcus, could you let her smoke just for this reading? Really, it'd be a bit sad if she fell out, 'cos you said there's one or two more scenes you want rewritten, and I do need her for that colour piece in *Woman's Own* next Saturday.'

'OK, OK,' said Marcus, feeling undermined.

Isobel made her way back to the table, satisfied. No victory was too small for her.

'Is it only Isobel who can smoke, or may I join her?' asked Richard in his most solicitous tone.

'No, go ahead,' said Marcus.

Richard lit up.

'Could I have one?' asked Marcia.

'I thought you didn't smoke anymore?' said Arlene.

'I don't really. I just smoke other people's.'

Janice lit up, followed by Neil and Tiffany.

'Oh, I'm dying for one,' said Corinne, taking one from Janice's packet. 'I'm going to take this one from you, Janice, without asking, because I don't want to burden you with the guilt of allowing me.'

'How long were you off them?' asked Janice.

'Three months,' said Corinne. 'My husband accuses me of poisoning the children, so I'm not allowed to smoke at home. He has threatened to get a barring order if I do, on the grounds that I'm doing violence to them. I have to hide behind the coal shed.' She shrugged.

'God, that's a bit heavy, isn't it?' said Janice.

Candy, the stage manager, went off to get the ash-trays which Marcus had previously instructed her to remove from the room.

Soon, great clouds of happy blue smoke were billowing up into the air. Arlene looked up as the smoke formed itself into various shapes against the dark-coloured ceiling. A fist, a horse, an unborn child. Random shapes. For a moment, Arlene was tempted, but she stopped herself.

'OK, now that you are all attached to your props, let us read,' said Marcus coolly, and then, recollecting himself, he beamed out a huge, shining, forced smile. Marcus, normally unruffleable, was feeling intimidated. He had never worked with anybody as successful as Richard Power. He wasn't sure that he would be able to take control of the rehearsal room.

Things settled down though, and people started to read aloud. It was exciting, this first reading, each actor getting a feel for the others. Richard was very low-key, barely interpreting the part, just reading. Marcia was giving it much more of a lash. So was Janice. Corinne took her cue from Richard, and read very gently. It was magical.

Isobel started to relax. Her nerves subsided, as she listened in awe to the actors bringing out a whole other dimension in her writing. She became so engrossed she forgot to smoke her cigarette and it burned away in the ash-tray, leaving a long round stick of ash. A cigarette cremated, rather than smoked.

the first evening of rehearsal

Arlene went back to her office at lunchtime, satisfied that the first read-through of the script had gone reasonably well. She beavered away for the afternoon. Things were getting hectic now. She was fighting with her insurance company who were slyly insisting on charging more than the quote which had tempted her custom. She was fighting with the bank, who wouldn't allow her to overdraw to the extent that she needed to, because her friendly bank manager was away on his holidays. August was the cruellest month. It was impossible to get anything other than an imbecile on the telephone. Only fools and half-wits worked in August.

The office hummed all afternoon. Five-thirty came and Carmel, the administrator, started to pack things up from her desk.

'I think, Arlene, that it's time for me to call it a day. My brain is feeling a bit fried. This heat!'

'Sure, Carmel, goodnight.'

Arlene looked at Carmel as she made her way to the door. Carmel was a Kelly girl. Arlene's favourite Kelly girl. It wasn't just anybody who could fit into Arlene's office as a temp, and she'd had other Kelly girls who had driven her to distraction. Carmel was a spectacular secretary. She could type at the speed of light. Knew her way around every sort of computer. Could even do repair jobs on them. Seemed to Arlene to practically have a degree in computer engineering. Was absolutely charming and confident in her dealing with people. And, was totally calm. Arlene wondered why she wasn't running a company, or a department, or a small republic, so mystified was she by Carmel's talents.

'Couldn't be arsed,' said Carmel. 'Don't like being in the same place for too long. Get sick of seeing the same faces. Temping suits me just fine. I'm the modern equivalent of the tinker.'

Carmel was a hippy in a suit.

'See ya tomorrow,' she said. 'Don't forget to unplug the computer and switch on the answering machine when you go.'

Gone, gone. Arlene was happy to have the office to herself again. She was used to it like that, and though she found Carmel particularly bearable, she was happiest alone. She crammed in another hour's work.

It was six-thirty. She had an arrangement to meet Isobel and Richard in Candel's restaurant for dinner at eight. Richard had arranged this several weeks ago, that he would take herself and Isobel out for dinner on the first day of rehearsal.

There was a gentle knock on the door. Marcia entered and sat down.

'Hi, Arlene, I just dropped by for a chat. We finished up at five-thirty and went for a drink, and I didn't fancy staying any longer.'

'How did the afternoon go?'

'Fine. It went very well. Marcus and Isobel seemed to be happy enough with it. The script really is good. Meaty. She's a very talented writer. I must read her novels. Have you read them?'

'No,' said Arlene. 'I must get round to them.'

Arlene put her finger on what was different about Marcia. She had lost a good deal of weight, and was wearing more figure hugging clothes than she used to. Single again, and there's no business without advertising. Arlene sighed.

'I wondered would you like to come and have a bite to eat with me?' said Marcia.

'Oh, well, I'm meeting Isobel and Richard for dinner at eight.'

'Oh, they never said,' said Marcia, faintly hurt.

Arlene would have been quite happy to invite Marcia along as well, but it was Richard who had invited her and Isobel, and it would be he who was paying for it. Besides, she knew she was being bullied, and wasn't going to give in to it.

'I'll have a scoop with you now,' said Arlene brightly, by way of compromise.

Cunningham's was quite quiet. Tea-time of a Monday. Not too much action. A few German tourists in a corner. Most of the regulars had shagged off for August.

They settled themselves in Arlene's usual corner. As the nineteen-twenties' glass ladies had aged over the last number of months, they had become friendlier looking. Twelve months of cigarette smoke had dulled their sharper edges. Put them slightly out of focus.

It was lovely and cool inside. 'I can't cope with this heat,' said Arlene fanning herself with her blouse. 'I'm definitely not moving to New York when the show transfers to Broadway.'

'I wanted to thank you,' said Marcia, 'for dragging me out of myself and offering me this. I know I was difficult, but thank you for insisting.'

'Hey,' said Arlene. 'Don't thank me. I wouldn't have done it if you weren't just right for the part. You thank me as though I was doing you a favour. I never do anybody favours.'

Marcia knew this wasn't true. Arlene hated, more than anything, being thanked. Yet, she needed, more than anything, to be thanked. Marcia knew this, because Marcia was an expert. She was an expert in the examination and interpretation of motivation and emotion. The science of feeling. The actors' science.

'OK, no more said,' said Marcia.

'Except occasionally I do people the favour of buying them a drink. Landlord!'

Sheila the barlady came over. Sheila was still here in August. She never took holidays. She had six kids, ranging in age from early twenties to teens, and they were spoiled out of their minds. They treated their hardworking mother like shit, came in to the bar and scabbed money off her all the time. Sheila adored them, was besotted by them, thought one was better than the next. Arlene wanted to give them a damn good clip around the ear. They should have a little more respect for their mother.

'A pint of the usual and?' said Sheila, looking at Marcia.

'Tomato juice and slimline tonic,' said Marcia.

Marcia most certainly was on a diet if she was drinking that

101

shit. Sheila went back over to the bar. Arlene watched her go. Sheila was about fifty-five, and had a slim and wiry body. Built for work. Boxer, the work horse. She seemed to have endless endurance, endless good humour. A smile constantly played around her lips. When Arlene's business really took off, and she was running a major empire of entertainment consortiums, she was going to hire Sheila. She wasn't quite sure what as, but as something.

'There's just one thing I'm a bit worried about,' said Marcia.

'What?'

'I don't want to seem egomaniacal, but–'

Here we go.

'–but I think that it's important that I get as many publicity opportunities as Richard and Isobel. I know she's a hot-shot and he's a big-wig, but I have my own little following. Small, but perfectly formed and faithful. I think I should be there on Saturday, for the magazines. They can do an "at home" piece on me. My house has recently been decorated. I'll look great in the white living room in my new green John Rocha.'

'Fine,' said Arlene. 'Two in the afternoon in my office on Saturday. I just didn't want to take up your weekend.'

'And–', Marcia paused.

What could be coming next?

'I notice in the contract we made no agreement about billing. Well, I would like it alphabetically.'

'Fine,' said Arlene, 'that's how I intended it. Well, yourself and Richard above the title, alphabetically, and Janice and Corinne below.'

'Me above Richard,' said Marcia.

'Well, no, alphabetically. Richard above you. P for Power. R for Range.'

'It's Range-*Browne*. That means B for Browne,' said Marcia.

'No. It's fuckin' R for Range-Browne. That's it.' So that was why Marcia had ditched the husband's name. To improve her position in alphabetical listings.

'Richard's name goes up top. I haven't dragged him over here at ludicrous expense to hide his credit under your new bloody stage name that nobody will recognise. You're pushing it anyway, with this new double-barrelled effort. Do you know that the typesetters charge me per letter? Richard's first, then yours. I don't want it mentioned again.'

'OK, OK,' said Marcia. 'Sorry. Didn't mean to nark you.'

This looked like a victory for Arlene, but in fact, it wasn't. The most Marcia had hoped for when she embarked on the discussion was to get her name above the title alongside Richard's. This she'd achieved.

'Let me buy you one,' said Marcia.

'OK,' said Arlene.

'Now, don't be upset,' said Marcia. 'Please don't be cross with me. I need to look out for myself. You know, I need to push myself professionally, 'cos, in this business, the big boys walk all over you if they get a whiff of doormat. I like having a reputation for being fussy about credit, because then, people are afraid to denigrate my credit in case I throw a wobbler.'

'OK,' said Arlene. 'Get me a drink.'

Marcia returned with the drink, smiling broadly, her hair escaping from its band. 'Marcus seems to be a nice little chap,' she said.

Oh no, what was coming now.

'Pity we have to have them.'

'What?'

'Directors.'

'Of course you need to have a director,' said Arlene. Jaysus. Marcia could be rough going at times. Everything had to be a fight or a drama.

'The theatre survived for centuries without them. It's a silly notion, imported from France via England.'

'Couldn't we talk about something else, other than the theatre?' said Arlene.

'What else is there?' said Marcia. 'My personal life is too tragic to talk about. There's nothing in the news. It's August. No news happens in August. People don't even declare wars in August. They put it off until their minister for foreign affairs returns from Biarritz. The news programmes have taken to reporting on the arts, for God's sake.' Marcia paused. She suddenly had an idea. 'Let's talk about you. Tell me about you.'

'There's nothing to tell,' said Arlene.

Richard and Isobel fell in the door of the restaurant half an hour late. Isobel was drunk. She really couldn't hold it. She was a scandal.

'Get some coffee into this woman,' said Arlene.

'Sorry we're so late,' said Richard. 'We couldn't get away. Isobel was in a major pow-wow with Marcus, and I hated to interrupt.'

'I love you,' said Isobel and gave Arlene a kiss on the cheek. 'Pardon me while I run to the ladies and screw my head back on.'

But she was charming.

'She's a bit of a whirlwind,' said Richard.

'Myself and Marcus call her Hedda,' said Arlene. 'So, Dick, how did the afternoon go?'

'Don't call me Dick. It's Richard.'

'Sorry. Richard, Richard, Richard. I'll drum it into my skull eventually.'

'The afternoon went very well. They're all great. Particularly Marcia. Hey! What a lot of charisma. And Isobel seems very energetic, very intense,' said Richard, nervously looking around. He looked like he was gumming for a drink, and was practically smoking two at a time. Arlene suspected that Richard might find Isobel vaguely trying. Isobel was the sort of person that people either fell for or they didn't. There were no half measures about her. In order to tolerate her excesses, you needed to be a little in love with her.

'Let's order,' she said, once Isobel had returned from the loo. At least this would give Richard something to do with his paws. Isobel looked less skew-ways now.

Once he had some stuffed mushrooms in front of him, Richard started to relax. Isobel as usual just picked at things. Arlene tucked in. She was starving, and had ordered steak and chips. Isobel had begun to despair of ever curing Arlene of her cholesterol addiction.

'That was a good day's work,' said Richard. 'I always find the first day of rehearsal particularly tiring. Here's to the show!' and he raised his glass of mineral water.

'Sláinte.'

'And to a very fine script, by a very exciting writer,' he said. Isobel bestowed one of her most brilliant smiles upon him.

'And here's to the finest actor in the land playing Daddy,' she said.

This was quite a mutual fan club. Interesting.

'I read your books, Isobel,' said Richard.

'Oh,' said Isobel.

'Well done,' he said.

'So, how much did you love them?' said Isobel, merry enough to make this remark.

'They're entirely wonderful. So, so dark. They're more satirical than the play.'

'Yes,' said Isobel. 'I found that the theatre is too honest a medium to be humorous in.'

'That's an interesting idea,' said Richard. 'What do you think, Arlene?'

Arlene was thinking that Richard was absolutely on his best behaviour, that he seemed instinctively to know how to charm Isobel, though they had met for the first time today.

'Uh huh?' she said.

'Miles away,' said Richard.

'Sorry, I was running over some old accounts. My concentration is always a bit dodgy when I've a show on.'

'Your fathers are all very odd,' said Richard. 'The father in *Candid*,' for example, 'being a weekend psycho-killer in County Kerry, and living the rest of the week as a typical suburbanite, even though he only has one eye. And the father in *In a Corner* having such a strange relationship with his dog, before getting cut in two by a speedboat. And the father in *Over the Moon*, my part, he is almost psychotic at times, a fanatic.'

Arlene perked up. 'In what way?'

'Well, in the way he makes his wife and daughter kneel down at six o'clock to say the rosary, for example.'

'But that was quite normal here for years', said Arlene.

'Yes, I know that, but somehow when you see it written down in black and white in the middle of the nineteen nineties, it looks like a chronic perversion.'

'Yes,' said Arlene, 'nothing like a bit of distance to give one a handle on perversions.'

Richard stared at Arlene. Isobel noticed.

'What is your own father like?' asked Richard of Isobel.

'He's dead,' said Isobel. 'He died over ten years ago, when I was twenty. Cancer. My first book is dedicated to him.'

'Oh, I'm sorry,' said Richard.

'I suppose losing a father at a relatively young age is difficult, and that might be why my writing reflects a paternal aggression,' blurted Isobel, uncomfortable with the question. 'Or maybe it's just that because he'd dead, I can write about terrible fathers, knowing that I won't upset him. Whatever about not libelling the dead, you certainly can't annoy the dead.'

'And your mother?' persisted Richard.

'She lives as a semi-detached recluse, sorry, a semi-recluse in a detached house in County Waterford,' said Isobel. 'I go and visit her every few months, but she isn't easy.'

'Oh,' said Richard.

There was silence for a while.

'My mother is still alive,' said Richard. 'She's eighty-seven and ga-ga and in a nursing home on the Southside. I'd lost contact with her for years, but when my father died eight years ago, I tried to make up with her. But it was kind of too late. She could never get the look of hostility from her face. I think she despised me for growing up. Or for not growing up. One or the other. Now, I just pay her bills.'

'Did you know her?' Isobel asked Arlene.

'Yes,' said Arlene and stiffened. Arlene hated any reference made to her previous intimacy with Richard. Isobel had previously squeezed a little information out of her on the subject, which had been surrendered with extreme reluctance.

There was another silence. Nobody volunteered anything else on the subject of parenthood. Arlene remembered Richard's mother. Nasty little woman. Had always looked at Arlene with an expression of contempt. Nobody was good enough for her Dickie.

the past II

Arlene had always wanted to be an actor. She had started stage-managing in the hope that she'd get a couple of little parts. She was going to acting classes in the evenings, and doing the occasional course at the weekends, in voice or improvisation, but she was having her major success as a stage manager. Talented twenty-one year old actors-aspirant were two a penny then. Hard-working junior stage-managers were in short supply.

Dick played parts for her amusement. He was hyper-energetic when he wasn't being lethargic, and sometimes she came home to Robert de Niro, once, Marlon Brando.

'Stella, you wanna play poker with me? One-eyed Jacks are wild!' and he dealt out the cards on the little kitchen table.

'Shore, Stanley, whatever you want.'

'But this is strip poker, Stella, so yaw'll have to put aside yaw good upbringin' and git down to ma level. How many yaw want?'

'Three,' she said, throwing in three cards.

'I'll take two,' he said, and dealt.

'Git us a Coke from ice box, Stell.'

'Shore thing.' She got up and poured two glasses of Coke from a large bottle in the fridge. She put copious amounts of ice in them.

'I bet one jumper,' she said.

'I'll see yore jumper, and raise yaw yore shirt.'

'I'll see yore shirt.'

He dropped his cards on the table. 'Four aces.'

Arlene dropped the accent. 'Ya shaggin' cheat ya.'

'You know what they say. Cheaty at cards, uncheaty in love,' he said, laughing. 'You owe me one jumper and one shirt.'

'No, you cheated, you're not getting them,' she said.

'Aw Stella, yaw not treatin' me right. Please.'

She took off her jumper.

'And the shirt, Stell, yaw raised me yaw shirt.'

'Yaw'll have to raise my shirt yawself, honey,' and she laughed loudly, and almost choked on the ice cubes in her Coke. He opened her blouse slowly and gently, but pretending to be rough. He fell on her young breasts and wanted sex.

It never occurred to Arlene that he was turned on by himself, not by her.

They played pool often, in a pool hall on O'Connell Street. It had started off as her idea, her way of taking him into a pub-like atmosphere where there was no drink. He took to pool with enthusiasm, fast developed the skill that comes easily to an addictive personality. She was tolerably good, but he soon outstripped her. This annoyed her. They were both competitive.

They played rounds of five, competitively, for sexual favours, the loser generally having to make the winner come with their mouth. It was a great laugh, a huge joke. Life was so sexy. Arlene looked at other people, standing at bus stops and so on, normal people, dull people, people who weren't living her super-cool life. It never occurred to her that she was arrogant. She considered herself simply superior.

Oh, life was a laugh.

Then Dick went through a quiet patch without much work, despite her efforts to hustle on his behalf. He always got moody if he was unemployed for a while. He became less playful. Did a lot of sitting and staring into space. Displayed symptoms of depression. She worried about him.

She came home one day to find him sitting in front of the typewriter. He said nothing in reply to her greeting when she came in.

She looked at the page of typing. *All play and no work makes Jack a dull boy*, was typed over and over again. Dick smiled at her with a wild look in his eye.

There was something familiar about the typed lines. *All play and no work makes Jack a dull boy.*

Suddenly she remembered.

Dick was holding a large axe from their toolbox, curling and uncurling his fingers up and down the handle, his knuckles whitening and unwhitening with the strain.

Arlene laughed. Uproariously. He really did look like Jack Nicholson in *The Shining*. She didn't believe that he was dangerous.

He stood in front of her with the axe, looking into her eyes. 'All play and no work makes Jack a dull boy,' he repeated, in Jack Nicholson's voice. He kept the look up for quite a while, his hair tossed over his face, just like Jack Nicholson when he used to have hair.

'You're the image of him.'

His throat muscles just tightened. He stared at her. 'Heeeere's Johnny,' he proclaimed, a huge bad smile stretched across his face.

'Stop messin', Dick.' Slowly she started to feel unsettled, her heart started to pound. She felt fear. And, as though sensing that, as though he'd been waiting for it, he put the axe down and laughed, and kissed her on the mouth. He put his ear down to listen to her heart, which pounded now with the same ferocity as it did after she came. He laughed, but not in a happy way. It was a dead laugh. She decided she'd have to find him a job.

He went through a very very bad patch then. He did a ton of auditions, and just missed a number of great opportunities. His temper got very raggy.

'They call me back and shortlist me for every job, and still, when the time comes, they offer it to some other cunt.'

'Dick, please, I hate that word.'

'It's just a word, like any other word. You never give out when I say bollocks.'

'It's a worse word than that.'

Just as things were looking desperate, when he had almost given up speaking or going out, he got a part in a show in London. He was all life and delight again. He had a great time over there; the show was a success, and he got rave notices. She went to visit for a while, and they set up in a fancy apartment in Covent Garden and went around the place like King Ferdinand and Queen Isabella. She got a stage management job in Dublin, though, and had to come home early. She worried if he would be able to manage properly on his own. She had taken over his life to such an extent that he was becoming increasingly incapable of doing anything for himself. She liked it like that. It would make it difficult for him to escape.

He came home thrilled with himself. He was on a high. She jumped on him when he came in the door, and ravished him. She had missed him terribly.

A few days later, she started to itch down there. She examined herself. 'I'm really itchy,' she said.

'So am I,' he said.

'I think we have crabs,' she said.

'So do I,' he said.

'And where might we have got them?' she asked.

'Eh, I don't know,' he said.

'You slept with somebody else in London.'

'Yes, I did.'

She calmly sent him off to a chemist to find a cure. Normally, she would protect him from the demands of life, but this time she put her foot down.

While he was out of the house, her anger rose. She could not believe what he had done to her. She had never been angry with him before, never spoken a harsh word to him. Now, by the time he came back with a green cream, she was hysterical.

'I feel filthy,' she said. 'Totally filthy, totally crawling.'

'You are crawling,' he said.

'I remember having nits in my hair when I was a kid. I didn't sleep for a week.'

'It's only a dose of pubic lice. They're just little fleas that were looking for a new home. Perfectly harmless.'

'And how do I know what else you've picked up on your travels? The lice are probably only the tip of the iceberg.'

'I didn't pick up anything else.'

'Jesus, there's lots of them are incurable. Herpes for one, and there's a new one called AIDS that kills you in weeks.'

'AIDS doesn't exist. It's a rumour dreamed up to whip naughty boys and girls into line.'

'How many people have you been sleeping with since we've been together? I'm sending you off to get checked out.' Arlene put her arms around her young body, in a hopeless attempt at protection from invasion.

'I wore a condom with this girl in London, but that doesn't protect against pubic lice. I don't have anything else.'

'You bastard,' she said, and howled.

'I never promised you I'd be faithful. This is the package. You either take it or leave it.'

'You bastard, you tramp. I never want you to lay another one of your filthy fuckin' fingers on me,' she screeched.

'All right,' he said. 'I'll keep my filthy fuckin' fingers to myself.'

'Yes, do.'

Arlene ran off to their bedroom and sat there and shook for a while. She contemplated throwing him out. But that was as far as it got. How do you throw out your whole life?

They didn't speak to each other for a while. They both used the cream, and it did its job. She was busy on a show at the time, and he had just started rehearsal for a film, so they were out a lot, and occupied. Dick stayed out later and later at night. Three weeks after, he was still chilly with her. Arlene started to panic. He was going to leave her. She shouldn't have overreacted to the bloody pubic lice business. He stared at her coldly when he came home at night. His expressionless eyes were like harsh slaps.

'I'm sorry,' she said.

'I'm truly sorry,' she said.

'How do I know you're sorry?' he said.

'I'm telling you that I am,' she said.

'I'm sorry too,' he said.

They didn't have sex that night. It would take a little longer to get over the revulsion. Arlene nearly cried. Her lovely sex life that she had been delighted with. That shiny special thing, was defaced, vandalised. It was like biting into an apple and finding half a maggot, an unseen worm.

That night, as he lay in the bed beside her, on his tummy, she got a blue biro and wrote on his upper back, 'This body is the property of one Arlene Morrissey. Trespass at your peril,' and she drew a little skull and crossbones beside it.

A few days later, he came home with a bunch of red roses. She asked him to marry her.

He burst out laughing. 'What on earth do you want to be married to me for?' he asked, stupefied.

'Because I've decided I want you. Will you do it or not?'

'But you're only twenty-one. You'll meet other men later.'

Arlene hated being patronised. 'Look, I'm not going to offer again. You either go for this now, or you forget it forever,' she said seriously, showing signs of the single-mindedness that would be so much a part of her nature as she got on.

'OK,' he said. 'Sure, let's get married.'

He'd grow out of his promiscuity, she thought.

They were married six weeks later: just enough time to put the advertisements in the papers. Because of the speed of the operation, everybody thought that Arlene was pregnant. Nothing could be further from the truth.

Because he was now hers, she dedicated herself almost entirely to promoting his career. She abandoned all her own ambitions to act, and put her energies totally behind him, continuing to take stage-management work, as it came up. She was his manager. She was his pusher. And he was her drug.

endings, happy endings

'That'll be three-fifty,' said Martin Campbell to Arlene, handing her a triangle of Roquefort, and smiling his huge smile.

She handed him the money, and smiled to see that the poster for *Over the Moon* was being displayed in the window.

'It's a lovely poster,' he said. 'I love the colour.'

'Yes,' said Arlene. 'I think it turned out OK.'

'So, I'm looking forward to the show,' he said. 'I'll be along with Aunt Isa, as usual.'

'Great, excellent,' said Arlene.

'Only a couple of weeks now,' he said.

'Yeah,' said Arlene absent-mindedly, and left. Martin was a real pain. He couldn't just sell you your slab of cheese or whatever. Felt honour-bound to chat to you every time you went into the shop, made you feel guilty if you hadn't the energy for small-talk. That was fine a lot of the time, but right now, she needed quiet. Her mind was totally occupied. She had an enormous number of things to attend to. Press had to be followed up. She had to do some major selling to the tourist market; September was still high enough season. Isobel had to be calmed down, she was at high doh.

When she got home, there was a message on her answer machine, from the weirdo. This was the first time she'd heard from him in ages.

'Hello, Arlene. It's a relief to find a machine here instead of the sorrowful mystery woman. One does get tired of human beings. Is she ever going to leave? Just watch yourself with her. Best wishes, from your well-wisher.'

The voice. It was uncannily familiar. He was becoming intimate now, calling her Arlene, not Ms Morrissey anymore. Hmmmn. She decided she'd better wipe the tape, because if Isobel heard it she'd go bananas. This weirdo seemed to dislike Isobel. Very strange. Arlene was very curious. It was the strangest thing ever, but she guessed that she was never going to find out. She put it out of her mind, because otherwise it would drive her demented.

It was six-thirty. Isobel wasn't home yet. The apartment seemed empty without her. She had brightened the place up quite a bit. There were fresh flowers in two vases in the living room. Isobel had an arrangement with one of the flower sellers on Grafton Street who gave her bargain flowers, and she frequently came home with great bunches that she got at discount. Cut flowers at cut price. She loved bargains. Everything was much tidier now, but everywhere Arlene turned she got pollen up her nose. It was like living with an opera singer.

Isobel had been here six months. Since February. The temporary arrangement had somehow become permanent. Isobel had made constant references in the first few months to flat agencies and newspaper lists, but she seemed to have given up all pretence of searching now. Arlene didn't know what she thought about the matter. She liked having Isobel around. She would miss her when she went. But she'd have to go sometime. Maybe she'd wait until the show went up and talk about it then. No point in unsettling Hedda at this stage.

She poured herself a glass of red wine, glad nonetheless of the peace and quiet and Isobel-less-ness to think a little. She closed her eyes.

Richard was behaving himself alarmingly well. He and Arlene had become quite pally. He seemed to be really enjoying the rehearsal period, loving his part, loving Marcus and everybody. He and Marcia spent a lot of evenings together; he expressing sympathy regarding her recent bust-up; she enjoying the opportunity to flirt a little, something she hadn't done in ages. Richard had become considerate and compassionate, openly thinking about other people's feelings. He seemed truly transformed, almost as if he'd had some training in niceness. Been to nice-school.

Arlene'd had no real love affair since him. The odd little dalliance here and there, like the Marcus episode, and various other little day trips into the territories of love, to the frontiers of fornication, but nothing involving any great psychic energy. She hadn't missed it, hadn't hankered after it. She wondered what Richard would be like now?

Then she stopped herself and gave herself a good sharp slap on her wrist. What nonsense. If she had any more ideas in that direction, she'd give herself more than a slap. Her instincts told her that Richard's conversion was well dodgy.

Isobel came through the door. Glowing. She seemed invigorated by the rehearsal period. She looked wired all the time now. She had a new energy.

Arlene poured herself another glass of wine. 'Do you want some?' she asked.

'Yes,' said Isobel. She sat on the sofa. Then stood up and paced the room nervously. She sat down again. She stood up again. Arlene knew that Isobel wanted to discuss something, but didn't want to bring it up herself. Arlene decided not to ask her but smiled inwardly at her discomfort.

Finally, she gave in. 'What's the matter?' she asked, handing Isobel a glass of red wine.

'I'm getting huge hassle from everybody about the ending of the play. Nobody likes it. Marcus doesn't like it. Richard doesn't like it. Marcia doesn't like it. What do you think?'

'I like it,' lied Arlene, 'but I try to be as hands-off as possible and let Marcus get on with it. At the end of the day, the script is yours, so you have final say over it.'

'Well, I find that Marcus *says* that my opinion is the bottom line, but then he doesn't listen to what I'm trying to get into his fat head.'

Oh, dear. This didn't sound too good. Isobel was very gnarly.

'He seems like a bright boy, but he is simply deaf to what I am trying to explain to him, and my only possible conclusion is that he is thick.'

Isobel was in a temper. Harsh words from Isobel were rare. Marcus must have really pissed her off.

'Do listen to Marcus, but don't be bullied by him. What does he say?'

'Well, he says that it's melodramatic.'

'And the others?'

120

'Richard doesn't believe that his character would do that. But then, he's interpreting him in a softer way than I intended. He's made Mark Delaney into a nicer person. I've said this to Marcus, but Marcus says I should let Richard explore the positive aspects of the character for the moment, and he'll pull him into line in time. But that was two weeks ago, and Mark Delaney is still a joy to all who know him.'

'Oh, this sounds like trouble.'

'Mark Delaney, as he is now being played by Richard, is such a gentleman, that I can fully understand Richard saying that he wouldn't do what the script says in the final scene. But if he was playing Mark Delaney right, he'd do what's in the final scene, and worse.' Isobel's voice had become very angry.

'Look, don't get yourself into a state about it, Isobel. It's natural that there are some problems. Things were going far too smoothly. I was getting nervous.'

'Richard himself is such a softie, he doesn't seem to have any real concept of negativity and evil.'

'Oh, I'm sure, if pushed, he'd manage to wrap his faculties round those negative concepts.'

'I'm not sure he's right for the part. We might have to fire him, like you said.'

Shit. Isobel was really at high doh. Firing actors was all very well, but they couldn't fire Richard Power. Arlene's firing homily didn't apply to international stars. She topped up Isobel's glass, hoping this might calm her down.

'Have you explained all this to Marcus?'

'No. Not properly. I've tried to get it across, but I tell you, he's not listening to me.'

Oh dear. Communication seemed to be breaking down.

'Maybe, would you come with me to talk to him? I don't think he takes me altogether seriously,' said Isobel, almost in tears.

'That's ridiculous. Of course he does.'

'Look, will you come and talk to him with me.'

'Well, I can't appear to take sides. But we'll see.'

A row. There was always a row. Arlene had yet to produce a show where a row didn't happen. This looked like it was boiling up to be a bruiser. A regular tornado.

showdown

Arlene climbed the four flights of stairs to the rehearsal room on North Great Strand Street. Marcus had asked her to come in and watch an entire run of the play. There was two weeks to go to the first preview, and he wanted to get all final script changes done over the following weekend.

The row that had been brewing was now imminent. Isobel was getting moody and defensive about her ending. Marcus was getting stroppy and hysterical. Richard was being all things to all men, trying to keep both Isobel and Marcus happy, and succeeding only in annoying them both. But in the last few days, he had started to slither over to Marcus's side.

Janice came down the stairs and grinned at Arlene.

'Hiya, Arlene. It's great you comin' in today, we really need a fresh eye. We're dying to see what you make of it.'

'Happy to do so,' said Arlene, trying not to stare at the new yellow ring through the girl's lip. 'How is it going?'

'Oh great,' said Janice. 'It's brilliant. I love it. I think it's going to be great.'

'Great'. The single most used word in Janice's vocabulary, if that was not too expansive a term for the number of words she used.

'What's going on at the moment up there?' asked Arlene.

'We're on a break. Marcus is out looking at some furniture in a warehouse somewhere. Candy is out getting a sandwich. Richard and Marcia are upstairs, just chatting. He's brilliant.'

'Who?'

'Richard Power, he's just *great*. I don't believe I'm working with him.'

'You better believe it, kid.'

'I've never met anybody like him. So much *charisma*.'

'Oh.'

'I'm going out to get a bottle of water. Frog,' she said making a face that indicated a sore throat, and with that she bounded on down the stairs. Arlene went on up. They always succeeded in winding her. She wasn't twenty-one any more.

She went into the rehearsal room, and saw Richard and Marcia sitting in the corner together. They seemed to be talking intently and didn't notice Arlene come in.

'I saw you looking at her,' said Marcia.

'Well, I am entitled to look at her. You are imagining things if you think that there is anything improper in my looking at her,' said Richard.

'Not while you sleep in my bed.'

What! Arlene couldn't believe her ears. Richard, sleeping with Marcia?

'Well, I'll stop sleeping in your bed. You are clearly deranged.'

'You've changed so much,' said Marcia, very meaningfully. She lifted up a hand to stroke his face.

'I haven't changed.'

'You have. When I knew you first, all those years ago, I used to watch you from a distance, and I thought, here was a man of genuine principle. Now, you've turned into a machine, no feeling.'

'I don't know who you think you are, woman, talking to me like that. I don't know what has come over you these days. You haven't been right since your last miscarriage. But what you forget is that it was my baby too.'

What? Richard had been the father of one of Marcia's miscarriages? Arlene thought they hadn't seen each other for ten years. She felt suddenly sick, shocked.

Richard stood up. 'You have always behaved as though it was just you that suffered loss,' and he walked over to Marcia's side. 'But remember, the one thing I wanted in life was a son.'

The penny dropped. They were running lines from the play. Arlene's heartbeat slowed down.

'And we lost three babies. Maybe three sons.'

'But we have Nuala.'

'I know. And I don't undervalue Nuala. But my pain has to be allowed too.'

'I wish I were back at home again, and you and I were just walking out under the stars, and us over the moon, and before us stretching our whole lives, like a magic carpet with different patterns. It just hasn't happened the way I though it would,' Marcia said, her voice cracking.

'I've disappointed you, everything I touch turns to death,' and Richard's voice cracked too.

Totally hammy, thought Arlene. Totally overacted. She hoped that Marcus wasn't encouraging them in this caper.

They appeared to have reached a pause.

'Hi, guys,' said Arlene.

'Oh, God, Arlene, I didn't see you come in,' said Marcia. 'We were just running some lines.'

'Hi,' said Richard.

Richard and Marcia looked at each other and then blushed.

'We were overdoing it a bit,' said Marcia. 'Frankly we were hamming it, but, it's very enjoyable. There's nothing more enjoyable for the actor, and excruciating for the audience than performing without restraint.'

'Too true!' said Richard.

This pair were obviously getting on all right.

'God, what I wouldn't do for a decent, over-the-top, Victorian melodrama. Once in a while. All this realism is *killing*,' Marcia proclaimed.

'Where's Marcus?' asked Arlene.

'Oh, out and about, attending to things,' said Marcia. 'Doing his little job jobs.'

There was obviously no love lost between Marcia and Marcus.

'By the way,' and Marcia handed Arlene an envelope and a little package. 'Happy birthday.'

'How, in God's name, have you remembered my birth date? I'm amazed,' said Arlene.

'I just remember, because I care so deeply about you.'

Arlene opened the gift. A little set of fruit flavoured soaps. 'I hate my birthday,' she said, 'but I do thank you for the gift.'

Richard shuffled a little uncomfortably. He had spent several birthdays with her.

Marcus appeared. 'Hello Arlene, you're a pet for coming in. Oh, a present. Whose birthday?'

'Arlene's,' said Marcia.

'Happy birthday!' said Marcus. 'Damn, I forgot it. How ancient are you?'

'OK. That's enough birthday. I don't want another word about it.'

'We'll get started at four sharp,' said Marcus. 'I have the lighting designer coming in as well. Where is everybody?'

With that, Janice and Corinne came in the door.

'So, we'll run the entire show, pausing at the interval, as normal, so people can have a cup of tea. Please be careful with pace, as I'll be timing the show and will need to get accurate readings. Will everybody be able to do it without scripts?'

'Sure,' said Marcia, 'with perhaps the odd prompt from Candy,' she smiled at Candy.

'I'm sorry,' said Janice, 'Can I keep the book in my hand until after the weekend? I meant to learn lines in the evenings this week, but I've had to work because everybody in the restaurant has gone sick, and they were desperate. I'm sorry, sorry.' Janice's lip quivered a little, having the disturbing effect of sending her lip ring bobbing up and down.

Oh no, thought Arlene. Janice is obviously a total flake. She'll be dropping lines like confetti all through the previews, and will finally learn them for opening night, after Arlene threatens her with violence.

'I'm afraid I can't learn them for you,' said Marcus, in the patronising-but-hurt tone that he reserved for just this sort of occasion. 'Otherwise I gladly would.'

'I promise,' said Janice, 'that I'll be off book on Monday.'

'Fine,' said Marcus, 'There'll be trouble if you aren't.' He was obviously getting tetchy too.

Everybody got into position. Candy set up the furniture and props and the run was about to commence.

'Where's Isobel?' asked Marcus.

'I don't know,' said Arlene.

'I assumed she would come along with you.'

'Well, I assumed she'd be here.'

'That's a bloody nuisance. I really wanted her to be here to look at that bloody final scene.'

'We'll wait for her.'

'I can't. We have to be finished by six. Janice has to be at her restaurant by six-thirty.'

'Sorry,' said Janice and grimaced. She knew she wasn't going down well at all with Arlene.

'Well, I need the run anyway. Shit! It's very annoying when people are not being cooperative.' Marcus was showing definite signs of wear and tear.

'Look,' said Arlene. 'Just run the show. I'll look very closely at the final scene, and we'll talk to Isobel later.'

The run went very well. Richard was truly magnetic. Marcia was forceful. Janice was indeed very good. Arlene mellowed towards the little waif. Her ridiculous hair and rebellious nose-rings looked great when she was Cathy. And she had all the exuberance of youth, an energy, a spirit that cannot be faked. A naked optimism. A clear belief in the future. She played and was a young person who thought that life would be fair to her, would give her the opportunities that were her birthright. Arlene was touched by her performance.

And Corinne was stunning. Totally stunning. When she acted, she seemed to switch off her hardness. She took Arlene's breath away. The depth of feeling she brought to bear as Nuala was amazing. The character had risen up from the page, like a phoenix. No, like a soufflé. No, like steam from tarmac after a shower on a sunny day.

When they got to the contentious scene, Arlene opened her script and followed it as performance and occasionally throwing an eye down onto the page.

Act 3, Scene 5

Nuala Delaney sits at the kitchen table. She stares blankly out front, occasionally, compulsively scratching her neck and her arm. Mark Delaney comes in, and shuffles round the kitchen. He wants to speak, but cannot open his mouth. This stiffness and shuffling continues for a while, then finally:

Mark: Tea, Nuala. I'd like some tea.

Nuala: Make it yourself. I'm leaving this house of horrors.

Mark: While you're in this house, you'll do as I say.

Nuala: Fuck off.

Mark: Gutter language. Where did you learn that? From that little prostitute I've seen you with?

Nuala: Leave her out of it.

Mark: Do you realise that everybody knows?

Nuala: Of course they do. But you can't blame me for that.

Mark: No. I don't blame you for everybody knowing. But I do blame you for doing it.

Nuala: You've never let me grow up.

Mark: Are you surprised? When this is what you get up to. I can't believe it.

His voice breaks and he puts his hands to his face.

Mark: You went straight from singing 'Ave Maria' at our Right to Life fundraiser onto an aeroplane to murder your own child.

Nuala: It was not a child. It was a squidgy red blob!

Mark: It was a human life.

Nuala: We're talking different languages here. It was not a child. What's important is a woman's right to choose, a woman's right to exercise jurisdiction over her own body.

Mark: Where did you learn that devil talk? And the referendum only a week away. All those photographers! Your forked tongue. Oh you are not my child.

Nuala: You pretend to be so holy, but I've seen you looking at me.

Mark: Devil's tongue.

Nuala: Looking at me in the way you should have been looking at my mother.

Mark: Stop trying to deflect attention from yourself.

The scene was going along nicely. Both Richard and Corinne were being very persuasive. Arlene looked over at Marcus, and he had an expression of pure concentration on his face. Poor Marcus. She knew that he concentrated so hard that it hurt.

The scene was building very nicely. Then, a loud noise as

(Richard) Mark Delaney banged both his hands against the table and bellowed. He was very good. A vast array of possibilities were created. There *was* danger there, but it was overridden by compassion. Arlene was shocked at how suddenly her admiration for his talent overcame her. His craft, his wizardry.

He went over to his daughter and grabbed her by the hair. Then he stopped, frozen, and said nothing for a moment. Arlene wasn't sure if he was still acting. He sat down on the floor.

'I'm sorry, it just doesn't feel right. I cannot do this scene until it feels right.'

'Sorry,' said Corinne, 'was I not being brazen enough? Marcus, eh, maybe, if I could crank up the brazenness, then he might be more goaded into it?'

'No Corinne. You are plenty brazen. I don't see you getting any more brazen.'

'I'm sorry,' said Richard. 'I've ruined the run. I'm sorry, Marcus, I'm sorry, Arlene. I've buggered the whole thing up.'

'No, Richard, it's not your fault. It just isn't right,' said Marcus. 'We have to fix this damn scene. Where the hell is Isobel?'

nee-naw

They all went into the pub down the street for a Friday-night-after-rehearsal scoop. All except Janice who had to run off to her restaurant, and Corinne who had to run home to her kids. And Candy, who had a Friday-night date.

'Oh, well, I have to run home to juniors. I can't wait till they're grown up and I can go back to being a juvenile delinquent, when I'm in my forties,' Corinne had said, gleefully.

'Don't knock them. It's great that you have them,' Marcia had replied, with a pained expression. Marcia had this knack of making everybody's life relevant to her own pain.

Corinne had gone beyond feeling sorry for Marcia's childlessness. They'd all heard about her husband and the young one from Fairview. The first time she heard the story, she had been sympathetic, but on the fifth telling, she'd got a pain down the side of her face faking a pitying expression. Marcia gave her the pip.

It was a nice little dark bar, unsullied by the influence of modernism or hygiene. Nobody mentioned that Isobel was still missing. She had disappeared. Arlene discreetly phoned her home number on her mobile, but just got the machine.

She wondered where else to try? Isobel's old number? Perhaps she'd run back to Conor.

Marcus sat in the corner sucking his orange juice and looking profoundly miserable.

'Well, it went very well, except for the end bit,' said Marcia, smiling weakly.

'I'm sorry,' said Richard.

'Don't worry about it. Hey! We've still got two weeks,' said Marcia.

There was a silence for a while. Everybody sipped their drinks.

'It was a very intense time, were you still here, Richard?' Marcia continued, brightly.

'When?' said Richard.

'1983. Around the time of the *Right to Life* anti-abortion campaign.'

'Yes,' said Richard, 'I didn't leave Ireland until 1984.'

'Do you remember the little gold feet that people used to wear on their lapels?'

'No,' said Richard.

'Oh, you must remember them. They were about this size,' and she indicated a centimetre with her thumb and forefinger. 'They were supposed to be replicas of an unborn child's feet at nine weeks'.

'I remember them,' said Marcus. 'My mother wore them.'

'This country was kind of hysterical, it was scary, anything was possible,' said Marcia.

'And you're saying that I'm not getting this in my performance,' said Richard, paranoid and defensive.

'God, no! I'm only making conversation. I'd never pass a

remark on a fellow artist's work,' said Marcia, getting defensive as well.

'But you think it anyway. You wouldn't pass a remark, but you'd insinuate one,' said Richard.

Richard appeared to be losing his rag. Arlene was surprised. Not a glimpse of his old temper had been witnessed since he'd reappeared in Dublin. Everybody was very tense. Things were looking a bit gnarly.

'Oh, for God's sake,' said Marcus, 'stop making a problem out of nothing.'

'I think Marcia should apologise,' said Richard.

'I didn't do anything,' said Marcia. 'I can't apologise when I haven't done anything.'

'Look,' said Arlene. 'I think we're all a little up-tight.'

'I want an apology,' said Richard.

'I'm not giving in to his tyranny,' said Marcia.

'Look!' said Arlene. 'We're all a little tense. The problem is that Isobel's disappeared. I know that's what's getting to all of us. But there's no point in taking it out on each other. I promise we'll have her back on side by Monday. She's hyper-sensitive. I'm surprised she hasn't thrown a wobbler before this.'

Arlene's mobile rang. 'I bet that's her,' she said, and she snook off to a corner to answer the call.

'Yes?'

There was silence for a minute.

'Arlene?' came a whisper.

'Isobel, is that you?'

'Yes.'

'Where are you?'

'I'm in your bathroom. I've just cut my wrists.'

'What! I'm on my way. I'll call an ambulance.'

'I've changed my mind, and I don't want to die,' came the whisper. 'Please save me.'

'OK, I'm coming.'

Arlene phoned 999 on her mobile and called an ambulance. She told them to ring the bell on the Cartwrights' apartment, and they'd be let in, but to break down the door if necessary. She gathered up Marcus, Richard and Marcia and they headed out into the street to find a taxi. Richard hailed one and they jumped in as he gave the driver the address.

'And please hurry. It's a matter of life and death,' said Arlene.

'I'm sorry love, it's only so fast I can go. The whole city is dug up. They never finish with the digging. I often wonder are they doing it for the fun of it. My wife, now, she's after going back to work now that the kids are raised, and she's working for the Corpo and –'

A chatty taxi driver! Arlene was not able for this at all. Richard chatted politely back to him, relieving the others of the burden. They approached the canal and turned into Arlene's street. Outside her building were parked an ambulance and a squad car.

Arlene jumped from the taxi while it was still moving, and ran over to the ambulance. Sergeant O'Hanlon, her phone call investigator, was there. Two paramedics were carrying a stretcher out of the building.

Richard, Marcia and Marcus followed her.

'Me fare! What about me fare!' said the taxi driver. Quite a reasonable demand, when you thought about it.

Richard ran back to pay him.

'That'll be five pound even,' said the taxi driver. 'I've given you twenty pee off, on account of the emergency.'

'Very generous,' said Richard. 'Do you take plastic?'

'Not on your nelly,' said the taxi driver.

'Marcia, have you any money?' called Richard.

Marcia came back to the taxi and took out her purse. She handed the taxi driver a fiver.

'Keep the change,' she said, imperiously, not realising there wouldn't be any. There was something innately grand about Marcia.

'I'm sorry about back there in the bar,' said Richard to Marcia. 'I was being paranoid. I think I smelt trouble in the air.'

'S'okay' said Marcia. 'Let's hope Hedda's all right.'

Sergeant O'Hanlon put his hand on Arlene's shoulder.

'She'll be all right,' he said. 'They got here in time, and she had missed the vein on her left wrist. Gave herself a nasty flesh wound all the same. They'll probably only keep her overnight for observation.'

Arlene went over to Isobel's side.

'I'm sorry,' said Isobel. 'I'm afraid I'm weak. You know when you plant saplings together, and some grow big and strong, and others don't thrive. Even though the soil's the same and they look the same in the beginning. I'm one of the weak ones. One of the ones that doesn't ever feel the sun on its branches.'

'Oh, Isobel, don't say that. You really are a stupid bitch,' said Arlene gently, but thinking, what a corny image, saplings. Isobel often expressed herself in bad metaphors.

'Thanks for saving me, Arlene. I changed my mind the minute I thought of you.'

The ambulance men carried her into the ambulance, and whisked her away.

'Will you be all right?' asked Sergeant O'Hanlon.

'Sure,' said Arlene. 'I have some friends with me. Sergeant O'Hanlon, would you and your daughter Rosa like to come to the opening of the play?'

'Love to,' he said.

'I'll send you tickets,' she said.

Arlene invited the others into the apartment and there Marcia took charge.

'Richard! I want you to go into the kitchen and make stiff hot whiskies for everybody. I'll attack the bathroom,' said Marcia. She put on rubber gloves and went in. It was covered in blood. She got out the bleach and the Dettol and started scrubbing. It was dirty job, but somebody had to do it.

'What'll we do about the final scene?' asked Marcus. 'I don't mean to be callous, but it is important, to Isobel as much and more than any of us.'

'I don't think that you're callous. I think *she*'s callous,' said Arlene.

In the rush of adrenalin caused by the emergency, Marcia had forgotten that she was squeamish about blood. Her stomach started to churn.

'The problem,' said Marcus, 'is that I'm afraid that I've been putting too much pressure on her. I don't want to be the cause of her going off the deep end.'

'Don't worry, Marcus, she's more resilient than you think. She constructs her own psychodramas. That is why she is a good dramatist.'

Marcia threw up, violently and noisily, into the toilet bowl.

She felt a bit better after that and continued with her scrubbing. There was blood everywhere in the otherwise immaculate bathroom. She'd never seen this amount of blood since *The Shining* with Jack Nicholson. 1980, that was. Marcia prided herself in her memory of dates of films. She was a buff, an expert at quiz entertainment questions.

'Resilient?' said Marcus. 'Those are not the actions of a resilient woman.'

'Yes and no. She phoned for help, didn't she? Isobel is like an elastic band. She stretches very, very far, but she bounces back. Like a human bunjee jump. I actually don't worry about her. Not really. She'll be fine.'

This wasn't entirely true. Arlene did worry about her. She was beginning to sweat very heavily under her arms.

Richard arrived into the living room with a tray, on which was a kettle of hot water, a bottle of whiskey, sugar, lemon and cloves.

Marcia emerged from the bathroom. Her face was a limey green. 'A large one of those. *Quick*!' she said.

Nobody spoke while Richard poured out the whiskies.

'How come the blood's only in the bathroom?' asked Marcia, noticing the spotless carpet under her feet. 'How did she get to the phone?'

'There's a phone in the bathroom. It's shaped like a fish, and it's just beside the sink.'

Arlene began to feel the tell-tale pressure on the front of her brain. A migraine. She'd been free of them for ages. Oh no! When the going got tough, she got migraine. She knew she'd have to go and lie down.

from the hospital bed

'I should never have written that play, or, having written it, I should never have allowed it be staged,' said Isobel from her hospital bed. She was surrounded by flowers. Everybody had sent her flowers, great bunches of them. The air was thick with pollen.

'Oh,' said Arlene, 'It's a bit late for that now. It has to go ahead, or we'll have to return all the investors' money, which is half spent at this stage.'

Isobel looked like a waif. Her wrists were bound. She had lost a lot of weight, and was dwarfed by the bed. How had Arlene not noticed the pounds slithering off her?

'Sitting in rehearsals for that play felt like running a razor blade over an open wound. I should have known I would crack,' said Isobel.

'What are you talking about?' said Arlene. Isobel was being entirely cryptic.

'The final scene. The one everybody hates. Tell me honestly, what do you think of it?'

'Well, I suppose I have to agree that it is a little over the top.'

'It's true.'

'It's true that it's over the top?'

'No, what happens in the scene really did happen.'

'How?' asked Arlene.

'It happened to me. My father beat me to a pulp after he discovered I'd had an abortion. I was hospitalised, and was on a life-support machine for a week. Damage to internal organs. I nearly died.'

'What?' said Arlene, incredulous.

'Yes. This play has a lot of autobiographical elements in it.'

'Jaysus, Isobel, you should have told me this.'

'My father was a harsh man. He was reared in harsh days and never learned to communicate. He made my mother's life a misery. My mother would be out in the garden hanging up washing, and rather than get up from the table to fetch the salt, he'd call her in and make her get it.'

Arlene watched Isobel. The reason for her hollow face and big sad eyes started to make sense.

'He was a huge man. Six-foot three, and he towered over us both. We were afraid of him, Arlene, both of us were just terrified of him. But, you can't really blame him for it. It was the way he was reared. He himself had two brothers and two sisters. The girls were kept at home as unpaid domestic servants to the boys, my aunts Carol and Miriam. God, they were wasted women, totally wasted, shadows of people. They never spoke. My mother started to become like them too.'

Isobel stopped and got herself a drink of water. Her thin little arms looked like the arms of a child, of a sparrow.

'He beat me, as far back as I can remember. Spare the rod and spoil the child. I don't think that it was especially hard or anything, just consistent. I was more afraid of the thought of it than the actuality. He stopped when I got to be about thirteen. I think he thought it improper to beat an adolescent girl. He never laid a finger on me from when I was about thirteen, until the abortion episode, when I was eighteen.'

'God, Isobel, that's a terrible story,' said Arlene.

'It's just one more terrible story. But everybody has terrible stories. Everybody is going round in the world putting a brave face on horror stories.'

'I don't agree,' said Arlene. 'Some stories are worse than others, and that is a truly terrible story.'

'You know, I'm not really surprised that he flipped his lid over the abortion. I had been helping him fundraise for his campaign, and at the same time I ran off and had one. I was running with the hares and hunting with the hounds. And I got caught. And there was publicity. Everybody knew that his daughter had had an abortion. I think he couldn't bear that aspect of it. The fact that everybody knew.'

Isobel smiled and then started to laugh. 'Everybody knew. It was hilarious. I had kicked his soapbox out from under him. I felt so bad about that.'

'How did everybody get to know?' asked Arlene.

'Well, I had told my parents that I was going hostelling with An Óige for the weekend. Things went grand in London, until I was getting my return flight at Heathrow. I had totally forgotten that I had a ten-spot of hash in my pocket. It had been sitting there for over a week, wrapped in tin foil. They had sniffer dogs, and I was sniffed out and arrested. I got done. Charged with possession. OK, I only got a suspended sentence, but my parents were informed. I had told the customs officer that I was having an abortion unbeknownst to my parents, in the hope that he would take pity on me and let me go. He was a youngish looking guy with an earring, so I thought he'd be sympathetic and it was only a ten-spot, for Christ's sake. But, unfortunately, he was one of *them*, and nailed me with even greater enthusiasm.'

'Oh,' said Arlene.

'It was in the evening papers the next day. My father went berserk. I recovered, obviously, but my father didn't. He just sank lower and lower. He never looked at me with love again. I did go to visit him in hospital, it was cancer he died of, a year later, but I reckon it was really a broken heart. We were never reconciled. He looked straight through me when I tried to speak to him. My aunts and uncles wouldn't speak to me either. He died, and I didn't go to the funeral.'

'The book, *Candid*? You dedicated it to him.'

'Yes, my stupid way of trying to reconcile myself to him and deal with my problems. I was trying to remember the more positive aspects of him. He was always proud of my achievements, I did very well at school, and he loved that but it didn't work. I was never happy about it. Then I thought if I explored my relationship with him through this play, I might set myself free from him, but I didn't realise how *real* it would be. I had thought that it would be like my books, but it's much more frightening, because the actors act it out and make it true.'

'Three dimensional, Isobel, not true.'

'I'm wrecked. Look at me now.'

'You'll be grand, Isobel. You'll be grand.'

'What really set me off, Arlene, was not Marcus's run-through and the row I was having with him. It was something else entirely.'

'What?'

'It sounds ridiculously melodramatic.'

'I think that we're in a pretty melodramatic situation anyway.'

'Well, the day my father died, in 1984, I was at home in my garden flat in Dún Laoghaire. I opened the back door, and there, on my back doorstep was a dead blue-tit. There were a lot of cats in the neighbourhood, and one of them must have killed it and left it for me as an offering. The culprit was a grey tom, who sat on the wall of the garden, and watched my reaction. It was the summer, and the poor dead bird was covered in ants.'

'Yuck,' said Arlene.

'I got out a spade, I remember every detail of this incident, a large yellow spade that was lying against the wall, and I picked up the bird with it, carried it to the bottom of the garden and dug a deep hole and buried it. All the time, the grey tom watched me. When I finished burying the bird, I put a cross over it, made of stones. And I went back inside to attend to bits and pieces. A few hours later, the phone rang, and it was my mother, she just said, "Your father's dead," and hung up. And all I could think of was the grey tom-cat, and the little dead bird.'

'Isobel, that's really pretty hairy,' said Arlene. It seemed now to Arlene, that though herself and Isobel were fairly pally, she really knew nothing about her. It wasn't Arlene's style, poking her nose into other people's affairs.

'And I thought that the tom was my father and the little

bird was me. Even though it was him that had died, it felt like it was me.'

Arlene breathed out a big sigh, and poured them both some water. It was very hot in the hospital.

'So, on Friday morning, I came home from getting some groceries, and on the doorstep to your building was a little dead blue-tit. I looked around, and one of the Cartwrights' cats, the grey fluffy one, the tom, was sitting on a tree looking at me. I couldn't believe it.'

'What!' said Arlene.

'It reminded me of the Mafia sneaking a dead canary into a high security courtroom to intimidate a witness. Because, if the canary sings, the canary dies. I suddenly thought that my play was an act of witness, and that I was a singing canary.'

'Jesus,' said Arlene, 'why didn't you call me?'

'There was no spade, so I got a soupspoon and carving fork from your kitchen, and I dug a little hole in the front garden, and I buried the poor bird, while the cat watched. And then I decided life was too painful, why live it? I was blind with emotion, and I went up to the bathroom, and cut my wrists.'

'And what made you call me?' said Arlene, very softly and gently.

'I just saw the fish shaped phone on the wall, and I picked it up, and something about the fish made me realise that if I died, I'd soon meet my father in the after-life. And the thought of that made me want to live. I didn't want to meet him, or any of his self-righteous cronies. I could imagine them all, sitting in a line, wearing their bitter expressions of perpetual joy. I thought I'd stay here for another little while. And sing my song.'

descent of chaos

Arlene walked home from St Vincent's private hospital to her flat. It was Sunday, but the roads were as busy as ever.

A good walk, nearly forty minutes, but she needed it. Needed to clear her brain. Blow away the internal cobwebs. Dust down the cerebral mahogany.

Isobel had a way of catching everybody up in her private psycho-dramas. You didn't need concerns of your own. You could have all of Isobel's. It was a bad omen, this episode. Maybe Marcia was correct about the Friday the thirteenth preview. Maybe that was responsible for attracting disorder. Arlene started to get angry. Putting on a show really was difficult enough without having to deal with – but then the thought of the pale creature lying there, dwarfed by the bed, brought a bizarre prickling to her eyes. A curious feeling. A feeling she resented. She paused to explore the sensation. But it didn't get beyond this oddness at the back of her eyeballs, and a small fleshy lump in her throat. When nothing further happened, she proceeded along the concrete path.

She made it home, feeling a little better for the walk. She passed a couple of the Cartwrights' cats on the landing, and stared at them mistrustfully. The cats stared back brazenly. Cats were in league with the devil. There was no doubt about that. Isobel's tale about the cats did not surprise her. She had never liked them anyway.

Her machine blinked a '1' at her. She pressed Play: 'Hello, Arlene, this is Janice Murphy at three in the afternoon on Sunday the first of September. I'm afraid I have some very bad news...'

More bad news, thought Arlene. Great! Just great!

'... I'm leaving the country today,' and then there was a loud clunk, followed by a pause, followed by: 'Sorry, I just dropped the phone, I'm on a public phone at the airport, and it's very hard to balance the receiver as well as my bags, and there's this ledge to put coins on that's too small and they keep dropping off. I know that I'm letting you down, but I'm afraid I have no choice. I've explained it all to Marcus, but he said I should ring you to apologise. I'm sorry. So, eh, sorry.' Click.

Great! That's just fantastic, Janice. Arlene had known that Janice was trouble from the start. She had been expecting something like this earlier, but since it hadn't happened, had put it out of her mind. Marcus would have to sort that out. Marcus and his little bloody fancies! Just bloody brilliant!

Arlene was beginning to lose her temper. Damn, damn, damn. She slammed some magazines on the table and made several loud thwacks! The buzzer went. No peace!

'Hello, who is it?' Arlene bellowed into the mouthpiece.

There was silence for a moment, then the tentative voice of Richard. 'Hello, is that Arlene?'

'Yes.'

'Are you OK?'

'Sure. Do I not sound OK?'

'Well, you were shouting.'

'Was I?' she roared.

'Can I come up?'

'Sure.'

She buzzed open the door with her newly repaired buzzer. She decided she'd better calm herself down, and took long deep breaths, during the time it took him to climb up the stairs. Richard gingerly entered the room.

He peered at her suspiciously. 'How are you?'

'I've been better,' she replied.

'So you saw Hedda?' he asked.

'I think we should stop calling her Hedda, you know. The girl has just made an attempt to top herself, so I reckon the nickname is now officially in bad taste.'

'You're right. But I got kind of fond of it.'

She put the kettle on. She felt totally exhausted. And a little bewildered. Suddenly she became conscious that she was alone with him. He'd never been in her apartment before without Isobel being there too. He was looking at her with an expression of pure sympathy on his face, his head slightly inclined to one side, his eyes wide and compassionate, his mouth upturned at the corners. She considered him for a moment, and slowly the sweet face of now withered into the bitter vicious face of the past. Turning her back on him, she went out to make the tea.

Richard sat and listened to the account of Isobel's delightful family life with his mouth open, making the occasional interjection of shock and horror.

'And you mean to say that her father hospitalised her?'

'Yes.'

'What were the injuries?'

'I don't know, I didn't ask her for her medical records. I felt I'd had quite enough details anyway.'

'The poor girl,' said Richard. 'I always had a feeling there was something distraught about her. Something traumatised.'

'In what way?'

'I couldn't exactly put my finger on it, but she couldn't write the way she does if she hadn't been down a few dark alleyways.'

'Yup. There's always been a ghost, all right.'

'I can see now how I'm going wrong with the part. I'm doing him far too nice. I'll have to change.'

'Just think about it.'

'I hate playing bastards,' said Richard, glumly. 'I've done a few of them recently – I did *Richard III* last year – and I find that part of them enters my soul.'

What rubbish, thought Arlene. So this was Richard's excuse for his behaviour: I became possessed by a devilish character. I suppose one of his psychiatrists had given him that lead.

'This must be all very hard on you, Arlene. After all, she is your flatmate.'

'Well, it's just that I have the show on at the moment, so I can't really give her my full attention. The show needs my care, for her sake, for all our sakes.'

'You overestimate your own necessity.'

'I wish I did.'

'You're very fond of Isobel.'

'Yes,' said Arlene quietly.

'It's very obvious. She's your pet, and you look after her.'

'Well, most people are fond of her. I'm sure you've noticed. She has this way with people. She's one of nature's charmers.'

'But you're especially so.'

That was quite enough from Richard. Arlene wished he'd shut up. He was giving her the pip. She was tired of everybody and everything.

'Why did Isobel write this play if it was going to do her head in?' he persisted.

'Why do any of us do things that will do our heads in? It's the human condition.'

'I don't agree. There are lots of people who aren't killing themselves over their work.'

'We're not happy until we feel pain.'

'That's a rather masochistic view.'

'Or, maybe it's the relief of pain that attracts us. Food always tastes better after hunger. Happiness feels like normality, unless it comes as a relief of misery.' Arlene felt she was beginning to reassert herself.

'True.'

'Perhaps it's not "looking over the edge" that excites us, but rather the "not falling" part,' Arlene said.

'Hmmmn.'

'You must know about the edge, Richard, you've danced on it.'

'I suppose I have looked over the precipice, all right,' he said, turning away from her.

Yes, you bastard, and you did your best to shove me in, she

149

thought, her guard of sweetness towards him dropping for a flash. Maintaining forgiveness was hard. It took up a lot of energy.

'Perhaps we'll have more tea?' she said, smiling as kindly as possible.

The piano phone rang. 'The Entertainer.' Terribly cheerful. Da-da-da-da, da-da, da-da, de-de– Arlene answered it. It was Marcus. He sounded awful. Arlene remembered she was still livid about the phonecall from Janice.

'Yeah, yeah, I got a message from the little cunt. I have only one thing to say,' said Arlene, 'and that is "replacement".'

'Can you believe it?' asked Marcus.

'Where's she off to? She said she was at the airport, but not where she was going. Tenerife for a little hol perhaps?' said Arlene.

'A kibbutz.'

'A kibbutz?'

'Yeah,' said Marcus. 'I didn't think anyone ran off to kibbutzes any more. I thought that had gone out in the eighties.'

'Odd.'

'She's up the pole. And her boyfriend is intent on going to live on a kibbutz. He's not Jewish or anything. I think he's a frontiers' man. Huge big guy, goes camping a lot, catches fish with his teeth. Anyway he gave her an ultimatum, come with him now and marry him out there or else he'd just bugger off and have nothing to do with her or the kiddie.'

'Great father potential. Compassionate. She's made a great choice.'

'So she said she was real sorry, but she had to put her child's parenting before the show.'

'Sentimentalists. Don't you hate them.'

'I don't need this right now,' said Marcus. 'I'm under terrible pressure, what with Hedda gone barmy –'

'I don't want her called Hedda anymore. I think it's bad karma.'

'I'm missing an actor,' Marcus's voice had slid into a higher octave, 'I don't have an ending for the script, everyone's throwing wobblers. I'll be next, I'm telling you.'

'Look, let's cancel rehearsal tomorrow,' said Arlene calmly, 'and we'll get on the case. You try phoning around tonight and if you can make a straight offer to somebody, go ahead. If you need to try people out, set up auditions tomorrow afternoon, you can use my office.'

'I'll do that.'

'And Marcus,' said Arlene, her voice replete with self-justification, 'I knew she was trouble from the start.'

'You are very cruel,' he said. 'Goodbye.'

Arlene went back over to the sofa and sat down.

'So,' said Richard, 'filling in between the lines, we've lost our Cathy.'

'Yup.' Arlene was embarrassed. She hated the way this reflected on her and her administration. She liked to run a tight ship.

'Things are beginning to unravel,' said Richard, 'the centre cannot hold. Chaos is descending.'

'So it seems,' said Arlene.

'I like that,' said Richard. 'I like chaos. It's creative.'

the past III

Arlene and Dick got married on 23 September 1981. She wore a tumultuous white dress borrowed from the costume department at the Gate Theatre. It had been used in a production of *Wuthering Heights* and was cut in the dainty lines of the late eighteenth century. She had to wear a basket construction under the skirt to make it sit right. It was covered in tiny teardrop-shaped jewels, individually hand-sewn, which shimmered in the light. Dick wore a frock coat suit that had been tailored for him for a production of *A Woman of No Importance*.

They met up with all their friends beforehand for a drink in the Shelbourne Hotel, causing chaos, spreading chaos, sprinkling chaos like confetti. They were a vision to behold as they advanced down Dawson Street towards the register office in Molesworth Street, accompanied by their motley retinue of stage-managers, jesters and jokers, actors and chorus girls.

Arlene's mother developed a migraine, and had to go and lie down, thereby missing the ceremony. She recovered in time for supper, though Arlene's two brothers attended the affair with a vague air of embarrassment. It was strange how they had grown up so embarrassable and Arlene had not. Arlene put that down to the fact that her mother had fussed over the boys, but let her do as she pleased, let her run wild. The boys were so embarrassable that they had emigrated to avoid further exposure. Left behind them the country of their embarrassments forever. Ran away from the site of their ultimate embarrassment, having been born of woman.

The ceremony in the register office was fast and dramatic. The entourage squeezed into the little room, overflowing out the doorway, into the hallway and out onto the street. Afterwards, Dick carried Arlene outside, and spun her round in the air. She was thrilled. He seemed to be enjoying himself. It was terrific. She laughed and laughed.

They invaded a bar on Duke Street. Everybody got drunk. Speeches were made. Dinner was had in the basement room of a restaurant on Wicklow Street. Finally they got home to her flat and fell in the door.

'Mrs Whelan,' whispered Dick in Arlene's ear, 'my wife.'

She knew he was turned on by it. He liked saying the word 'wife'. It was erotic for him. He stood behind her, caressed her body, kissed her neck and started to unzip her white satin dress.

'Did your mother explain to you about sex?' he asked.

'Why no, sir,' she replied, as the white dress fell to the floor. He picked up the dress and threw it over the back of a chair. The fabric snagged a little, and a few of the teardrop jewels came loose and dropped to the floor.

'What is sex?' she said wide-eyed, standing in her white underthings.

'You don't know anything about it?' he asked.

'Nothing, sir,' she said.

'Well, I'll have to give you a few lessons.'

'Like maths and geography?'

'More like geography.'

So, he started his geography lesson, and she was an attentive student.

'I always wanted to marry a virgin,' he said.

They moved to an old red-brick house in Donnybrook, to a larger flat with a spare bedroom. When she opened the front door of the building, the familiar smell hit her, that smell of flatland, of damp, and cigarettes, of poverty. But their rooms were at the back, and the smell didn't penetrate there. Their windows got the sun in the evening, and they flung them open for air.

His drinking lessened. They took it in turns to cook meals. After dinner he would bark loudly and jump all over the furniture, signalling that he wanted to go for a walk. His energy was boundless. Their walks inevitably took them past several bars, and outside them he whined a little and pawed her arm, but didn't seriously want to go in. Most of the time, that is.

One of the problems with his career was that he was too proud to do a lot of hustling. So, she hustled on his behalf, got him auditions for everything. She wasn't too proud. Things started to improve for him. He got a lot of gigs. Was making a lot of money. She took less and less stage-management work, as it proved financially more expeditious for her to be working on his behalf.

'You should be on ten per cent,' he said and laughed.

Ten per cent? She stared at him.

She got him a very lucrative gig on a movie. An American financed and produced story filmed in County Clare. It was a horror story based on the Irish legend of the banshee. They both thought the script riotously funny, but the cheque serious and handsome.

They decamped to a hotel in Clare. Great fun was had on expense accounts and in bars that knew no licensing laws and thus stayed open all night long. Arlene had nothing to do during the day, so she lolled in the bath, went for walks, took a holiday. It was so unlike her. The winds of County Clare lifted her sails. The film was total and utter tosh, but Dick managed to be very convincing in it and he got very good notices when it was shown. Arlene pirated a copy of it on video to make him a showreel. They both felt that the big break wasn't far away.

The big opportunity came. A decent grade-A film. About the IRA. Arlene went down to the Berkeley Court Hotel one morning and found the casting director tucking into his sausages and eggs. She sold Dick to him, leaving a copy of the showreel. The casting director was impressed. Dick was sent the script. It was fabulous. His part was that of the best friend of the lead, very juicy. He was thrilled. A fee was negotiated. A retainer was paid. Advance publicity was released. He did some interviews in the press about how he felt it would be to work with such major stars. He turned down other offers.

Then there was a row between the director and the production company. The director left, and the casting director was fired. Dick was dropped.

Depression.

Drinking.

Money got tight again. Accustomed to poverty, they weren't scared of it, and when money came in, it was spent rapidly. No concept of the rainy day. Nothing turned up for Dick, so Arlene took a stage-managing job on a production of *The Playboy of the Western World* which was touring Ireland and the UK.

It was the first time since their marriage that they had been separated, and Arlene missed Dick terribly. She missed him during the day, but most of all at night. She phoned him from hotel rooms where her body ached for want of his. So bad was this feeling, that when they played Athlone, a two-hour drive from Dublin, she decided to try and make it home. Once the show came down, she rapidly put away all her props and effects. She jumped into a borrowed car and put her foot on the accelerator, hardly looking to left or right as she drove to Dublin.

She made excellent time on the road, and hit the city by a quarter past one. Her imagination was playing havoc with her, and she was dying for sex. She abandoned the car on the road outside their flat, almost ran up the path, and slid her key through the hall door. She quietly made her way up the stairs, out of consideration for the other occupants of the house. She was about to put her key in her own door, when she heard laughter coming from inside. A woman's laughter. She opened the door, and walked into her kitchen.

On the table was Dick, doing an Elvis impersonation, holding a bottle of beer as a microphone, with his shirt opened down to his chest. Sitting in a chair, helplessly laughing at him, was Elisabeth Dunne, an actress that Arlene knew by reputation.

For a moment, Dick didn't see Arlene and continued with his song, treat me like a fool, but Elisabeth saw her and stopped laughing and sat up straight. When Dick did see her, he didn't flinch, but continued singing, this time to her, treat me mean and cruel, but love me. He was obviously going to brazen his way out of it. When he finished his song, he jumped down from the table.

'Fancy a beer?' he said to Arlene and opened a couple of bottles, cool as could be. 'Have you met Elisabeth? Elisabeth, this is my wife, Arlene.'

Elisabeth held out her hand and Arlene took it and, after a moment's hesitation, shook it.

Elisabeth was equally cool. 'So Arlene, you're on tour with *The Playboy*... How's it going?'

'Fine.'

'Where is it now?'

'Athlone.'

'Athlone's a grand spot. It's in the middle of everywhere. I remember playing there when I toured with *Measure for Measure*...'

And Elisabeth was away. Lots of chat. Blah blah blah. They were so innocent in their behaviour that Arlene began to relax, began to think that she was a fool to have thought they were up to something. Elisabeth seemed to be a nice person, friendly. Dick was putting his arms around Arlene and pulling her onto his knee.

After about ten minutes of chat Elisabeth said, 'I suppose I'd better be off. He dragged me back here to keep him company, because he said he was mortally lonesome with you away.'

Elisabeth put on her coat and headed out to the hall. Dick went to walk her down to the front door. Arlene looked after them mistrustfully, but she wasn't sure. Were they innocent? They were actors. Were they acting? How many people did he sing his Elvis songs to, did he do his Marlon Brando acts for? Did he bark like a dog for walks with? She put it out of her mind. She had no wish to think these things.

He came back, skipped into the flat. He was a little drunk, a little, but not a lot.

'Welcome home, darling, I've missed you terribly.' And she believed the sincerity she heard in his voice as she melted like butter, and he laid her down on the table, tickling under her arms and down her sides. She laughed that terrible involuntary laugh of the tickled.

'Ah, stop,' she shouted, but still laughing, teetering there on that brink where laugher meets terror, meets tears. Then he started to tickle her inner thighs, and this was unbearably sensitive, but still she laughed, and before she knew it he was about to come into her and she said, 'No, not on the table, me back's killin' me. Bed.'

'I love you,' he said, 'my Arlene.'

'I love you too,' she said.

They meandered off to the bedroom, removing what clothes remained as they went. Arlene was delighted to be home, even if only for one night. She would have to be up early in the morning to get back to Athlone in time for a call at ten-thirty. Dick was still attached to his bottle of beer. She hated that. He took a bottle of beer with him to bed frequently.

She pulled back the covers and was horrified. There, in the

158

middle of their bed was a stain of menstrual blood. Not hers. It was fresh, probably from last night or the night before.

He saw her seeing it.

'Who?' she said.

He put the beer bottle to his lips and took a long drink. 'Does it matter?' he said.

'Yes. Was it Elisabeth? Was it *her*?'

'Look, it doesn't matter who it was. You must know by now that there will always be somebody else. But it doesn't mean that you're not the most important.' His drunkenness made him misjudge her mood, and he went to put his arm around her shoulders.

She slapped it away. 'What is wrong with you that you need all these other women? What are you trying to prove?'

He took a sullen gulp of his beer. She gave him a sharp shove, which startled him and made him spill the bottle.

'Was it Elisabeth?'

'Yes.'

'And she has the cheek to sit in my kitchen and chat to me about shit when she has just poked my husband, and was planning on doing it again tonight, if I hadn't come home.'

'You know the deal,' he said. 'I never promised you anything.' He walked out of the room.

Arlene ripped the sheets off the bed and brought them into the kitchen where she stuffed them in the bin. She fetched fresh sheets from the cupboard and went to put them on the bed, when she noticed that the faintly brown liquid had permeated through to the underblanket. She pulled this off in a fury, and yes, the stain had gone through to the mattress. It was indelible.

She bellowed, and remade the bed with a fresh underblanket and the fresh sheets, while he sat in the kitchen and opened a new beer from the fridge.

She slipped into bed, still naked, and started to shake and then it happened.

A ferocious headache. Her brain started to vibrate and shards of electricity passed through her head. Oh no, she thought, I am going mad. My mind is snapping. She tried to call for help, opening her mouth, but she knew nothing came out. She switched on the light, and the brightness assaulted her eyes. Then, terrifyingly, the room splintered into zigzags, and lurched to left and right. She closed her eyes, but the zigzag image remained imprinted in her brain. She tried to call out again, and this time was conscious of making a little groaning noise, like an animal. Then, her stomach heaved, and she threw up all over herself and the bedclothes.

Dick had heard the groaning noises and came in just in time to witness the vomiting. He fetched a basin of water and some tea-towels. He held her hair back from her face as she retched.

She tried to say brain, but all that came out was, 'Ain, ain.'

'Pain?' he asked.

Yes, she thought, a pain in the brain.

'Ain,' she said again.

'Migraine,' he said, realising what was going on.

Through the hallucinations, she heard his voice and it became clear to Arlene what was happening. She was having one of her mother's migraines. She grabbed on to him, hoping that it would anchor her, but her arm felt strangely elastic, and when she put it around his shoulders, she could have sworn that it wrapped several times around him, like an octopus.

He eased her into a lying position, and wet a towel which he put on her forehead. She had stopped retching, but was shaking and sweating profusely. Dick panicked. His drunkenness left him. He ran out into the hallway, and was about to phone an ambulance, when he thought to phone Arlene's mother.

The phone call woke Mrs Morrissey up, but she was very soothing and reassuring. 'It's all right Dick,' she said. 'I was twenty-two when I got my first attack as well. It's very shocking to begin with, but it's really no trouble at all when you're used to them. Light aggravates the attacks. Get her to turn off all the lights when it starts, and if it's daytime, pull all the curtains.'

'And are you sure I needn't call a doctor? She seems very sick.'

'Wait until the morning. Get her to sleep if possible. If you can get to sleep before they really take hold, you can cut them off at the pass.'

Dick went back into the room where Arlene was still shaking in the bed. He turned off the light, and in the darkness, pulled away the bedcovers that were soiled with sick, and got a fresh eiderdown from the cupboard. He got into bed beside her and cradled her. The shaking subsided, and soon her breathing acquired the consistency of sleep.

The next morning she remembered every detail of the attack, and she remembered also the joyous feeling of calm after it, this nerve-storm, had passed.

And she remembered the dream she had while she slept

afterwards. She dreamed that his penis had withered and turned into a gnarled and rotten twig.

Migraine established a residency in her brain. After she got over the shock, she got used to them, these janglings, these parodies of sensation. The attack itself was always difficult to handle, but the aftermath was quite pleasant. A joyful sense of relief, of release.

She saw a doctor who monitored her, but was essentially unalarmed. 'Classical migraine. A benign, though inconvenient psycho-physical condition,' he called it. 'It is a symptom not just of illness, but of health. It reminds us that human beings may *need*, from time to time, to be ill.'

It manifested itself most often when she was experiencing rage. It was as though she had developed a pathology of tension. But sometimes migraine visited for no reason, just paid a courtesy call on her, to remind her of itself, and of the dark side.

back to work

On Monday evening there was a message from the Weirdo. 'Hello, Ms Morrissey. I heard what happened to Ms Coole. I'm terribly sorry. I hope it hadn't anything to do with my calls. I hope she didn't hear the last one. I'm hopelessly sorry. I won't call again. 'Bye.'

Hmmmn, thought Arlene, he sounds real upset. He feels bad about it. It wasn't his fault though. Her instincts had been right about the Weirdo. He had no badness in him. He was just a lonely soul floating about on the telephone lines. A person adrift.

Isobel came home from hospital, with a strong warning from her doctor to avoid anything likely to render her excited. This was an impossible instruction. She was bang in the middle of the show. She couldn't run away and leave it. She was going to have to be excited.

'I think I'll be OK,' she said as she sipped weak tea in the kitchen.

'There was a message from the Weirdo. He said he hopes that you're OK.'

'How did he know?'

'I dunno, Isobel. The only explanation is that the Weirdo is somebody who knows us quite well.'

'How odd. Nice of him though,' said Isobel, who seemed to be imbibing strength with the tea.

Arlene thought she looked much better, much larger than she had in the hospital bed. 'We have a kindly Weirdo,' said Arlene.

'That's something.'

'Maybe you ought to see someone,' she suggested, 'someone that you could talk to about your thing with your father, and this abortion business. It was obviously very traumatic. Someone professional, who knows what they're talking about.'

'I have in the past,' said Isobel. 'It helped a little bit at the time, but really, this current ambush is only to be expected. I should've known that the play would bring everything up again. Still, I feel a lot better now. I feel I've stopped pretending that there is nothing wrong. And that means a lot.'

'Yes,' said Arlene.

'I can talk to you about it, pal,' and she put out her hand and gave Arlene's hand a little squeeze.

I'm not very good at this kind of thing, thought Arlene, always a great believer in calling in the professionals. She looked at the little skinny hand trying to squeeze her own large robust one. She smiled at Isobel.

'Dear Arlene. Such a sweet smile. I'm sorry I've stayed here so long, without so much as a by-your-leave, and foisted all my problems on you. You are endlessly patient and kind. I'll start looking for a flat as soon as the show goes up. I promise.'

'Don't worry,' said Arlene. 'You are no trouble here. In fact, I enjoy having you around. You can stay as long as you like.'

'Thanks, Arly, you're a pal,' and Isobel smiled.

Arlene wondered if she had walked into that. You could never be sure with Isobel. So sweet, so vulnerable, yet so calculating, so cool.

Marcus phoned, having located an actress that he was happy with to play Cathy. 'Paula Costello. She's free, and she'll be dynamite. She'll be different to Janice, she's older, less innocent, but she's very strong.'

'Good news indeed, my friend.'

'She's free from tomorrow. She was intending to go on holidays to Spain later in the week, but I've talked her out of it.'

'Holidays? Who needs 'em?'

'We'll have to pay for the holiday though.'

'Okay, okay, we're desperate.'

'And her mother's. She was supposed to be going with her, and if she's not going, her mother won't go. Her mother has angina and is afrai –'

'Look, Marcus, do I need to know all this? I have no interest in Paula Costello's mother. I do not care what she is suffering from. I don't know why I am having a conversation about her at this moment in time.'

'There is no need to get shirty with me,' said Marcus, and he hung up. Dammit. Arlene would have to soften him up tomorrow. Damn! She'd better do it now. She dialled his number.

'Marcus?'

'Speaking.'

'It's Arlene.'

'What can I do for you?' he said in a cool, professional, but slightly injured, tone.

'I'm sorry,' she said.

'That's quite all right.'

'And well done.'

'About what?'

'About getting an actor, any actor, with or without an hereditary heart condition.'

'OK,' said Marcus and laughed. 'See you tomorrow.'

Phew! Arlene spent so much time keeping everybody happy.

'What was that?' asked Isobel.

'Oh, yeah, I forgot to tell you. Janice dropped out of the show.'

'Not because of me?'

No, Isobel, not everything revolves around you.

'No. She's up the pole and she's running off to a kibbutz with her boyfriend.'

'Oh.'

'Marcus has found a replacement. Paula Costello is her name. A fine actress. She'll be very good.'

'Oh. Shouldn't I have been consulted? My contract says that I'm to have approval on all casting decisions.'

'Hardly, Isobel, were we going to drag the woman in to audition at your hospital bedside.'

'Point taken,' said Isobel.

'Besides, we've no choice. We're so stuck for time, we're desperate. I know this actress though, and she's very good.'

'Have I seen her in anything?' asked Isobel.

'You'll see her in the rehearsal room tomorrow morning,' said Arlene.

*

The next morning, Arlene escorted Isobel to the rehearsal room, to make sure she was all right and to smooth things over for her. Isobel was wearing a long-sleeved shirt, to cover up her wrists and had put make up under her eyes to cover the grey hollows.

Candy had a chair ready for her with a big cushion on it. There was an ashtray on a small table by its side.

'How kind,' said Isobel, and lit up a cigarette.

Marcus gave a private grimace at the cigarette.

'Would you like a cup of tea?' Candy asked Isobel.

'Thank you, Candy.'

Marcus came up to Isobel, almost on tippy toes. 'How are you feeling?' he asked her in a hushed tone.

'Fine, Marcus, I'm sorry about everything. I'm grand now, absolutely grand. Don't worry about me. Just concentrate on the show,' and she smiled one of her least human smiles.

Seeing that Isobel was well set up, Arlene went out to the bathroom. Whilst in the cubicle, she heard Marcia and Paula Costello come up the stairs, and stop outside the bathroom to finish their conversation. Marcia was doing the talking.

'And you can see that it's a bit of a hornet's nest. Isobel Coole is clearly deranged, keeps topping herself. Apparently she's been doing this for years, and her literary agent keeps having to fly over from London to haul her out of psychiatric institutions. Marcus is a nice enough boy with plenty of charm and energy, but no real imaginative authority. Richard Power is okay. He does at least have the advantage of being a famous star. And Arlene, well Ar –'

Arlene did not wish to hear any further, so she pulled the chain, and the conversation was drowned by the flush. When she emerged, they were gone. It unsettled her, this loose talk. People making free with information. Marcia. Sweet as sin, but disloyal. It was strange that this bothered Arlene today. She knew that people could be disloyal, could be two-faced. Normally she didn't care at all what people thought about her, what they said about her behind her back. But today? Today she cared.

She came back into the rehearsal room. Isobel was further propped up in her chair, having acquired an extra pillow. Paula was being introduced to everyone. Arlene noticed a stiffness to Corinne Cooper's reception of her. Ancient rivalries, she thought. Corinne and Paul had gone to drama school together and had ended up competing for the same parts. Corinne had generally come out on top, but she had surrendered a few parts to Paula, and was the more bitter about it. Typical. Those who can most afford magnanimity least display it. Arlene shook herself. It wasn't like her to get judgmental. She wasn't feeling quite right. Exhausted, she was.

Everybody seemed to be settled, so she decided to make her escape and leave them to it. Isobel could lead them all in a ritual jump out the window, for all she cared. She wanted to go home.

There was a man sitting at the bottom of the steps. Long hair and unshaven. Unkempt. Arlene was about to walk past him, when he greeted her.

'Arlene!' he said as he jumped to his feet and stretched out a bony hand to shake hers. Arlene stared at the figure. She didn't recognise him.

'It's David Range,' he identified himself. 'Marcia's husband.'

No wonder she didn't recognise him. He usually looked cleanshaven, and smart as a new pin. He had always been tall and thin, but somehow you didn't notice it so much when he was well dressed. Now, kitted out like a hippy, he looked skeletal. He must be trying to keep up with the young ones, she thought, but he hadn't got the look quite right. Chic Seventies' retro was in fashion, but David didn't look chic. He looked like the *genuine article*; a real Seventies relic, circa 1972.

'What are you doing here?' asked Arlene.

'Coffee?' he asked her and without waiting for a reply, steered her across the road to a coffee shop, and sat in the window where he had a good view of the entrance to the rehearsal space.

'I am so pleased to see you, Arlene,' said David.

'So,' said Arlene, 'where's Miss Fairview?'

'Who?' asked David.

'The doxy from Fairview.'

'Arlene, I've made a terrible mistake. I need you to help me. I need Marcia back.'

'Oh,' said Arlene.

'Please say you'll help me. Marcia worships you and will do anything you say.'

So Marcia worships me? Huh! 'So things haven't worked out for you and the young wan?'

'That's putting it mildly. She's too, too, too young. I don't know what I was thinking of. She's not really grown up.'

'Yeah, well, if she's only twenty-two –'

'She's too, too,' – he searched for a word – 'too young. I don't know what got into me. I think it must be the male

169

menopause. I don't know how I could've left Marcia.'

'Look, David, I don't think you'll have a problem getting her back.'

'Believe me, I am having a problem. She hangs up when I call.'

Poor David. He looked like he hadn't had a square meal in ages.

'So that is why I'm reduced to coming here to her rehearsal room, in the hope I'll intercept her coming out.'

'How did you know we were rehearsing here?'

'I followed her from home one morning.'

This was obviously a sad case.

'Look, David. I'd suggest you get a large bunch of red roses from the florist on O'Connell Street, and wait for her to come out for lunch. You know Marcia. No gesture too large.'

David took Arlene's advice, but the bunch of flowers was so spectacular he got the inspiration to bring them up into the rehearsal room, without waiting for lunch.

Meanwhile the rehearsal was going reasonably well. Paula was settling in nicely. She had a calm and confidence-inspiring air about her. Isobel was amazed to see how different the part of Cathy was in Paula's hands. She was so used to Janice's perky friskiness that Paula's languid, cynical teenager was quite a shock. But she didn't say anything. She didn't want to rock the boat, shipping water as it was, all the time.

There was a knock on the door. Candy answered it.

'Can I speak to Marcia?' said the visitor in hushed tones, staggering under the biggest bunch of red roses Candy had ever seen.

Candy tip-toed over to Marcia, trying her best not to disrupt the rehearsal.

'Marcia, there's a man outside wants to speak to you.'

'If it's my ex-husband, I'm not speaking to him. Tell him he'll be hearing from my lawyers.'

Candy tip-toed back to the door.

'Sorry, she won't speak to you. She says you'll be hearing from her lawyers.'

David burst into tears. Candy, a soft-hearted girl at the best of times, felt very sorry for this half-man, half-rose bush. She said she'd try Marcia again. She tip-toed across the room again and made an appealing face at Marcia.

'Under *no* circumstances,' said Marcia.

Candy went back to the door and delivered her message to David, who, weeping, asked Candy if she would bring the flowers in to Marcia, and tell her that he'd be in the coffee shop across the road at lunchtime, waiting for her.

Candy came back into the room, smothered by the huge bunch of flowers.

Marcus, who had been making an heroic effort of concentration, finally lost the rag when the mobile rose-bush appeared. 'What the hell is going on? Candy? My concentration is shot to hell. You're in and out of the door like a bleedin' yo-yo.'

'Sorry,' said Candy. 'A floral delivery for Marcia.'

'Sorry,' said Marcia. 'I have a deranged ex-husband wandering around out there.'

'Oh, so David's trying to get back with you?' said Isobel to Marcia.

'Well, you see, he called a fortnight ago and since then –', said Marcia.

'Jesus H. Christ!' said Marcus, his face getting redder and redder. 'I don't believe this. Why don't we just shut down rehearsals and have a nice little gossip for ourselves, like a bunch of bloody housewives. I'm sure we all have plenty of scintillating personal details that would rivet the room. Corinne, I'm sure you'd like to tell us all about your husband and children, and Paula, you must have a nice little man tucked away –'

'–Woman,' said Paula. 'I'm a lesbian.'

'Oh, even better,' said Marcus. 'Juicier. We could all have a good chat about that, and I'm sure you all want to know what I've been doing all weekend with that nice Spanish boy you saw me with, but –' his voice was getting louder and louder, '–at this stage, I think I need a ten-minute break,' and he walked out the door, slamming it behind him.

The room was stunned. Everybody looked at everybody else.

'Strain,' said Marcia. 'He's obviously feeling the strain.'

'Sure,' said Isobel, feeling guilty.

'I didn't like the "housewife" reference though,' said Marcia. 'You see, these new-fangled men are all very well, but when you put them under pressure, you really see what they're made of. Then you see their genuine contempt for women.'

'Coffee?' asked Candy. 'Maybe we should all have coffee.'

That evening, at six-thirty, Isobel arrived home in a taxi with the red roses. Marcia had refused to take them, and wanted them put in the bin. Isobel thought this was a terrible waste, and said that she'd bring them home to brighten up the apartment. Marcia acceded to Isobel's request on account of Isobel still being a bit of an invalid.

So, the red roses ended up under Arlene's nose.

'There must be at least fifty roses in that,' said Arlene.

'Sixty. Five dozen. I counted them.'

'Did she meet him?' Arlene asked.

'Yeah, she did finally. They had lunch together. It seems that he's sick of Miss Fairview. She's not sophisticated enough for him. Marcia told me this with great glee. Miss Fairview buys wine for £3.49 in Quinnsworth and apparently he came home one day to a dinner of spaghetti covered with tinned spaghetti.'

'Is Marcia going to take him back?'

'I don't think she's going to give in too easily. I think she's enjoying her freedom. She'll make him suffer for a bit.'

'I've a surprise for you,' said Arlene.

'What? What?' and Isobel jumped a little.

'A nice surprise,' said Arlene. She led Isobel into the kitchen, where the small table was set for dinner, and bubbling on the stove was an interesting-looking casserole, dispersing smells of garlic and herbs.

'Dinner,' said Arlene. 'Lamb casserole. I cooked us dinner.'

This was not entirely true. Arlene had bought the casserole from Martin in the deli, but she had heated it up by herself. She had also done some boil-in-the-bag rice and she'd thrown the ready-washed lettuce in a bowl with the Paul Newman salad dressing, adding extra salt to taste. She poured them each a glass of wine.

Isobel slumped down on her chair.

173

'Kind. It's very kind,' and big tears started to run down her face.

'What's wrong?' asked Arlene.

'I don't know,' said Isobel. 'I'm overwrought. I can stand anything but kindness.'

Arlene stared at Isobel, aghast.

'C'mon. You're probably starving. Get some grub inside you. It'll do you good.'

This was, in fact, true. Isobel settled as she ate the dinner. It massaged her ragged nervous system from within.

'How did you find Paula Costello as Cathy?' asked Arlene.

'Fine, eventually. She's so different from Janice, it took me a while to get used to her. Janice brought an innocence to that part, but Paula brings something darker. There is a lot of underlying tension coming out in the friendship between Cathy and Nuala.'

'In what way?'

'Well,' continued Isobel, 'you know that kind of youthful schoolgirl envy? You see it all the time. Young girls, who are ostensibly best friends, but who would knife each other in the back and pinch each other's boyfriends given half a chance. That's what the friendship is like now.'

'Oh. Is that all right?'

'Yeah. It works. It darkens the relationship somewhat, and I like that. It was a tiny bit idealised before.'

'Yes, I agree,' said Arlene.

'I suppose that Cathy does love Nuala, but somewhere, mixed in with that love, is a resentment and jealousy of Nuala's talents.'

'Sure.'

'And Nuala resents Cathy's energy and capacity for happiness,' continued Isobel. 'In fact, though they are best friends, their love for each other is very conditional, like, I suppose, all love is conditional.'

Isobel's gloom was permeating her work.

'Paula and Corinne are rivals,' said Arlene. 'They keep pitching for the same parts, so they're very uneasy around each other.'

'Is that what it is?' said Isobel.

'As simple and as complex as that.'

'I knew there was something going on, but I wasn't sure what. It's funny,' said Isobel, 'I thought I had written a play and that it meant something independent and tangible, but then these actors appear with their own concerns and their own lives and suddenly my play is a different thing. A generous friendship becomes a competitive one because the actors playing the parts aren't too fond of each other.'

'Fascinating, isn't it?' said Arlene.

'Sure,' said Isobel.

finishing touches

Carmel was a wonderful presence in Arlene's life. Her calmness and capability had a soothing effect on her. The phone was hopping. The interest in Richard Power's presence in an Irish production was immense. Booking for the show wasn't due to open until Monday 9 September, but already, the Lunar Theatre box office was being swamped with calls. The press was swarming. The summer was past, and there hadn't been a theatre opening for a number of months. The journos had returned from holidays with great energy, happy to go chasing stories in their tans.

'For you,' said Carmel, and handed the phone to Arlene. 'It's Shirley Hastings, producer with that new Jeff Jones chat show, *Samson* on Friday nights. She insists on talking only to you, and she's phoned three times. I gave her your mobile number, but she keeps calling here.'

Arlene took the call.

'Arlene, how are you?'

'Fine, Shirley, fine.'

'We haven't seen each other in ages, we must "do lunch" as they say.'

'Sure.'

'When was the last time we got together? asked Shirley.

Get to the point, thought Arlene. 'Ages ago. It's such a busy world.'

'I just love the sound of *Over the Moon*,' said Shirley. 'It sounds entirely fascinating.'

'Yes.' The point, Shirley, let's get to the point.

'And it'll be great for Irish audiences to see Richard Power.'

'Yes.' The point, Shirley. You *can* do it.

'And you really *do* do interesting projects, Arlene, I admire you so much.'

'Yes.'

'I admire your independence, your being a freelancer.'

'Yes.'

'And I've had a wonderful idea for the *Samson* show.'

Here it was!

'You've got Corinne Cooper playing the part of the girl who has the abortion, don't you? Well, I thought it would be a *super* idea if she came on the show, and discussed the experience of having an abortion with Jeff. We wouldn't let on that she was an actor, we'd just launch into the questions. Jeff would be very sensitive, of course, he's very good with women, as you know, very into women's issues. He'd ask her very sensitive questions, things like what exactly was going through her mind at the time, and so on. We'd go into all the details. A real "in your face" piece. We'd shirk nothing because, on the *Samson* show, we're not afraid to grasp the issues. Nothing simple. Everything very complex. You know what I mean?'

'Ye-es.'

'The interview would last about ten minutes, and then, at

the end, we'd tell people that this wasn't a real person, it was an actor, and she was in *Over the Moon* in the Lunar Theatre.'

'Hmmn.'

'It'd be a wonderful item. Abortion is very sexy at the moment,' said Shirley.

'It's original,' said Arlene.

'So shocking. So vibrant. Such good TV. It'd be an absolute media event!' Shirley sounded very excited.

'Let me think about it.'

'Can you get back to me by ten AM tomorrow? I've a production meeting at eleven. It'd be this Friday. And it'd be great publicity.'

Arlene strolled across town to the rehearsal room. She steered Corinne off for lunch, and put the proposal to her.

'Under no circumstances,' said Corinne. 'If you think that I am going to be a media tart, you've another think coming.'

'Don't react too fast.'

'I can't believe you'd cooperate, Arlene, with such a charade.'

'Hey, don't come over all judgmental. We need publicity, and publicity is a dirty business. You can't sell a show unless you're prepared to get your hands dirty.'

'No way. My husband would have a fit. Imagine all his work colleagues watching their televisions on a Friday night and seeing me there chatting away about abortions I haven't had.'

'You could explain to them beforehand.'

'The people at my kids' playgroup?'

'We-ll.'

'My mother in Leitrim! She'd probably have a heart attack before they got to the revelation bit.'

'Yes.'

'Nobody goes on national television to chat about their abortions, and I'm hardly going to do it either, especially since I've never had one.' Corinne was coming to the boil now. 'And Arlene, I do not appreciate your even asking me to do this. I may be an actor in your employ, but I am also a human being. And you can tell that to Shirley-bloody-Hastings.' Corinne downed her tea, stood up and turned on her heel. She flounced off.

Arlene didn't blame her. Her reaction was absolutely right. Arlene's own judgment had been off.

She followed Corinne back to the rehearsal space. Give her an hour or two and she would calm down. Arlene winked at her when she entered the room. Corinne gave her an indignant look.

'What are you doing here?' asked Marcus.

'I crossed town to have lunch with Corinne, so I thought I'd watch rehearsal for an hour or so. Is that all right?'

'Sure. Make yourself comfortable.'

They were working on Act 2, Scene 2. It was a piece between Mark and Colleen Delaney. Arlene sat beside Isobel and watched.

Richard and Marcia were working without books, and the scene was well developed. Marcia's Colleen had come on a lot since Arlene had last seen it. She had a sunken, defeated expression on her face, and her shoulders cast a curve of dejection. Richard was transformed. He was playing, riding the negative aspects of his character, surfing high on those harsh waves embedded in the writing. Having ceased to deny the darkness, he indulged it. Played it. In his fingertips there was potential violence. The explosion in the final scene would now work.

All of this seemed clear to Arlene as she watched Richard and Marcia act out the scene. But also, she now saw him as he used to be. This was the black Richard, the black Dick that she had known. The cruel volatility of him. Those hands, pulsing with a desire for revenge unspecifically directed. He gorged himself on vile energies. It was so ugly, so sad. Arlene shivered.

'Great,' said Marcus as they finished the scene. 'Very, *very* strong.'

Isobel smiled sadly and a little sigh seeped from her. Arlene could tell by Isobel's face that this was what she wanted. Richard had altered his interpretation to suit her.

'How does it feel?' Marcus asked Richard.

'Good. It'll help with later on, the final scene.'

'Yes, it feels really creepy,' said Marcia. 'It really makes me feel scared.'

'It's very good,' said Isobel, 'very sad and very good.'

Richard smiled at her. Since Arlene had privileged him with Isobel's secrets, he knew what she was really saying. He went over to her and gave her shoulder a little encouraging squeeze.

'I'm glad you're happy with it,' he said.

Richard had taken to calling round to Arlene's apartment frequently in the evenings. Isobel had gone back to cooking, and he occasionally joined them for dinner.

Arlene noticed that Isobel gave Richard man-sized portions of whatever she was cooking. 'Isobel,' she said one day, after he'd gone home, 'you always give Richard the largest piece of meat or whatever.'

'Well,' said Isobel, 'he is six-foot two, and underweight for his height. He needs more food. You are five-foot five, and overweight, so naturally you need less food than he does.'

Defeated, Arlene didn't push it any further, but continued to make her clandestine forays to the chipper. She seemed to get on better with Richard now, enjoyed his visits to the flat with Isobel present to prevent any unpleasant intimacies.

She flip-flopped on the subject of Isobel: some days she was almost unbearably thrilled to see her and talk to her, other days she felt crowded by Isobel's all-invading emotional personality. Sometimes she snapped at Isobel, to distance her, to test her.

'Arlene, are you happy?' she'd asked one evening.

'What?'

'Happy. Are you happy?'

'What sort of a foolish question is that?'

'It's just a question.'

'Sure. I'm fine.'

'Fine! What kind of a way is that to be?' said Isobel laughing.

'Well, what about you Isobel? Are you happy?'

'Leave me out of this. We're talking about you.'

'No,' said Arlene, riled. 'You try to top yourself a week ago and then you have the gall to interrogate me about whether or not I'm happy.'

'This isn't an interrogation. It's just a chat. I just want you to be happy. You don't think about yourself very much, I'm just encouraging you to.'

'There's such a thing as thinking about yourself too much,' said Arlene.

'Sure,' said Isobel, 'but you're hardly guilty of that.'

'No, I wasn't talking about myself,' said Arlene. 'I was talking about you.'

'Oh,' said Isobel, stung.

'Well, let me tell you, I'd be a lot bloody happier if you hadn't carved up your wrists last week,' said Arlene, shortly, sharply.

Isobel lifted her head and looked at Arlene. Her eyes had that hunted look in them. Stung. She took her napkin off her lap, folded it neatly, stood up and went off to her box-room.

Arlene sat there and stared after her. She poured herself another glass of wine. Why on earth had she done that? She knew it was nasty, sadistic. Why had she let Isobel get on top of her? Poking at her. Prodding her. Upsetting her at every turn. She'd better go and apologise. She tapped on Isobel's door.

No answer.

'Isobel, I'm so sorry.'

Silence.

She continued, 'This is a preliminary apology. I'm going for a walk and I'll come back later with a proper one.'

The canal always worked. It was like a long straight knife wound in the heart of the city. Humanoids tried to pave over the earth, citify the ground, cover over nature. But it broke through, and in this case, with its lush vegetation and its population of ducks riding on its back, it was like a long glimpse of the flesh of the earth.

She arrived at Paddy and sat down. He knew she'd done a

bad thing. He felt truly cold and stony. She didn't have the energy to talk to him.

Back home, she knocked on Isobel's door.

'Come in,' said Isobel.

She had been crying. Her eyes were red. Arlene felt awful. She felt as though she had just terrorised a small child.

'I'm so sorry, Isobel.'

'It's all right,' sniffed Isobel. 'You're right. I am selfish.'

Arlene didn't want this. She would be much happier if Isobel told her to fuck off. The martyr act was a total killer.

'It's just,' said Arlene, 'I must have been hurt by what you did.'

'What do you mean?'

'I care about you a good deal, and I thought you cared a little about me. I don't know how to put this, but, but, I thought that if you had any feelings towards me, you wouldn't try to kill yourself, because you'd not want to upset me.'

'I guess I'm not used to having people care about me,' said Isobel.

'I s'pose I'm not used to caring very much about people.'

'You are right,' said Isobel, 'I do spend too much time thinking about myself.'

'No, you don't. I shouldn't have said that. I'm under pressure with the show. I shouldn't be taking it out on you.'

'You're upset about Richard, aren't you?'

'What makes you say that?'

'I just know you are uneasy around him. It isn't only myself I spend a lot of time thinking about.'

'Not really,' said Arlene, 'though I reckon he is some part of the strain. It's got more to do with the pressure of the show.'

'Sure,' said Isobel.

'You see, I'm used to living on my own, and when work gets too much, I generally take it out on the furniture.'

'And I have become part of the furniture,' said Isobel.

'I didn't mean it like that,' said Arlene. She knew by Isobel's eyes that she had lost her trust. 'I am so, so sorry Isobel. I have no right to take things out on you. Please forgive me.'

'Sure,' said Isobel. 'I shouldn't be here. You are meant to be on your own, Arlene. Your spirit is such that you don't make sense in the context of anyone else's company.'

Isobel wasn't trying to be cruel. She was simply trying to explain Arlene's behaviour to herself. Arlene was chilled.

'I'll be moving out, I promise, just as soon as the show is safely up.'

Shit.

Isobel gave her a friendly little smile, and squeezed her arm.

Shit!

previews

Arlene was depressed for an evening after her row with Isobel, but soon toughened herself up.

She didn't have time to engage in Isobel's games. She had a show to open.

Despite Marcia's misgivings, the first preview went ahead on Friday 13 September. Arlene had hired a wizard production manager, Daniel O'Connor, who could work magic, and into his capable hands were consigned the logistical problems of the fit up. He decided that they'd have to work through Thursday night in order to get everything done.

The Lunar theatre was a converted cinema, seating three hundred and fifty. A good, middling size. The original structure had been built during the Thirties, and its facade had the bold, smooth lines of that period. It had closed as a cinema in the sixties, and been used as a furniture display room until it had been bought in 1984 by its current owner, one Aengus Hennessy. Hennessy was a philanthropic businessman, whose love for the entertainment world knew no bounds. He had restored its function as a place of entertainment, despite advice from his accountant to turn it into a car-park. Car-parks were where the money was nowadays. But Aengus Hennessy was not to be deflected and persisted in his dream of opening a theatre. The accountant just threw his hands up in the air and sighed. Arlene and Marcus were both very fond of the Lunar Theatre. You could do what you wanted with it. Turn it this way or that. Move the stage and seats around. It had a good, comfortable foyer with a bar, and decent sized accommodation backstage.

On Friday morning the crew was beginning to show signs of strain. The actors had been called for ten AM. It meant they would get a chance to settle into the dressing rooms and walk the space in the morning, before the tech, but the crew were exhausted, and a bit ragged, and they were behind schedule. Nothing was as far along as it should be.

Neil O'Mahony, the designer, was feeling very stressed, and sat down to drink a diet Coke and contemplate the work. This was his most difficult phase, this final drawing together of all the elements. It required total concentration. He hated doing all-nighters.

He felt very hard done by. Why was it always the designer's work that got short-changed in terms of time? He was supposed to have had three hours clear on the set after construction had finished and before lighting got going, but the construction people had over-run and the lighting simply couldn't wait, so he'd had his time shaved at both ends. Because he was quite young, and though talented, inexperienced, he hadn't quite got the hang of asserting himself during a get-in. I bet Robert Ballagh doesn't get shoved around like this, he thought.

The actors entered the auditorium.

'It's a padded cell!' said Marcia, in a loud voice.

Everybody went quiet.

'And those things over there. They look like giant loo rolls,' and she giggled a little.

'Let me take you all to your dressing rooms!' said Arlene, before Marcia had a chance to say anything else insulting.

Neil stared after the retreating actors. 'I hate people commenting on the set before it's finished. That Marcia Range is a bit of a bitch,' he grumbled. 'I know it looks like a padded cell now, but it'll look like the interior of a womb by tonight. I promise you.'

'Neil, how do you know?' asked Candy.

'What?'

'How do you know what the interior of a womb looks like?'

Neil stared at her. 'I remember, OK?'

Arlene led the actors off backstage to their quarters. They were nice comfortable dressing rooms, spacious.

'Okay, who wants a room to themselves, and who wants to share?' said Arlene. Normally she would assign Richard and Marcia separate rooms and request that Corinne and Paula share, according to seniority. But under the circumstances, she thought it wiser to keep the two younger women apart. For a moment Arlene thought that Marcia was going to demand a separate room, so she gave her a sharp look.

Marcia took the hint and piped up. 'Richard how about you and I share. We've a lot of scenes together, and we can run lines.'

'Sure,' said Richard.

'Fine,' Arlene said. 'You can have room one, as it is the

biggest. You two can have rooms two and three.'

'Fine,' said Paula.

'Grand by me,' said Corinne.

Excellent, thought Arlene. Happy actors in their dressing rooms.

Arlene returned to the auditorium. Marcus and Neil were in deep discussion.

'*I* know it's the interior of a womb. *You* know it's the interior of a womb. What I want to know is, how will the *audience* know it is the interior of a womb?' said Marcus.

'I don't mind,' said Neil, 'if they don't have an absolutely clear sense that that is what it's supposed to be. It should be more subliminal. They should get womb-like visual vibes from the set.'

'Womb-like visual vibes,' repeated Marcus, his voice a tad uneasy. He had loved Neil's concept right through rehearsals, but now, staring at the yet-to-be-painted white-padded structure, he wasn't so sure.

'What do you think, Arlene?'

Arlene knew that Marcus's crisis of confidence had been prompted by Marcia's stray comment.

'I think it will look like the interior of a womb when it's painted,' she said, backing Neil up.

'Maybe,' said Marcus, 'if the fallopian tubes were less abstract and looked more like fallopian tubes,' gesturing at two long papier mâché structures lying by the wall.

'No, the whole point is that it should look abstract. Nobody wants to see realistic-looking fallopian tubes.'

'Hmmmn,' said Marcus.

'But you liked all of this in the model,' said Neil, upset now.

His was a nature that got sad rather than angry.

'I know I did,' said Marcus.

'Wait until I put up the ovaries,' said Neil, indicating the two cubic structures that were lying to the side of the auditorium.

In a flash, Arlene saw it. The entire structure coloured pink and lit splendidly against the blackness. This odd structure; you couldn't be sure what it was, but part of you would suspect that it was indeed a woman's womb. It was going to be magical.

'I think that it's going to look fantastic!' she said and she jumped to her feet and clapped her hands together. 'Worry not, Marcus. Your judgment hasn't failed you yet.'

Arlene's attention was caught by the playing space. One of the stagehands, just hired for the day, was balancing precariously on a ledge as he reached out and attempted to screw a light fitting into place on the wall. What he was doing was dangerous, and if he fell, he'd get a nasty tumble.

Arlene called Daniel O'Connor over. 'Who's the guy in the green jumper?' she asked.

'Johnny Mack is his name,' said Daniel.

'Is he aware that what he is doing is totally dangerous?'

'He's just a little too keen,' said Daniel.

'I want him sent home,' said Arlene. 'Pay him and send him home.'

'Oh.'

'And please explain to him that putting himself at risk is a stupid thing to do. Not because I have the slightest concern about him breaking his neck, but because he will mess up the stage and take up all our time as we try and look after him and his injuries. Also, he will probably sue me, and make my insurance premiums go through the roof. If he likes thrill-seeking, he should take up stock-car racing or rock-climbing, but whatever he does, I want him to get the hell out of here.'

This was all delivered in a cool, semi-distracted, dispassionate tone. Daniel made the mistake of thinking that her voice indicated only a casual concern.

'He's just inexperienced. I'll get him down off that ledge. I don't really want to send him home. I will need the extra body later on, when we've stuff to hump around.'

He was wrong.

'Send him home,' said Arlene. 'It will be the best lesson he has ever learnt.'

She handed him her mobile. 'Here. Phone another body, if you need one. Half the country's unemployed.'

Carmel entered the auditorium from the foyer and waved at Arlene. Arlene left Daniel with her phone and his unpleasant firing task.

'All the previews are sold out!' said Carmel. 'The office opened at 10 AM and the phone literally hasn't stopped. I had to man a phone for them, it was so busy. They're making a cancellation list now,' and Carmel put a Styrofoam cup of coffee into Arlene's hand.

'Great,' said Arlene. She lifted the lid and smelt the coffee. Delightful. Carmel was so efficient she even knew how to buy good coffee in a Styrofoam cup.

Candy came bounding up to them. 'Arlene, we're about to start the tech. Is it OK if I call the actors?'

'Candy. Marcus is your boss in here. Don't be asking me,' said Arlene.

After Candy bounded off, Arlene turned to Carmel. 'Carmel. Do you think that I am a bossy person?'

'Yes,' said Carmel.

'Inordinately so, or just as much as is necessary?'

'No, you're over-the-top bossy.'

'Oh.'

'But don't worry about it.'

'Do you know, I think it's in my nature to be bossy. I've always been like that. Once I was in a supermarket, and I saw two sales assistants trying to stack various cartons on top of each other. They were making a mess of it, because they weren't getting the base right and it was all coming apart as they got to the top. And I, for some reason, decided to intervene. I gave them instructions, and supervised them until they got it right. They did exactly as they were told. The fact that I wasn't an employee didn't seem to enter their heads.'

'More fool you,' said Carmel.

The actors were duly summoned, and Arlene sat at the back of the auditorium while Marcus worked through all the cues. He did one after another, going over each cue several times.

Arlene watched Marcus work, and was impressed. He was an absolute perfectionist. Wouldn't leave a cue until it was perfect. Worried those damn cues to death. And he was endlessly patient and courteous with everybody. Even when Corinne went missing and Candy had to go off and find her. She'd just wandered outside for some air. Marcus was totally polite to her.

After a while Arlene couldn't bear to watch. It was such a slow process. She knew that it was necessary, this endless redoing of cues, but its slowness and cumbersomeness did her head in. She went back to the office.

*

Arlene sat beside Isobel for the first preview. It was indeed a full house. It did her soul good, to see all those paying customers streaming into the auditorium.

Richard was spellbinding, dynamic. But they all were. Marcus had toned down the melodramatic elements of the text and delivered a smooth and modern whole. But Arlene was distracted throughout the performance by Isobel, who was so tense she sat on the edge of her seat and chewed her hair throughout. Her body made small involuntary shudders as the play hit its dramatic peaks. Arlene watched her reactions out of the corner of her eye. Isobel seemed to have forgotten that she was there. During the scene of violence at the end of the play, Isobel's face distorted into an expression of intense pain.

After the curtain, Arlene looked over, expecting Isobel to be distraught, but she wasn't. She was totally calm. Like a lake after a storm.

'That was fabulous. I was so moved,' she said.

'Well done,' said Arlene.

'No, not me,' said Isobel, 'It's them. Those actors, those magicians. They've made it sing.'

opening night

Arlene made Isobel agree to her doctor's suggestion that she take some tranquillisers to stop her bouncing off the ceiling on opening night.

'Look, you're like a helium balloon. I can't keep a hold of you all night.'

'Yes, Mammy,' said Isobel, too pleased with everything to be annoyed at Arlene bossing her around. They had had breakfast together, Isobel allowing Arlene a feed of sausages considering the day that was in it.

The piano phone rang. Arlene dived on it.

'Yo!'

'It's Candy. Sorry to call so early, but disaster has struck.'

'Ye-es.' Disaster was due.

'I put all the whites in the washing machine last night and there was a red napkin in the pocket of one and–'

'And they're all ruined.'

'They're not *all* ruined. The shirts and blouses I can bleach and I'll have them right as rain by lunchtime. I wouldn't be bothered phoning you if it was just the shirts, but Nuala's white dress, for the *Ave Maria* scene, that fabric won't take a bleach.'

'Can't we get another one?'

'It was 'specially made.'

'Can't we get another one made?'

'It cost a fortune.'

'How much? No, don't tell me, just do it, Candy. I don't care how much it costs.'

'The material was imported from Paris.'

'Have you spoken to Tiffany?'

'No. I wanted to talk to you first. She'll go mad. Tiffany loved that dress. It was her favourite thing in the costume design.'

'Just tell her to do her best with a replacement.'

'I'm terribly sorry. I feel awful.'

Arlene settled back to her breakfast. It occurred to her that Candy was great to be in the theatre finding out that she'd ruined the wash by eight-thirty in the morning. She'd buggered everything up, but she was in on time to put it to rights. Now, there was a stage-manager worth her wages. Sausages were the most delicious thing in the world when you were hungry.

'What's the problem? asked Isobel.

'Nothing serious,' said Arlene.

'What do you do today?' asked Isobel.

'Well, normally I have lots of last-minute details to attend to but, for some reason, this time, I have nothing to do. I think it's because Carmel is so on the ball.'

'Let's go to the pictures in the afternoon,' said Isobel.

'Sure,' agreed Arlene.

*

Arlene had scheduled a reception for six-thirty, so guests could have a few drinks before the show. The foyer swarmed with people. Isobel held court, looking buoyant and terribly dramatic in a long figure-hugging red dress, and folks flocked around her like bees round honey.

Sergeant O'Hanlon and his daughter Rosa arrived. Rosa was a lovely little thing, as slim as a whippet, and quite small, but with huge grey eyes that seemed to devour everything, and the longest eyelashes Arlene had ever seen. Arlene brought them over to meet Isobel, and Rosa was so pleased, you could see she was almost going to burst.

'I'm so thrilled, so thrilled!' said Rosa.

'That's very kind of you,' said Isobel.

'So thrilled, so thrilled.'

'Maybe you'll sit beside me tonight?' said Isobel to Rosa. Rosa went into transports of joy. Hero worship. Arlene had never witnessed it close-up before.

Sergeant O'Hanlon was clearly moved. 'You see, Rosa wants to be a writer. Ever since she saw Isobel Coole on the telly, she has been saying to herself, that'll be me. I'll be a writer like Isobel Coole, and I'll be on the telly,' he said, with tears in his eyes.

There *was* something special about Isobel, thought Arlene. She had some power or other. She held a strange attraction for others. Arlene looked at her now, moving expertly and gracefully through the crowd, yet finding time to single out little, sick Rosa. As Isobel gestured with her hands covered in fishnet gloves, Arlene forgot that they were there to cover the scars on her wrists, so very cool was this Isobel.

David Range arrived in the door. His hair was cut and he

was neatly dressed. Marcia had relented and sent him an invitation for opening night. She had decided to take him back, and had scheduled her dramatic forgiveness scene for after the evening's performance, so it didn't put her off her stride. David didn't know this yet, and he was still very nervous.

'Good luck,' he said to Arlene.

'Well, we can't turn back now,' said Arlene.

'How's Marcia?' he asked.

'Nervous, but fine.'

'Did she mention me?' he asked.

The sooner Marcia put him out of his misery the better.

'You'll see her after,' said Arlene reassuringly and patted him on the shoulder.

David wasn't sure how to take this cryptic statement. It might mean Marcia was going to welcome him back on the one hand, but on the other hand, it might mean he was for the chop. 'Arlene, what do you mean –' he said anxiously.

But Arlene was gone.

Martin Campbell arrived, this time on his own. No Aunt Isa.

'Where's Aunt Isa?' asked Arlene.

'Not well enough to come, I'm afraid, so I'm on my own.'

'Well, you're welcome,' said Arlene.

'You look splendid! That's a lovely suit.'

'Thank you,' said Arlene and twirled in her new green suit. She called it a tit-and-thigh suit, because it had a plunging neckline covered in sparkly diamante, and a deep slit up one side of the skirt. Isobel had picked it out for her a week previously, and made her buy it.

'Here, for luck,' and Martin handed her a small package wrapped in yellow paper.

'What? You shouldn't have.'

'Please, Arlene. Take it.'

'But I couldn't.'

'You invite me all the time, and I accept your invitations. Allow me my thanks.'

How strange. Martin giving her a little gift. How odd.

She slipped into the darkened auditorium and opened it. It was a silver pendant denoting the masks of comedy and tragedy. It looked expensive, she thought, but was totally tasteless. An ideal gift for a seventeen-year-old drama student. She was going to put it in her pocket, but on an impulse, hung it round her neck. Might as well get into the spirit of things. Heigh ho!

Candy sidled up to Arlene, who suddenly remembered. 'What did you do about the dress?'

'We got a new one made. The material isn't as nice as the first, and Tiffany went into quite a rage. Marcus tried to calm her down though. She was looking for my blood all morning, but I lay low. Finally she tracked me to the Spar supermarket where I was getting the edible props, and let fly at me.'

'Oh, dear,' said Arlene.

'I was so tense I burst into tears. When I got back here, Marcus was raging at how upset *I* was, so he in turn laid into Tiffany, told her she'd no right to be upsetting the stage-manager when I had so much to do to get ready for opening night. But then Tiffany got *real* upset, and I ended up having to get her tea and tissues.'

Arlene was glad she'd been in the cinema, and missed all of this kerfuffle.

'So finally, Tiffany apologised and I gave her a Twix bar, and we made up.'

'Good.'

'Quite a lot of wasted energy, really,' said Candy.

'Where is Tiff now?'

'She's in the back putting the final touches to the dress. It's not needed until the second half, so it's not quite finished yet. She says she'll have it ready though. I'd better get back to my chores, I s'pose.'

Arlene watched the retreating Candy, her curly hair bobbing along. It had a life of its own, that hair. It made Candy look strangely startled, almost electrocuted.

It was now after seven-thirty and the actors were scattered about the stage and auditorium, all doing their warm ups.

'La-la-la-la-la, tra-la-la-la-la, fa-la-la-la-la-la,' went Marcia in ascending octaves. Corinne was singing scales. Paula was doing stretching exercises. For a moment Arlene couldn't see Richard, but then she spotted him, sitting in the back row of the auditorium. She went over to him.

'I like to sit quietly and concentrate before the show,' he said in a hushed voice. 'It's funny, no matter how many shows I do, I'm always nervous before the curtain goes up on opening night,' he added with mild but real panic, an actor's panic, showing in his eyes.

'I'll leave you in peace so,' she said in an equally hushed voice, and she went to go, but he grabbed her arm and gave it a squeeze.

'Thanks,' he said. 'It's done me a lot of good, being here, and doing this,' and he smiled at her.

'Thank you,' she said. 'It's done the box-office a lot of good too. And good luck.'

'Fifteen minutes! Clear the auditorium please as the house is about to open,' came Candy's bright tones over the loud-speaker.

Arlene went back out to the foyer. She spied Marcus sitting in the corner against the bar. He gestured to her. 'Are you going to watch the show? Or are you going to sit here at the bar with me and drink gin and watch the proceedings on that monitor over there?'

'I'll stay here,' she said.

The audience filed into the auditorium, and Marcus ordered a bottle of gin and a bowl of lemons.

'Cheers!' he said.

The opening music sounded and as the lights went up, on the monitor appeared the actors, in the medium of play.

The Corkscrew, a nightclub near the theatre, was the venue for the after-show party. Everybody was as high as a kite, and energy bounced off the walls.

Arlene watched at a distance as Marcia forgave David. David wept. It was touching, almost. She was glad Isobel had taken the tranquillisers, because if she hadn't, she didn't know how she would have been able for the excitement.

The two women took a taxi home at around three o'clock, and fell in the front door. Isobel tripped over one of the Cartwrights' cats in the hall and her own screech drowned out the screech of the cat.

'Jaysus, you've put the heart crossways in me,' said Arlene. They made their way up the stairs, the smell of cat piss beginning to reassert itself again, as Isobel's vigilance had lapsed a little.

'I have us a private bottle of champagne in the fridge,' said Arlene. She produced the bottle and opened it with a resounding 'pop'. She poured it into two wide-brimmed, shallow champagne glasses.

'Did you know, Isobel, that this style of champagne glass was designed from a cast made of the shape of one of Napoleon's mistress's breasts.' Arlene held the glass up to the light. 'Pretty,' she said, as the glass wobbled. She was a bit drunk.

Isobel picked up her glass, but she too was a bit the worse for wear, and her hand was unsteady. The champagne sloshed out the side of the shallow glass.

'A pity she didn't have larger breasts, because I'm having difficulty balancing the stuff in this,' and she giggled. She put the glass down on a little table, and attempted to lap up the champagne, with limited success.

'If you were a dog, Isobel, you'd be a poodle.'

'If you were a dog, you'd be a sheepdog.'

'Why a sheepdog?'

'You'd chase sheep around, and worry them.'

'Oh.'

'Let me tell you a secret, Arlene.'

'What is it? I like secrets.'

'I never took the Valium.'

'Oh.'

'I thought that it would be a pity to waste any of this feeling tonight. I'll take the Valium tomorrow when there's nothing to feel anyway.'

'Oh. That's good, Isobel.'

'So, it's up,' said Isobel. 'The baby is born.'

'Yeah. A healthy birth.'

The buzzer sounded.

'Who the hell could that be?' asked Isobel, startled. 'It's after half-past four in the morning.'

'It's Timothy. My paperman. I engage him to get me the papers first thing in the morning when I've a show on.'

'Whyever for?' asked Isobel.

'Reviews, of course,' Arlene said as she greeted Timothy through the intercom, and buzzed him up.

'Reviews! I forgot all about them,' said Isobel. 'Maybe I'll need those Valium after all.'

Timothy arrived in no time at all, as he'd taken the stairs three steps at a time, scattering screeching cats to left and right. He jogged in the door. He worked for his uncle Pat, and it was with Pat that Arlene made the arrangements, but it was Timothy who did the hard work. That's capitalism for you.

'Here y'are, Elaine,' said Timothy, handing over the two daily papers.

'Thanks, I'll fix it up with your uncle next week, and by the way, it's Ar-lay-nah, not Elaine.'

'So, is it a theatre show yis are after doing?'

'Yes. In the Lunar Theatre. I'll get you tickets if you like.'

'Can I've a glass of water?' he asked, ignoring her offer.

Isobel went to the kitchen and came back with a glass of water.

'Thanks, doll-face,' he said, and winked at her. He downed

the water in one gulp. Picked up his bag and jogged out the door, calling 'See ya again, Elaine.'

'Doll-face!' said Isobel.

'I think he's on speed,' said Arlene. 'It's the only possible explanation for it.'

'Doll-face!' said Isobel once again. 'I'm old enough to be his mother.'

'Here,' said Arlene, and she handed the papers over to Isobel. 'You can read them first.'

'Not bloody likely,' said Isobel, and dropped the two papers as though they were hot coals.

Arlene picked them up and expertly found the review pages. She read the first one.

'This one's a rave,' and she handed it over to the shaking Isobel. 'And so is this one,' and she handed that over too. 'I'm afraid we have a winner on our hands.'

Isobel's nervous eyes scanned the columns. 'Phew!' she said. 'They're great. Do you know, Arlene, that I've never had a bad review for any of my books? It's extraordinary, but somehow, I've been terribly lucky.'

Arlene poured out more champagne.

'They say wonderful things about the actors. I'm sure they'll be pleased. And Marcus gets a very nice mention here: "the hand of Marcus Harmony's fluid direction is felt throughout." Marcus'll like that,' said Isobel. 'Or will he? What does "fluid" mean?'

'No, it's good,' said Arlene. ' "Fluid" is good.'

'But it might mean watery?'

'No, no, "fluid" is good.'

'Or sloppy.'

'Believe me.'

'And this one refers to "Neil O'Mahony's undulating, womb-like set." Neil will be pleased. He told me he wasn't sure anybody would know what it was supposed to be,' said Isobel. 'I'm glad that they knew. I'm glad they knew it was a womb.'

saturday night

Isobel went to the show each night. She sat in the audience, going through the play as intensely as the actors on the stage. She felt Nuala's trauma, Mark's pain, Colleen's numbness. Each night as the lights went down and the first few notes of the pre-show music played, her emotional system triggered the replaying loop of her own pain. She loved it. It made her feel. As she sat in the darkness she underwent the most profound catharsis.

Arlene, on the other hand, could never bear to watch a show after it had opened. She wasn't entirely sure why.

On the Saturday night of the first week of the show, she was at home and determined on an early night. Ten-thirty saw her tucked up in bed with the light off. She must have fallen asleep straight away, because when she woke up to a fuming Isobel standing by her bedside, she had no idea what time it was.

Isobel was waving a newspaper at her. 'I'm furious!'

'What's that?' asked Arlene.

'It's the *Sunday Echo*. I picked it up it town.'

'Oh,' said Arlene. 'I never get them until the morning,

because the country editions sometimes don't carry the Dublin reviews.'

'Well this one does,' said Isobel and slammed a newspaper down on the bed. Arlene picked it up.

REVIEWS

Over the Moon, a new play by Isobel Coole, is on offer at the Lunar Theatre. It tells the story of Nuala, a precocious nineteen-year-old who leads a double life, being the dutiful daughter fundraising for her father's anti-abortion campaign by day and going to discos and taking hallucinogenic drugs by night. It is set in 1983 during the 'Right to Life' campaign, and against a background of terrible early-eighties' disco music. The play presents the titanic conflict between tradition (rural) and modernity (urban) which has shaped individual destinies on this island, but it never actually engages with the pluralism of the present; at no point is there any co-incidence between the destiny of the community and the destiny of the individual. Because the author has taken leave of cultural contexts, the play becomes meaningful only as an aspect of the human condition, and thus descends into hopeless melodrama. The plight of the Irish girl, sandwiched between English abortion clinics on the one hand, and American popular music on the other, is never intelligently excavated. No real sense of the early eighties in Ireland is conveyed (where are the hunger-strikers, for example?) The father, a narrow minded gombeen-man, never rises above a limited stereotype.

I felt compassion for the actors, condemned as they are to act out this travesty of emotion night-after-night act out this travesty of emotion night-after-night. Only the sardonic Paula Costello as Cathy emerges with any dignity. The others are sucked down into a quagmire of histrionics. The last scene between Nuala and her father is comical. Never was a final curtain more merciful or kind.

Tommy Hatchett

Arlene looked up. 'Phew!' she said. 'He didn't leave a tooth in it.'

'How can anybody have written something so cruel?' said Isobel, tears in her eyes.

'He isn't called Tommy Hatchett for nothing.'

'Tommy Hatchett? What kind of a name is Hatchett?'

'It's his real name. There's a Mrs Hatchett and some sharp little Hatchetts.'

'But he can't get away with this,' fumed Isobel.

'He can and he will. There's nothing we can do about it. It's his job to review, and if he doesn't like a show, he has to say so.'

'You sound like you're on his side.'

'No, Isobel. I'm just being practical. The two daily reviews were good, and the two other Sundays will be good. Four out of five. A good average.'

'How do you know that the other two Sundays will be good?'

'I know. I have moles in all the papers who let me know things.'

'Did you know about this Tommy Hatchett demolition job?'

'Yes. Not in so much detail. I hadn't realised it would be *so* bad.'

'The other reviews used the term "melodramatic" to describe the play, but they use it more positively. In fact, the other reviews are very complimentary about the actors and about the direction and all that stuff but they don't say too much about the writing at all.'

'Oh, Isobel, you're overreacting. It's just a bad review. You're obviously not used to them.'

'No, I'm not. Everybody says that my writing is good. Who is this Hatchett guy? What's he ever done?'

'Nothing. He's a sad hasn't-been who fancies himself as the Frank Rich of Dublin. Fortunately, his influence doesn't extend beyond the parameters of his own office.'

'I've never read anything worse. It's in the paper. Everyone will read it. I won't be able to go out.'

'Don't give it another thought. I've had millions of bad reviews.'

'Well, it's all right for you to be cavalier. It's not your guts that are up there on the stage.'

'True.'

'You haven't risked anything.'

That wasn't entirely true.

'Look, Isobel. The show is sold out for all of next week. The phone is hopping all day and the next couple of weeks are booking heavily. This guy is just an asshole and you must pay no attention to him.'

'He repeats "travesty of emotion" twice.'

'That's just gremlins in the newspaper's layout machine. Don't take *that* personally.'

Arlene sighed and got up out of bed. She went into the living room and poured out some red wine. 'Here, get this into you. It's a narcotic.'

Isobel took the glass of red wine.

'We'll have to get you a thicker skin, Isobel. You can't take life so damn seriously. You'll wear yourself out.'

'I suppose you're right.' Isobel seemed to have calmed down a little now. She was very volatile, and suffered major storms, but they did seem to pass, to blow themselves out.

'That's a lovely little silver pendant in the bathroom.'

'What? Oh that thing. I think it's totally naff. Martin Campbell gave it to me.'

'Oh, it's delightful. Unusual.'

'It's not unusual. It's common as muck. Every sixteen-year-old who wants to be an actor owns a brooch of the masks of comedy and tragedy.'

Isobel sprang up and went into the bathroom returning with the pendant in her hand.

'But it's not comedy and tragedy,' said Isobel. 'Look!'

Arlene looked at the silver piece. No, Isobel was quite right. It wasn't comedy and tragedy. Arlene had only looked at it in the darkened auditorium, and had subsequently worn it around her neck. She had not examined it. It was, in fact, two comedy masks. There was something strangely disconcerting about it. It seemed like a disruption of the established order of things. Each clown mask smiled up at her, beaming positive vibes. Like smiling spirits, like fools.

dinner party A

'I have no idea why Isobel cancelled. She was all set to come but at seven o'clock she developed a mild headache and decided to stay at home,' said Arlene by way of apology, when she arrived at Marcia's house bringing with her a bottle of ancient and very good red wine, that Martin had dusted down for her from his back-room hoard.

'Oh, I do hope she's all right,' said Marcia.

'Yeah, I think she's fine. I reckon she needs an early night.'

Number 13 Hope Street was cheerier-looking now than it had been on Arlene's last visit. There was a big fire burning and lots of bits and pieces lying around, giving the place a friendlier air. The very grateful David had been re-installed.

'What'll you have to drink?' asked David.

'A glass of red,' said Arlene.

David went off to fetch it. He was on his best behaviour, and was fussing about, helping Marcia in the kitchen.

'Thanks,' said Arlene when he gave her the glass. The doorbell went and shortly, in came Richard.

'Sunday nights! I just love them,' said Richard. 'I enjoy doing the show every night during the week, but I think I enjoy *not* doing it on Sunday more than I enjoy doing it on any other night, if you get my drift.'

'Peace is merely the postponement of friction,' said Arlene.

'Here you go,' said David, putting another glass of red wine into Arlene's hand. She already had one, but decided not to mention it to the over eager David, who was exhibiting several of the signs of stress.

'Thanks!' and she smiled and put one glass down beside the other. David and Marcia went off to the kitchen to attend to the cooking.

'I had lunch with my agent today. He flew over to try and talk me into taking a film offer in December. To begin with I demurred, but he started threatening me, telling me I was ruining my career,' said Richard.

'So are you going to do it?'

'I finally said yes. This run will finish in the last week in November. I feel I've been here long enough, got a good feel of the old sod.'

'Sounds good,' said Arlene. 'What's the movie?'

'*Mansfield Park*. The Jane Austen novel.'

'Is there another Jane Austen novel left to film?'

Marcia came in and spoke in hushed tones: 'David has gone to great trouble to make these "puréed" carrots. He picked up the recipe from Sophie Grigson in last Sunday's paper, apparently. I think it's muck, like bloody baby food, but please, don't say anything mean about them in front of him.'

'Sure,' said Arlene. 'What? Me mean? Get out of here.'

'I much prefer a carrot to have a bit of damn crunch in it, but anyway,' and with that Marcia exited again. Arlene could feel domestic tension in the air.

'Well, that's good,' she continued, 'that you've got something else lined up now. And you'll return to London?'

'Yes. It's done me a lot of good, being here. I feel much better, much stronger. It's been nice to work on this project, low-key and intimate, and not a lot of the major public pressures that I'm used to having to deal with.'

Patronise me, why don't you, thought Arlene.

'Sorry, that sounded a bit patronising.'

'S'okay – I've got thick skin,' said Arlene.

'So, Isobel didn't come tonight?'

'No.'

'I hope she's not staying at home on account of that silly review.'

'I doubt it,' said Arlene, though in fact she thought Richard's interpretation was correct. Indeed Isobel was staying at home, sulking.

Marcia and David arrived in with a tray of steaming starters, and they adjourned to the dining table, which was located in the corner of the room. Though Arlene hadn't been to Marcia's house often in the recent past, she used to be a frequent guest, and knew they were in for a culinary treat. Marcia was a superb cook. When she started out as an actress, before she was making any money, she had worked at night in a fancy restaurant. But while her peers were waitressing, Marcia, embarrassed by being seen to be out of acting work, insisted on hiding out in the kitchens, where she acquired skills that she thought might stand to her should she need to pursue an alternative career. Happily, that didn't happen, though she often threatened to 'abandon this ungrateful profession and retire to Kerry to open an exclusive restaurant, where she'd get a bit of bloody appreciation'.

They all tucked in to the starters with enthusiasm. It was a delicious fish pasta.

'So Isobel has a headache,' said Marcia tartly. 'She really is given to the vapours.'

Nobody rose to the bait.

'It's great the way the show is booking so well,' said Marcia changing the subject. 'I jut love playing to the texture of a full house. My performance expands on a per capita basis.'

'Speaking of full houses or otherwise,' said Richard, 'I remember the most embarrassing moment of my career. It was in 1982, or was it 83? Early eighties anyhow, and it was an experimental poetry and movement show I was involved in in an art gallery in Temple Bar. We knew there was a big international agent coming, and it meant a lot to us, we were all dying for the big break. We had only one booking that night, a party of four, and they phoned the gallery to cancel at a quarter to eight because they'd missed their bus. It looked like we were going to be playing to the lonely agent. There were three of us in the show, and we were debating whether or not to go on –'

'– Until I arrived,' said Arlene, 'with a gang of twenty people. I'd hijacked them from a gallery opening up the road, they were being turfed out of there, and I promised them free drink after the show –'

'– So the agent came, and sat there in the middle of a gang of art college types, and he seemed to enjoy the show, and indeed, he invited me to audition for a few things after, in fact, he was the one who gave me my big break eventually, or am I right about that? My memory is so hazy. At the end of the show, we went out front and the agent shook our hands and then went, but the thirsty art students were there, looking for their free booze, and Arlene was nowhere to be seen –'

'– but just as the crowd were beginning to get disgruntled, in I arrived with a crate of red wine.'

'It was the most embarrassing moment of my life,' said Richard. 'I still remember it. I'm glad they've knocked down that gallery. It always gave me the heebie-jeebies afterwards. By the way, where did you get that wine? You must have told me at some stage, but I've forgotten.'

'I bought it,' said Arlene.

'Oh,' said Richard, 'I'd thought that you'd magicked it up from somewhere, just like you magicked up the crowd. It's funny that.'

'No. I bought it,' said Arlene. 'With money.'

Marcia and David stared at Arlene and Richard. Suddenly it seemed real that they had been together, had been a couple. Marcia and David glanced at each other and surreptitiously collected up the starter plates and left the room.

'That was so long ago,' said Richard.

'Yes,' said Arlene.

'I'm so impressed by what you're doing now, Arlene. I admire you.'

'The past,' she said, 'is long ago. I was a different person then.'

'Yes.'

The main course arrived, complete with accompanying puréed carrots.

'Mmmm! Delish. Mushy carrots. My fave, second to mushy peas,' said Arlene.

David gave Marcia a supercilious look. 'They're called puréed carrots,' he said.

Richard thought better of remarking on the carrots, seeing as Arlene had done it so elegantly. Otherwise, they chomped their way through an old-fashioned meal of meat and roast spuds. Once they were all relaxed, Marcia stood up to make a speech.

'The guest of honour here tonight is Arlene,' she said, 'and I want to thank you, Arly, for coming round here and making me do this show, because, as you all know I was totally depressed and Arlene here, came along and invited me, no bullied me –'

Arlene's mobile rang.

'I don't believe,' said Marcia in a furious tone, 'that you've left your mobile switched on.'

'Sorry,' said Arlene. 'I'd better answer it,' and she went over to her bag in the corner of the room to fetch her phone, while Marcia muttered furiously in the background about getting that damn phone surgically removed from that foolish woman.

'Hello, Ms Morrissey?' came the voice. 'It's Sergeant O'Hanlon here, I'm afraid we've got a bit of a situation on our hands. I've just had a call from a Mister Tommy Hatchett, and apparently Isobel Coole is over at his house, causing an obstruction and refusing to leave. He called us to get her removed, so, naturally, I thought I'd better ring you first.'

'Thank you, Sergeant.'

'Sorry about this now,' said Sergeant O'Hanlon, 'if you want us to handle it, there's no problem, but I thought you'd like to look after it yourself.'

'Thank you, Sergeant.'

Arlene switched off her phone and looked round at the others. They sensed something was up.

'Isobel's round at Tommy Hatchett's causing trouble. Richard, will you come with me to extricate her?'

'Sure. All in a day's work.'

'This Isobel Coole seems to be very demanding,' said David.

'What about dessert?' said Marcia. 'I've made a pavlova. If you think you're escaping without admiring my pavlova, you've another think coming.'

'We'll be back shortly,' said Richard.

'With an extra mouth,' said Arlene.

dinner party B

Isobel walked up the driveway to a modern house in Bushy Lane, Rathgar, home of Tommy Hatchett. She had got the address by stealing a look at Arlene's diary. There were lots of interesting names and addresses there. The Willows was a detached house and the number of large trees in the front garden gave it an impression of Gothic privacy.

She hesitated a moment on the doorstep, but then boldly rang the doorbell. After a few seconds, a young girl, about fifteen years old, opened the door.

'Yeah?' she said. She was all dressed in black, had black hair and black lipstick, with a very white foundation.

'Is this Tommy Hatchett's house?' asked Isobel.

'You're late. They've already started,' said the girl.

'Where is Mr Hatchett?'

'The Patriarch is in the dining room, seated at the high table of modernism with his fellow capitalists, eating murdered cow and vegetables.'

Isobel stared at the girl.

'I'm upstairs preparing a funeral service for the dead animal,

216

hence the black lipstick,' she said pointing to her lips, 'you may join me if you wish. I'm Melissa.'

'No, thanks,' said Isobel, gently.

'When the aliens arrive,' said Melissa, 'it'll serve us right if we get battery farmed. Did you know that cows aren't allowed to fall in love any more? They get sexually assaulted by a machine which squirts bulls' semen – the dining room is through that door there – and the feminists aren't doing anything about it. They're doing nothing for the bovine sisterhood.'

'I suppose I'd better knock,' said Isobel.

'Nah, just barge in,' said Melissa. 'And remember, funeral service is upstairs. I've scheduled it for after they've eaten dessert. It's a Hindu service. Cows are sacred in India, or is it Pakistan?'

Isobel was struck by this intense girl. She was interested in this funeral service, but decided against it. She was not to be deflected. Isobel slipped into the dining room. There were six people seated round the dining table, and at the end of it was a small squat man with a round shaped head, carving a joint of roast beef. Tommy Hatchett looked about fifty. Mrs Hatchett sat at the other end. The other guests looked the same age. In front of them they had empty plates, having obviously had a first helping. Tommy Hatchett was carving for a second round. Slowly, one by one, they noticed her. The last one to look up was Tommy, engrossed as he was in the business of carving.

'Hello, dear, you must be one of Melissa's pals? I heard the doorbell going,' said Mrs Hatchett.

'I'm not one of Melissa's pals,' said Isobel.

'Oh,' said Mrs Hatchett.

Isobel gave a half apologetic smile.

'Who are you then dear?'

'I'm Isobel Coole.'

Tommy Hatchett stood up straight and put down the carving knife. There was silence. Then he picked up the carving knife again, just in case.

'You're the writer. Yes, I've seen you on television,' said Mrs Hatchett, who appeared a little tipsy. 'I thought you were one of Melissa's friends, because they all have that black hair, like yours, that the young people all like nowadays.'

'What are you doing here?' asked Tommy Hatchett.

'That's rather a good question,' said Mrs Hatchett.

'I've come to talk to your husband about his review of my play.'

'Oh, was he unkind?'

'Unkind isn't the word for it,' said Isobel, Mrs Hatchett's kindness wrong-footing her somewhat, and making her feel vulnerable. 'He annihilated it.'

'Tommy, why did you do that?' asked Mrs Hatchett.

'I don't believe this,' said Tommy Hatchett.

Isobel turned her full attention on him.

'I just do not believe this,' he spluttered.

'Why?' said Isobel in her most injured tone.

'Excuse me please, but could you leave my house, Ms Coole, or I will have to call the guards. This is a private house, and we are entertaining guests for dinner, as you can see. If you wish to discuss my reviews, I'll be happy to do that in my office on Monday morning, or indeed, you may correspond with me or the paper.'

Hatchett's stuffiness got Isobel riled again. She snorted,

tossed her head and bared her teeth. She looked transformed, from the opaque austere beauty she was usually. 'You think you can write stuff like that in the newspaper and get away with it? Well, I've come here to tell you that you can't.'

Mrs Hatchett turned in an aside to one of her guests. She and Tommy Hatchett were going through a period of readjustment in their marriage. Vera Hatchett had recently returned to work outside the home, and tensions were high. 'Typical, he writes these awful harsh reviews, and she's such a nice girl.'

'I am a person,' said Isobel, 'with feelings. I put my heart and soul into my work. My play represents a year's toil on my part. For you, it was only a couple of hours in the theatre after you had a few whiskies too many in the bar.'

This was true. Hatchett had had a couple of whiskies before the show. Only two. But he suddenly remembered that he'd had a third one at the interval. Isobel had got the details from Nick, the barman at the Lunar Theatre.

'You cannot legally drive a car on a few whiskies, what makes you think you're entitled to judge my year's work when you're tanked up?'

'Won't you sit down and have a bite to eat, dear?' said Vera. 'I hate to be pass-remarkable, but you don't have a pick on you. Here, I'll make you a plate.' Vera started to load up a plate with some meat and potatoes.

'I want you to know, Tommy Hatchett, that I have nothing but contempt for you,' hissed Isobel. 'Your understanding of creativity is this small,' and she held her thumb and forefinger together.

'Do you like puréed carrots? I did them for the first time today, they were in last week's paper,' said Vera. 'I'll just fetch them from the hostess trolley where they'll be nice and hot.'

'Vera, please stop making her a meal, I'm going to call the police.'

'Now, Tommy, nobody calls to my house and doesn't get a bite to eat. Sit down there, dear, beside me, move over, James, to make room. Where was I, Oh yes! The puréed carrots. Everybody else was most complimentary about them.'

'For me,' said Isobel, 'creating a piece of writing is like a conflagration. An act of pyromania performed as a compulsion and executed as a life sentence. Don't you see? You can't just casually piss all over my work, because to do that is to piss all over me.'

'It's my job. I get sent by my paper. I'm doing my job.'

'In fairness, Tommy, you ought to answer the girl's, sorry woman's criticism,' said Jeffrey Cohen, one of the guests.

'Not bloody likely, I'm going to call the police,' he said getting up from the table.

'Answer me one thing,' said Isobel, 'what, in God's name, have the hunger-strikers got to do with my play?'

'Absolutely nothing. And this was precisely my point!' and Tommy threw his hands up in the air. 'I don't believe I'm even discussing this. Now, I am going out that door and I'm going to phone the police.'

Tommy Hatchett crossed the room, went out into the hall and made the phone-call as threatened.

'It's a very interesting question,' said Samantha Cohen, 'the right of reply of the artist to the criticism of the critic.'

'I have no problem with that,' said Tommy, coming back into the room, 'but all in its proper time and place, and not in my private home.'

Melissa came in the door and stared at them all.

'Hello Mel,' said Vera Hatchett, 'aren't you going to do a party piece for us?'

'Mummy, I haven't executed a party piece since 1991,' said Melissa, 'nor do I intend regressing at this moment in time. I just want to open the curtains, so you can see the view.'

Melissa went over to the curtains and pulled a cord. The curtains went swish, revealing a large banner which was suspended from her bedroom upstairs.

```
BEEF IS BRUTAL
MEAT IS MURDER
SPARE A THOUGHT FOR THE TORTURED UDDER
SUPPORT THE BOVINE SISTERHOOD!
```

'I'm performing a funeral service for your dinner tonight,' said Melissa.

'That's very thoughtful of you, dear,' said Vera, 'and very creative.'

'I wondered would any of you like to attend?'

'I think the guests would rather stay down here with the grown-ups, dear.'

Melissa sighed and walked out of the room.

'I think she looks very like you, Vera,' said Jeffrey.

'Do you?' said Vera.

The doorbell sounded.

'Ha! That'll be the police,' said Tommy and jumped up.

'This is very embarrassing,' said Vera, 'the police being called to remove one of our guests.'

'I want him to promise to print a retraction, after coming

to the play a second time and watching it without his glugful of whiskey.'

'I'll try and persuade him, dear,' said Vera.

Tommy came back in from the hall, followed by Richard Power.

'What are you doing here, Richard?' said Isobel.

'Is that Richard Power?' said Vera Hatchett.

'Yes,' replied Jeffrey.

'He looks very well, doesn't he. I hear he's fifty. Doesn't look a day over forty to me,' said Vera confidentially.

'I've come to take you away, Isobel,' said Richard. 'I'm to invite you to Marcia's for dessert.'

'How did you know I was here?'

'I think Mr Hatchett here phoned Sergeant O'Hanlon, because he in turn phoned Arlene, so we came by.'

'Where's Arlene?'

'She's outside in a cab. She wouldn't come in.'

'Is she cross?'

'Very.'

Isobel turned to Vera Hatchett.

'Thank you very much, Mrs Hatchett, for your hospitality.'

'I just do not believe this,' said Tommy Hatchett, losing the head now. 'Mister Power, could you please take this hysteric out of my home, my evening is ruined.'

'Poor Tommy. He gets high blood pressure. He finds things like this very distressing,' said Vera.

Richard finally bundled Isobel out the door.

'My hat!' said Isobel.

Richard went back in to get it. He passed Melissa in the hallway who was going out to Isobel.

'If you're looking for her hat. I've just given it to Mel to take out,' said Vera.

'Please allow me to apologise again,' said Richard. 'She has an artistic temperament.'

Melissa came out to Isobel on the doorstep.

'Don't forget to care for the beasts,' said Melissa, and she put the black-and-white dalmatian-spotted hat on Isobel's head.

'It's fun-fur,' said Isobel, 'not made from real dalmatians.'

'Fake fur,' said Melissa. 'Fur is never fun.'

Richard led Isobel down the driveway to the taxi that was waiting outside. Arlene was sitting in the back seat, fuming.

Richard got in first, so he could sit between the two women.

'Where are we going?' asked Isobel.

'To Marcia's for pavlova,' said Richard.

Arlene said nothing.

The taxi pulled up outside Marcia's house. Arlene paid the driver, thanked him, and all three got out.

'G'night now,' she said to the taxi-driver, who pulled up his window and whizzed off.

She rounded on Isobel. 'I can't believe you did that!'

Isobel stared at her.

'Where did you get his address?'

'I just found it out,' said Isobel.

'You rooted through my diary to find it.'

'No, I didn't.'

'Don't lie.'

'All right, I did.'

'It is so bloody stupid and childish, so immature.'

223

Richard shifted from one foot to another. 'Shall we go in?'

'I can tell you, Tommy Hatchett will think twice before he writes such a nasty review again,' Isobel said haughtily.

Arlene had reached boiling point. 'You are pathetic, Isobel. You are so absorbed in yourself, you think you've a right to go and disturb somebody's home in order to indulge your own precious ego.'

'Don't you lecture me! I won't have it,' and Isobel snorted. 'It's all very well for you, as you add up your box-office takings, stack your pennies one above the next. You don't take any risks, Arlene. You're a parasite.'

'You wouldn't be here if it wasn't for me.'

'And you wouldn't be here if it wasn't for *me*,' returned Isobel.

'Look,' said Richard. 'I think that you're both a bit over-wrought, let's go inside and at least get warm.'

'If you ever touch my diary, or anything else of my pro-fessional things ever again, I will never forgive you,' said Arlene. 'You've got to understand, Isobel, that as you make your life meaningful through your writing –' Arlene broke off.

Isobel was weeping now.

'– I render *my* life meaningful through my profession,' Arlene finished the sentence.

'He was only a dumb low-life critic,' said Isobel.

'To you, perhaps, but to me he's a valuable professional contact.'

Isobel started to wail louder.

'Stop it, Arlene, that's cruel,' said Richard.

the past IV

the theatre of cruelty

'I want a baby,' said Arlene.

Dick continued to munch his spaghetti, and stared at her.

'You'll grow out of it,' he said, slurping up a stray strand.

'Let's do it,' she insisted.

'Arlene, you persuaded me to marry you in the hope that it would fix us. It didn't. You are not going to talk me into having a child with you. Can't you just face the fact that we're not normal? Never going to be normal.'

'I want to have kids, Dick.'

'You think it'd be OK to introduce a kid into this mess?'

'Don't call it a mess.'

'But that's what it is. You can hardly be civil to me, and I can't stand the sight of you.'

'That's not true. We just say those things, but they're not true.'

'They're true.'

It was almost two years since Arlene and Dick had married. The early attempts to turn the flat in Donnybrook into a love nest had failed. Flypaper, put up in enthusiasm two years earlier, had congealed along with its victims, and hung in the air from the ceiling with the cigarette smoke. Now, they mostly slept in different rooms, though occasionally, in the black of night, one of them would creep into the other's room and steal pleasure, like a thief. A perverse appetite for each other.

Save us, Arlene would think. There is something the matter with us. We do not know how to do it, how to be human.

Their bodies would twine nakedly together, as close as possible, and into her ear he would whisper sweet hatreds, and she would bite his neck, a sharp sour nip of dislike.

Dick was doing very well. He was getting a lot of work, and was having to turn stuff down. Arlene still did most of his negotiating for him, kept his diary, organised his appointments, his clothes. Booked his hair-cuts for him. Polished his shoes. Ironed his shirts, his underwear. His drinking continued, in bursts, in binges. He became helpless, like a baby. Then, he had so much work on, that it became more difficult for him to find time to drink, and he steadied, he sobered, he mellowed. He got some time off around their second anniversary, and sweetly he asked her to come away with him for the weekend. 'I want us to talk.'

They went to a country hotel, a big fancy place, surrounded by nature, and seemed to be communicating quite well. Then, over dinner, he put it to her.

'Arlene. I think that we need to stop this. I think that we need to split up.'

She hadn't ever thought he would come up with this.

'I think that we have to admit we've made a mistake.'

'We could make it right, if we tried,' she said, 'if we wanted to.'

'No,' he said. 'We aren't the right mix. Right now, I am not fit to share my life with anybody else. And particularly not with you.'

'Why not me?'

He looked at her coolly. 'You have taken me over. I have lost my self, my self-respect. I need to regain it. I want to go away.'

They ordered drinks and went up to their room for some privacy.

'Your self-respect! You never had any,' snarled Arlene. 'I dragged you out of your alcoholic stupor and got your career on track. There'd be no fancy offers from England if it hadn't been for me.'

'I don't deny any of that,' said Dick, 'and I do owe you a lot, but I am suggesting this for your sake as much as mine.'

'Stop it,' she said. 'Stop it,' and she thrust her hands down the front of his trousers. He was always in the mood for sex. He was insatiable. He was predictable. Seducing Dick Whelan was one of the easiest things in the world to do, as half Dublin was well aware.

'I have done my best,' he said, 'I cannot leave you on my own, without your help. I have tried to save us, but we are finished. We will drown in this.'

The lights were turned down and the game began.

'I hate you,' she said, as she caressed his body.

'I hate you,' he said as he entered her. 'You disgust me with your bossy ways and your cloying nature.'

You are my prisoner, I own you, you are nothing, she thought.

'I wish that this hurt you,' he said.

'But it doesn't,' she answered.

Their sexual intercourse was energetic and enthusiastic, as usual. No different from normal. It was though they had always hated each other, they knew how to do it so well.

This existence lurched on, a downward spiral, until it reached dark places, undreamt of. He brought other women home to their flat, a thing which they had previously had an unspoken bar on, and made noisy love with them while Arlene sat in her room, and masturbated.

She still wouldn't countenance defeat. 'You can't hurt me,' she said to him. 'I will enjoy your delinquencies, because you devalue yourself, not me, when . . .'

Arlene looked at herself one night in the mirror, her twenty-three-year-old life in ruins about her. I hate my present, and I have no future, I am not impressed by the past I have accumulated. I am too smart to be in this situation.

The key sounded in the door. She waited standing in the kitchen, trying to gauge his mood. Silence generally meant either viciousness, or more silence, then bed. When he was drunk he could be tender, or he could be awful. Tonight he hummed. That was generally a good sign. He would talk to her.

He came into the kitchen with a six-pack and put it on the table.

'Why do women have a cunt and an arsehole?' he asked, with a smile.

'Dunno,' she replied.

'So you can pick them up like a six-pack,' and he laughed out loud and put his arm around her.

She laughed too. 'That's disgusting,' she said, cheerfully.

'Jimmy the barman told me that. It's disgusting, but it's hilarious,' he slurred, and laughed some more.

'Do you want a coffee?' she asked.

'I'll have another beer,' he said.

'Do you want me to open it?'

'Woof,' he barked in assent.

He *was* in good form.

'You are in good form,' she said.

'I was taken out for dinner by this American director guy.'

'Who?' she said sharply.

'Just a guy. I didn't get drunk until after he'd gone. Don't worry.'

'Who?' she said again. 'There's nobody in the diary.'

'No. He was a secret.'

'Has he a name?'

'A secret name.'

Arlene opened a beer for herself also.

'Woof,' he said.

'Woof,' she replied.

'Woof, woof.'

'And this secret person, with his secret name. Has he a secret film on the go?'

'Woof, woof.'

'And have you got a part in it?'

'Woof.'

'Is that yes or no?'

'Wo-of.'

'It's maybe?' she asked.

'Woof.' he agreed.

'If you were a dog,' he said, 'you'd be a Terrier. Yap! Yap! Yap!'

'You'd be a Rottweiler,' she said. 'Grrrrrr.'

He got a saucer out of the press and poured his beer into it, and started to lap it up, like a dog. Then he hopped up on a chair and started to howl loudly.

She threw back her head, and she laughed.

He continued to howl, but quieter this time. Then he started to pant and nuzzle her neck.

'It's a werewolf movie,' she said.

'Woof.'

'And you're to play the werewolf.'

'Woof, woof.' He started to open her blouse with his teeth. He got one button undone. He managed a second.

She jumped onto the table, and crouched and howled . 'Ow, ow, ow, ow, owwww.'

He opened another bottle of beer.

'Ow, ow, ow, ow, owwww,' she continued.

He looked at her and smiled. She saw the smile, and she knew he was about to turn vicious. 'You're pathetic,' he said. 'Why are you sitting on the table, showing off your knickers, and howling like a stupid dog?'

He opened the fridge, and took out another bottle of beer.

'Open it,' he barked, handing her the bottle.

She wanted to refuse, but her instincts told her to do as he said. He was six-foot two, and she only five-five. When he was in a mood like this, she did as she was told.

She got down off the table, opened the cutlery drawer, and

rooted for the opener. 'I can't find it,' she said.

'I'll give you until ten. Ten, nine, eight –

'You had it last,' she said as she looked around the room.

'Six, five, four –'

'Dick, I can't find it.'

'Three, two, one. Forfeit time,' he said and jumped up, laughing.

'Dick, please stop,' said Arlene.

He grabbed her hair in a fistful, and manoeuvred her head down into the basin of cold greasy water that had been standing in the sink since that afternoon's wash-up.

'Stop,' she called out just as her head went under. He held her under, and she tried to kick him with her feet, but to no avail. Her arms flailed and delhft scattered from the sideboard and smashed on the floor. He lifted her head out again, and she gasped for breath as air rushed into her lungs once more. She gasped and choked, and tears started to fall down her face.

'Bastard,' she said, regaining her breath, and her control of herself. And then, he pushed her head under once more. This time, she was in such a state that she immediately swallowed the dish-water, a mixture of washing-up liquid and bits and pieces of food.

He'll kill me, she thought. He'll kill me, and I don't care.

He let her up again, and she gulped and gulped, and coughed up the dish-water. Dick laughed.

'Woof, woof,' he said.

Arlene said nothing. She sat down on a kitchen chair and breathed heavily. She knew if she said anything provocative she'd end up in the basin again. She knew they were finished.

*

231

She sat at the table all night long, and tears galloped down her face, so many that she wondered where the water could possibly be coming from, wondered was she getting dehydrated with all the crying. She thought she would never stop.

The following morning he breezed into the kitchen. Her eyes followed him around the room. He seemed terribly cheerful. Relieved.

'You bastard,' said Arlene.

'And good morning to you too, dearie,' he said.

'You'll have to leave, you'll have to go.'

'And to what do I owe this delightful greeting this morning?'

'You know damn well.'

'What are you talking about?'

'Last night,' said Arlene.

'What about last night?'

'You don't remember?'

'Well, I was out, talking to that director guy. And then I came home and went to bed, you were already asleep, so far as I recall. What are you talking about?'

Arlene looked at him closely. Did he really not remember? He looked innocent enough. But he was an actor, after all.

'Nothing,' she said finally. If he wouldn't remember, neither would she. 'You'll just have to leave. You'll have to go. We'll have to stop.'

When he came home later on that day he had a suitcase with him, borrowed from somewhere. 'OK,' he said. 'I agree. England. I'll got to London this week.'

'But you've stuff coming up here. You're due to go into rehearsal in two weeks' time.'

'I'll cancel it. They'll replace me. As they're so fond of reminding us, actors are always replaceable.'

'What makes you so sure you'll get work in London?' She wanted him to go, but she didn't want him to go.

'I know an agent there. She said that if ever I came over, she'd get me set up.'

He'd been planning this for a while, she thought. He'd wanted his escape.

'I have a problem,' he said.

'A drink problem,' she answered.

'No, it goes deeper than that. It is a life problem. I need to get away from you. You are killing me.'

'That's not true. It's not me killing you. You're killing yourself and me. You're killing us. You treat me like a doormat.'

'How can I treat you any other way? When you've spread yourself at my feet, how can I treat you any other way? I can't go out the door without stamping on you.'

'I've been trying to help you.'

'Nobody asked you to. I didn't want a house-maid, a fucking laundry-maid.'

'How can you say this to me? You'd be nothing without me. I've built you up, your career. I've slaved for you.'

'I wanted a wife, a partner. Not a slave.'

He had this knack of turning everything to his advantage. She was the one who had been nearly killed last night, yet he was the one who managed now to act the injured party. He'd been looking for a way out for some time, she thought. He'd got it now.

He left. Arlene stayed in for a few weeks. She didn't want to meet anybody, talk to anybody. She was so ashamed. With him gone, so was everything else. She had done so much work on his behalf, she had no profession without him. She had been turning down stage-management jobs for the past while, and now she was no longer the first on anybody's list.

Word got out in the theatrical community that he had gone, and people called to ask how she was. She hated this most of all. Pity. To be on the receiving end of it. She would much rather have been left alone.

She got a job, ironically from one of Dick's previous lovers, but she took it. It was nice to be back working again. People liked working with her because she was totally reliable and frighteningly efficient. She put the head down and worked away quietly.

He wrote to her enclosing a cheque, saying he was aware that he owed her a lot financially. She considered calling a lawyer and arranging some sort of separation deal, but finally she tore up the letter and the cheque and wrote to him saying that she never wished to hear from him again. Let him use his cheques to buy a clear conscience elsewhere. Join bloody Amnesty International or something. She would not do him the favour of spending his money for him. Another cheque arrived a couple of months later, with a very formal letter from his agent. She tore that up too. Let him get out of her life.

She changed all her documentation back to Arlene Morrissey. She started again. She got her hair cut. Her birthday was coming up, and it was time for change. She would be twenty-four.

*

A few months later, she switched on the television and there he was, smiling out at her from an English soap, speaking in an English accent. She shivered. She watched the credits roll. He was billed as Richard Power. He'd changed his name too. Mr and Mrs Whelan were no more. Neither component still existed. She shivered again, and switched off the television set. Fool, she thought.

the present

'**Y**ou never talk about it,' said Isobel.

'There isn't anything to say.'

'There must be, Arlene, you need to transact things.'

'It's the past, Isobel. It has no meaning now. Stop getting at me.'

'But, Arlene, it can't mean nothing. A marriage, however brief, can't mean nothing.'

'Oh, shut the fuck up.'

'Fine. I'll not mention it again,' said Isobel. She had long ago given up taking offence at Arlene's brusqueness. 'Dinner's ready.'

Arlene and Isobel had made up after the Tommy Hatchett episode. They finally apologised to each other, and peace broke out. Isobel was still living in Arlene's flat. She was, however, actively and ostentatiously looking for a place. Evening papers were strewn about the living room with circles drawn around prospective pads.

They sat down to dinner. Isobel had ceased to cook meat at all now, citing something odd about the beef at Tommy

Hatchett's house, so Arlene was being treated to a diet of various beans and pulses.

'Are you going to the show again tonight?' asked Arlene.

'Sure,' said Isobel.

'It's amazing. Don't you ever get bored with it?'

'No. It's fascinating. It's different every night. There are different moments and nuances. And there's only a week to go. I'll miss it when it's no longer there. I've become very fond of everybody, the cast and crew.'

After dinner, Isobel put on her hat and coat and slipped out. Arlene sat there, feeling a vague discontent. She wanted something, but wasn't sure what. She knew she was going to miss Isobel when she went. She should never have let her move in. It had upset the old equilibrium. The flat seemed empty now, with Isobel gone out.

Stop being such a sap, she said to herself, and decided to go out for some chips.

It was late November, and though the day had been wet, the evening was now fine enough. Damp leaves stuck to the ground, to the paths. The lock of the canal had trapped the fallen leaves, so in the darkness it looked like the water had a leafy crust.

Arlene bought her chips and went to sit beside Paddy. 'How's it going?'

'Fuckin' damp,' answered Paddy.

'Do you know what he did?' asked Arlene.

'Who?'

'Old Dick-face. He burgled my bank of youth.'

'I hate that,' said Paddy, 'when they burgle your bank of youth.'

'He keeps coming round now, and it gives me the pip, but I can't help entertaining the notion of falling for him again . . .'

'Bad idea,' said Paddy.

'Because I think if I went back there, I might find some feeling that I've lost.'

'Feeling nothing isn't so bad,' he said, 'speaking from the point of view of a statue.'

'Oh.'

'Bad idea,' said Paddy.

'You're right, Paddy. Always the sensible pundit.' Arlene went on her way, tossing her chip bag into a bin. She wandered down to the off-licence, and decided to treat herself.

'Hello,' said Martin. 'How is the show going?'

'Great. It's a sell out.'

'The magic touch,' said Martin, 'you have the magic touch.'

'Martin, I want a really good red. Something that you've had hidden away for a special occasion.'

'And what, may I ask, is the occasion?'

'There is none,' said Arlene dryly. 'That's why the wine has to be so good. The wine is the occasion.'

Martin winked at her awkwardly. 'I think I have just the thing,' he said, and went into the back, emerging after a few minutes blowing dust off a bottle. 'And have you company for the occasion?' he asked.

'Mind your own business,' she said in a friendly but firm tone.

He bowed his head in assent. 'For you, ten quid. From anyone else, I'd be looking for eighteen.'

'A bargain,' she smiled as she handed him the tenner. She scuttled out of the shop, her booty under her arm and went on home to her appartment, feeling vaguely self conscious about going home to sink a bottle all on her ownsome.

There was a message on the machine.

'Hello Ms Morrissey, it's your well-wisher again –'

The Weirdo! He hadn't phoned in ages. She was glad to hear from him.

'I haven't called for a while, but I saw you by the canal, and I thought you should know that your flatmate and your ex-husband are conducting a very discreet affair. I'm sorry if this is bad news, but I thought you shouldn't be the last to find out. Click.'

What? Arlene sat down in a chair. Richard and Isobel? Richard had been coming around a lot, but she had thought it was to see *her*. What? How the hell! And then it started to make sense. Isobel was a lovely creature, Richard would of course take a fancy to her. And Isobel was so hungry for love.

Arlene opened the bottle of red wine. She felt such a fool. How had she not seen this coming? So *that* was why Isobel went to the show every night. But why hadn't she told Arlene about it?

She felt terrible, betrayed. She drank the wine, then put on her hat and coat, and took a cab to the theatre.

When she arrived, the audience was leaving, spilling out onto the street in hordes, many of them dabbing their eyes. Melodrama or no, people were truly moved by this play. Another full house, three hundred and fifty seats at twelve pounds a head, with a hundred seats at discount added up to – Arlene stopped herself. Her brain had this automatic habit of becoming a calculator.

She went inside and sat in the bar. She ordered a gin and tonic. She was a little pissed now.

Marcia came down. 'Hello Arlene, what are you doing here?'

'I just thought I'd drop in to be sociable,' said Arlene.

Corinne and Paula came down.

'Hello, Arlene,' said Corinne. 'It's lovely to see you. Since *you're* here, I'm going to stay for a drink. The show went great tonight. You know my final speech? Well, I can always tell by the sniffs at my first pause how it's going, and it went *brilliantly* tonight. They were very upset, there was one woman sobbing profusely in the front row. It put me in great form, and I gave her a big smile in the curtain call.' Corinne was very high. 'I'd just better phone him indoors to say I'm staying out. Hopefully he won't threaten to divorce me. Can I borrow your phone?'

'Sure,' and Arlene handed over the phone. 'Drinks are on me,' she said. 'Where can Richard and Isobel be?'

'I left Richard behind me in the dressing room,' said Marcia.

'I'll just nip upstairs so,' said Arlene.

She made her way along the passage to dressing room one. The door was a tiny bit ajar and she paused outside to listen.

'You have disappointed me so much,' came Richard's voice from the room. 'I thought I could trust you.'

'Well, you couldn't,' came Isobel's voice in return.

'I know that now,' he said.

'You've been looking at me for a long time now, and I know what your eyes mean.'

'You look so like her, so like she used to look when she was young. I can't help looking at you.'

'You are jealous, because you know that I've been with lots of men, and it bothers you.'

What on earth were they talking about? wondered Arlene. Then it dawned on her. The play. Richard was playing Father and Isobel daughter; this was the scene; the final scene. The one there'd been such a row about.

'Please don't hit me. I love you,' she said.

'Spread your legs for Daddy, then.'

Arlene's heart started to race. Isobel was getting her ending. Her *real* ending. The one in the play was only temporary, a stop-gap to hold the situation. In the meantime, Isobel had found her daddy to love.

pas de trois

'I'm sorry I didn't get a chance to tell you before you came in last night, but every time I brought Richard up you just changed the subject. I've been trying to tell you for ages,' said Isobel.

Arlene had tried and failed to regain her composure overnight. Instead she'd opened a bottle of red wine for breakfast.

'S'okay,' she said.

'I'm going to move out now,' said Isobel. 'I'm going to go back to England with Richard. We're going to get married.'

'That's great. How romantic!' said Arlene, gritting her teeth.

'I knew you'd be pleased, Arly,' said Isobel totally misreading her reaction. 'To begin with I wondered if you might find it difficult, but then, when I thought about it, you are always so cool to Richard, I guessed you wouldn't mind. I'm so happy.'

'When did it start?' asked Arlene.

'The night at the Hatchett's. He was so understanding, so gentle with me. He didn't think I was crazy. He seemed to think I was being reasonable.'

Arlene didn't know how to react, so she opened a second

bottle of wine. It was the middle of the afternoon, but these *were* exceptional circumstances.

'I am so happy,' said Arlene.

Isobel Coole. Mrs Power.

'Mrs Power,' said Arlene with a little laugh.

Isobel blushed at this.

'He's a bastard, Isobel. Don't do it. He'll kill you, like he killed me.'

'Arlene. What are you talking about?'

'Don't you realise, Isobel, that I'm dead? Haven't you noticed that I don't have any life in my body? He is a vampire. He sucks your life-blood, and you end up being one of the undead, like me, going round the place with nothing in your veins,' and she gestured with the hand that was holding the glass, sloshing red wine over the carpet. 'Salt emergency!' she said and jumped up to fetch the salt-cellar.

'Arlene, stop that. He's a lovely person, Richard. He's gentle and thoughtful and considerate. He's always asking how you are, for example. He cares an awful lot about you.'

'But vampires always seem to be very nice. That's how they seduce all the townspeople into bringing them their groceries.'

Isobel stared at Arlene. She realised that despite the early hour, she was drunk.

'But you're a vampire too,' continued Arlene. 'You go places and suck blood from people. You even look like a vampire, with your long black hair, and your silver nails.'

'Arlene, you're drunk.'

'Yup.'

'You *are* taking this badly.'

'Isn't it about time that I had my little drama, my moment

243

of climax? Haven't I as much of a right as anybody to roar and shout and do a jig?'

'Sure you do.'

'Don't do it, Isobel.'

'You're jealous!'

'I'm not shaggin' jealous, you fool. I don't care what happens to him. It's you I'm worried about.'

'Arlene, you're talking to me as though I'm a child. I'm very well able to take care of myself.'

'You could've fooled me. You're a wreck. Haven't I had to rescue you from all sorts of scrapes?'

'But they'll be with me anyway. My demons follow me about, regardless of whether I'm here with you, on my own, or with Richard. I'll always have them. He can't possibly make them any worse. In fact, he has made them better.'

'Richard Power, the Florence Nightingale *de nos jours*.'

'He is the most absorbing and entertaining person I've ever met.'

More entertaining then me? You ingrate. 'Spare me the eulogies, please, before I vomit,' said Arlene. 'Would you like a glass of wine?'

'No,' said Isobel, 'and I think you've had enough.'

'I haven't had barely enough.'

'Think of your liver.'

'I rarely do.'

'I'll have some tea,' said Isobel.

Arlene collected herself while Isobel was in the kitchen making the tea. It was very hard to behave properly, now that she was drunk, but she tried.

'I'm sorry Isobel, I'm being terrible. In fairness though, this is all a bit much for me to be dealing with.'

'I understand. Arlene, I didn't think it would matter to you at all. I'm sorry, I've been very cavalier. But you seem to care so little about anything,' said Isobel, flashing a little steel.

'It doesn't really matter. I'm just having an identity crisis at the moment.'

'Arly, I don't think this is the best time to ask you, but I'm going to anyway. Would you be my bridesmaid?'

Arlene couldn't believe what she'd just heard. She was so flummoxed, she couldn't speak for a moment, as into her brain swept a vision of herself in a pink bridesmaid's dress. She started to laugh.

'Better not,' she said.

Arlene met up with Richard in a coffee shop in town. He had rung that afternoon.

'I need to talk to you,' he had said.

'Talk away,' Arlene said now, sitting down.

'Things haven't exactly turned out as I expected,' he said.

'I hardly think even you would be depraved enough to *plan* this.'

'What are you talking about?'

'Leave her alone,' said Arlene. 'Leave her. I won't let you do it. I'll stop you.'

'But she wants me, Arlene.'

'She doesn't want you, and you know it as well as I do. She wants her father's love, and you're play-acting it for her.' Arlene produced a battered brown paper envelope from her handbag, and took out a page of typescript from it.

'What's this? asked Richard.

'It's the first draft of the play that Isobel originally gave me. This was the final scene. She cut it in the re-writes. Marcus wanted her to alleviate some of the more mawkish elements.'

Act 3, Scene 6

The stage is in darkness, and the voice of Nuala comes from OFF, ghostly (if possible) and slightly distorted.

Nuala: My father used to sing to me when I was a child. I remember the songs, they were full of joy. And I was so proud, and I loved him so much. I wondered how I would ever find a man who would measure up to him. Who would be worth more than the tip of his finger. Daddy, daddy. I know you are gone, yet I know you are still here. I will find you someday, and you will love me. I will hold you, and forgive you, and you will forgive me. And together, we'll be, and together we'll stay . . .

'So?'

'Oh, stop acting so innocent, Dick, I know damn well what you're up to and all I can say is that if you do her any damage, you'll have me to answer to.'

Richard took a long drag on his cigarette. 'It's weird to think,' he said, 'that I came back here to see if you were all right, to make sure that you had survived. And here you are now, so strong, so tough. Nothing fases you.' His dulcet tones made her hair stand on end.

'One thing, Arlene, that you have been right about. Isobel is as tough as nails. I'm under no illusions. I don't think you need fear that I'll damage *her*. If you have some spare concern, it could be for me.'

'The difference between the two of you,' said Arlene, 'is that she is trying to reconcile herself to her life through art. This may be a dumb strategy, but it has the advantage of being pure. You, on the other hand, are trying to re-adjust your life to indulge your art. This may have its aesthetic rewards, but it is a somewhat less-than-human course.'

'I don't suppose there's much point in my saying anything,' said Richard, 'as you appear to have the whole thing worked out.'

'Do you remember, Dick, way back,' and she hesitated a moment, then continued, 'the night before you left all those years ago. Do you remember what happened?'

'I remember very little from my drinking days,' he said. 'I remember very little about anything. And I'm glad about that.'

'I remember everything,' she said. 'I didn't think I did, but I do.'

the last night

'Well, since you insist on being so damn civilised about this, I'm just going to have to be outraged on your behalf,' said Marcia. 'I didn't mind them having a bit of an affair, everyone's entitled to have an affair, we have to do something with our sex organs, for God's sake. But getting married is a bit much. I don't believe she had the cheek to ask you to be bridesmaid.'

'Marcia, calm down. I don't give a fuck.'

'I talked it over with David last night, and he agrees. You'll have to stop them. At least stop them from doing it here under your nose. Get them to shag off to the Channel Islands or something, where they can get married with due discretion and appropriate quietude.'

'Isobel wants a big church wedding, in the parish church where she grew up. Apparently, there's some padre there that she was fond of as a kid. Discretion isn't her thing.'

'How can they get married in a church if he's divorced?'

'We were married in the register office.'

'Does that make a difference?'

'Yes. Maybe *I'll* go off to the Channel Islands for a holiday, and leave this island clear for them.'

'Can't you at least take him for a few bob. It'd make you feel better if you stung him where it hurts a bit.'

'Nah, it wouldn't.'

'Well, it'd make *me* feel better on your behalf.'

Arlene and Marcia were having a gin and tonic and a cup of tea respectively, in the bar of the Lunar Theatre. It was six o'clock on the last night of the show. Arlene had that sinking feeling she always got when a show was about to close. It felt like somebody was dying, but you weren't sure who. 'The poor old show is going to its eternal rest,' said Arlene. 'It has certainly been an eventful one.'

'Indeed,' Marcia agreed.

Richard came in, his face covered in a huge smile. He looked very happy. When he saw the two women, his smile withered for a bit, then rallied.

'Hello,' he said warmly.

'Hello,' said Marcia coolly.

'Hello, Richard,' said Arlene sweetly.

He tried to read her humour.

'Have a cup of this mighty fine tea. Nick! Another pot of this delicate brew.'

Marcia continued to sit there with a puss on her.

'Last Night!' said Arlene. 'As you know I've booked a room in the Corkscrew again, so we can party, party, party!'

'I do think that nightclub is unfortunately named,' said Marcia. 'It makes me think of hordes of Munster men having an orgy.'

Arlene sat beside Isobel for the last performance.

The house lights went down, and the audience hushed in expectation. Silence hung in the theatre for a moment, a secret velvety moment of anticipation, then the lonely cry of a single sax, soaring like a bird through the auditorium. Then, gently, the lights lifted to reveal the stage, the space for play, the saxophone died and the action began.

Arlene watched as Richard acted off Corinne Cooper. Corinne really did look like Isobel, especially from this distance. Corinne's rendition of the 'Ave Maria' was beautiful. So slim she looked like a child, in the beautiful replacement white frock, opening her mouth and out flowing the voice of an angel. Nuala, torn between remaining Daddy's little girl, and the biological imperative to grow up.

'Ave Maria
Gratia Plena
Dominus Tecum
Benedicta tu in mulieribus
Et benedictus fructus vestris tuae, Jesu.'

And when Richard/Mr Delaney cried and clapped after the song, you could easily see how this man could love this daughter. Why this man *should* love this daughter. How this man could not live if he did not love this daughter. The stage was alive with imperatives.

Arlene had a sense, for the first time, that Corinne was singing Isobel's song, night after night, locked in this repetition, this acting out of the past; this irretrievable past which the character is condemned to repeat, on Isobel's behalf. Arlene stole the occasional look at Isobel during the show, who sat there rapt, scarcely breathing.

The curtain came down for the interval.

Isobel smiled at Arlene.

'C'mon, I'll get you a drink,' said Arlene.

The bar was thronged with people. Arlene surveyed them. All dressed up in their good clothes, on dates, out with their husbands or wives, their families. An occasional group of pals. They were here to enjoy themselves, had set out this evening, costumed themselves for enjoyment. Even though the play was sad, it was that wonderful heady sadness that is so exhilarating to experience. Once the audience journeyed with it, went through the darkest chambers of it, they would emerge refreshed. Firstly, because having felt so deeply, they renewed their humanity. And secondly, they would be thankful that the tragedy wasn't their own.

'I'm sad,' said Isobel. 'Sad it's nearly over. I've loved it,' her eyes shone brightly.

'So have I,' said Arlene. Her eyes weren't given to shining.

The second half proceeded, action following pre-ordained action, towards its ending. Its horrible violent ending, its hopelessness. Arlene was suddenly appalled by the play. It was so sad, this parade of personal trauma in a public space. This public confession which would free Isobel up for private forgiveness. Then she could quietly reach her conclusions amongst the scattered costumes and tissues that make up a dressing-room's debris where she would arrive at congress with him. The shape-shifter. Uggh! The shiver down Arlene's back, which had abated, returned in force.

The last-night party unfolded. The mood was high and happy, bordering on the hysterical.

'I'm going to miss you all,' said Carmel, unusually drunk.

'Until the next show. Promise me you'll be free for me when I need you next,' said Arlene.

'I promise,' said Carmel.

Marcia and David were together, acting out their marriage. Its constants, its patterns. They were indeed happy, like two comfortable old sofas. Isobel shone like a star, constantly at Richard's side, smiling delightfully, spreading cheer. Marcus was sitting in the corner, looking a bit disconsolate, a little black cloud hovering over his head.

Great, thought Arlene. Marcus seems to be in my kind of form. I'll go and talk to him.

Marcus was indeed wrestling with a little black cloud. 'Arlene, I'm thinking of giving up.'

'What! Suicide? You can't be serious.'

'Not life, you idiot. The theatre. This caper.'

'But I can't imagine you outside of the theatre. You wouldn't make sense. You'd be like a goldfish out of his bowl.'

'It's so unreal.' Marcus gestured at the surroundings.

'Well, that's the whole point of it.'

'S'pose so.'

'What else would you do?'

'Follow Manuel back to Spain, and work in his hotel.'

'I just don't believe you've been having an affair with a Spaniard called Manuel. I think that's unbelievably tacky of you.'

'He can't stomach the cold and damp here.'

'The fact that he works in a hotel is even tackier.'

'He says that this is no climate for love.'

'Sensible chap, and he's absolutely right.'

'Chilblains. He suffers from chilblains.'

'Not very erotic.'

'No.'

'If he can't stomach a drizzly Dublin November,' said Arlene, 'I don't think he's one for the long haul.'

'Probably not.'

'Forget him.'

'Probably just as well, since he has a wife and child.'

'That's terrible, Marcus, you can't be having affairs with men who have wives and children.'

'Why not? Women have affairs with married men all the time.'

'S'true.'

'Why can't I, just because I'm queer?'

'No, of course you can. I'm sorry. I said something prejudiced. Pardon me. But you're only half queer. I should know.'

'I'm queer enough,' he said.

She smiled at him.

'But, notwithstanding, I think the Manuel chapter is closed,' he said, 'not because he's married, you understand, but because he's not able for the cold.'

'What are you doing later?' asked Arlene.

'It's later already,' he answered, 'it's half-past two in the morning.'

'No, later-later.'

'Nowt.'

'Will you come with me for some grub?'

'I'd love to. I've missed you, Arlene. I've missed our chats. It seemed that Hedda took you over.'

'Please don't call her Hedda.'

253

'Is it not all right to call her Hedda now that Mr Power has turned into a frog? Or rather, turned into a prince.'

'No. It's not all right to call her Hedda. It was never right to do it.'

'I'd love to come for grub.'

Arlene and Marcus went for a late-night feed of chips and sausages. Arlene had lost about a stone since Isobel had moved in with her and taken charge of the cupboard. As she chomped her way through the sausages, she delighted in the thought of putting it back on again.

Marcus came home with her, as she knew he would.

'I'm high-risk, because I'm bi-sexual,' he said, as he fell into her bed.

'I'll wrap you in cellophane and smother you in kisses,' she replied.

It occurred to her that she hadn't had sex with anyone since Isobel had moved in with her. And that was over eight months ago. She had forgotten all about sex. It had slipped off the menu.

Marcus beamed his huge smile up from under the duvet. What a nice person you are, Marcus, she thought. She knew he wasn't wild keen. But she knew he'd never show it. It was very kind of him.

'I'm too tired,' she said. 'I think it's time for sleep.'

christmas and new year

Decembeer kicked in with a sharp chill. Arlene went back to her life of work and sleep and solitude. She packed away all of Isobel's stuff into the small room, which had rapidly reverted to being a junk room. Lots of papers arrived from Richard's lawyers, and she signed them all. Why not? Closure. Closure was a good thing. It gave you a sense of finality. Of eh, closure. Bury the corpse. Don't leave it out in the open, decomposing, where it causes discomfort. Where it starts to produce a bad smell.

Isobel was living with him in London now. She had promised to come back for her stuff, but never had. Arlene suspected that Isobel had left the stuff there, the pink duvet and the hat boxes, so that she'd have a place to crash land, if and when the time came.

Arlene had a multitude of invitations for Christmas dinner. Marcia and David – nice and welcoming. Corinne Cooper and her husband – heroic, since she wasn't that friendly with them. Marcus, at his parents' house in Westmeath – fine but civilised. Her brothers in California – they invited her every year; one of these days she was going to take them up on it and they would die of shock. And of course, Isobel, on behalf of herself and Richard. She decided on Marcia and David's house. It was likely to be safe.

She spent the rest of the holiday period reading through the pile of scripts which had accumulated while she had been busy. She was in the mood for getting another major project off the ground, but somehow there was nothing that rang her bells, got her juices flowing. She thought perhaps she'd better wait until the new year to start anything fresh.

After Isobel's departure, the dust and untidyness began to re-assert themselves in her flat. The smell of cat-piss from downstairs became worse and worse. Tinned food re-colonised the cupboards. Hairs collected once again in plugholes. Dirt reigned.

New Year's Eve arrived with a playful blizzard. Arlene looked out her window at the snow whirling about. The trees along the canal were covered in white, and the road below took on a magical look. There was something absolutely delightful about snow. It reminded her of when she was a child. The buzzer went. There on the little TV screen was Isobel. Smiling sweetly, speckles of snow on her blue hat. The ice queen cometh, mused Arlene.

'Hello,' she said.

'Surprise, surprise!'

Arlene's heart began to beat faster. She pressed the buzzer, and went out to the landing to wait while Isobel walked up the stairs.

'Bastard cats,' said Isobel, as she stood on the tail of one and it screeched loudly. She sniffed at the unpleasant smell. 'You are the only person on earth I would chance being at home on New Year's Eve,' and she held out a bottle of red wine. 'Specially got from Martin in the deli.'

Arlene took the bottle and looked shyly at Isobel. 'What are you doing here?' she asked.

'I've come to see you.'

'Oh,' said Arlene brightly.

'And pick up my computer.'

'Oh,' said Arlene less brightly. 'Where's Richard?' she asked, the oddness of Isobel's solo appearance just dawning on her.

'He's doing a live New Year's Eve Euro-Broadcast. I could've gone with him, but I didn't. I decided to come here instead,' she said brightly. 'We can look at him later on the telly if you want. What's the time difference between Prague and here?'

Isobel took off her hat and coat, a blue wool ensemble that suited her very well. 'What are you doing tonight?' she asked.

'Nothing planned. I don't go in for all that auld-lang-syne crap. Let old acquaintances please fuck off, I say,' said Arlene.

'Do you really mean that?' asked Isobel, gently mocking.

'I make the exception for you, Miss Coole.'

'Can I stay with you? We could go out to eat or something, and then come back here.'

'Sure, Isobel.'

'I wanted to spend New Year's Eve with you, because you have been such a major part of this past year, and you're such a great pal.'

'Great! I had nothing planned, so –'

'So –'

'So, let's.'

Arlene got on the blower and persuaded the booked out La

Corsica to give her a table for two for the night. 'They've got lots of vegetarian things on the menu there. All that tofu shit.'

'How's things with Dick? Sorry, Richard,' enquired Arlene, slurping her soup.

'Well.'

'Still treating you all right?'

Isobel laughed.

'Have you a date for the big event?'

'No. Richard's lawyers are working on it. There are some legal problems about doing it here.'

Arlene poured out the wine. 'So, how's London?'

'Fine. I'm busy. I've started a new novel.'

'What's it about?'

'It's about a guy who makes anonymous phone-calls. It's about the Weirdo.'

'Get your paws off him. He's *my* Weirdo,' said Arlene, a sharp edge to her voice. 'You're not allowed to rob him and incarcerate him in your fictions. He's *mine*.'

'It'll be nothing like *the* Weirdo. He's just a point of departure. I'll be imagining my own Weirdo.'

'I'd say he'll be mightily impressed to find himself turning up in one of your novels, because I'm sure he's read them. I'd say he does his research.'

'Has he called recently?'

'Not telling you.'

'Oh.'

'No, not since he called to tell me you were shagging Dick,' said Arlene, slowly, swirling wine around the bottom of her glass.

'He told you that!'

'Yup.'

'Oh. How did he know? We were very discreet.'

'So, how are things with Richard?'

'You've already asked me that. They're fine.'

'Sorry.'

'I'm pregnant,' said Isobel, and blushed.

'What!'

'And I am *so* pleased.'

'Jaysus. That's a bit fast out of the traps.'

'Well, I'm thirty-two and Richard's no spring chicken. I thought we might as well get the show on the road.'

'I'm speechless.'

'I haven't told him yet. I did the test yesterday, and I'm only four or five weeks gone. It's really been quite a year.'

'For you, it has.'

'It's funny, Arlene, I needed this relationship with Richard to be creative. I needed this union to be celebrated by a child. To make up for the past. I need a baby to love, Arlene.'

So, the play continues. The union of father and daughter produces sinisterly early issue.

'Isobel. Are you sure *he* wants it?'

'Yes. Definitely. He really wants to be a daddy.'

'But whose?'

Isobel blushed and looked up at Arlene. She knew that Arlene knew. 'I wonder if my father can see me now?'

'Isobel, you do know he's acting. He's playing a part.'

'Stop it.'

'Isobel, come back to Ireland. You can stay here in the box-room for as long as you want.'

'You don't get it, Arlene. I'm totally happy with him.'

'You want a father figure, and he's willing to play it,' said Arlene.

'But what else is there, Arlene? We want something in life and we find somebody who will act it out for us. You wanted a friend, and I have acted that out. I have performed that task, that part. And that isn't to suggest falseness or insincerity in my behaviour, because, as with the best acting on the stage, emotion expressed in a spirit of purity and with noble intention is one of the most beautiful things on earth. So, too, with our acting out in life.'

'Oh.'

'Remember you said to me, that if you cast a person in the crucial drama of your life, and they don't shape up, you have to fire them?'

'Yes.'

'Well, I think that Richard is perfect in my life, and I don't want to fire him.'

Arlene didn't like having her psychology lessons repeated back to her.

'Plus he's kinky as hell, and it really turns me on,' Isobel said, smiling her ruthless smile. 'No guilt! I've done with guilt.' Isobel started to laugh.

Arlene started to laugh also. 'Do you know, when we were married, I wanted to have a child with him, but he wouldn't?'

Isobel started to giggle helplessly. 'You made the mistake of telling him. You should have just gone ahead, like I did. Presented it to him as a *fait accompli*.'

'I hated him in the end.'

'Why?'

Arlene pondered a moment, not on the question, but on how she would articulate the answer.

'I just did and I still do.'

Isobel stayed on the sofa. Arlene woke her with a cup of tea the following morning. 'Happy nineteen ninety-seven!' she said.

'Happy nineteen ninety-seven!' returned Isobel, then she looked at her watch. 'Shit! Nine-thirty. My flight's at eleven!' She jumped up, gulped her tea as she ran around the room gathering her things.

'I'll come back again for the stuff in the box-room,' she said, pulling on clothes over her delicate grey underthings. She picked up her computer, neatly packed in a travel case.

Arlene walked her out to the landing.

''Bye, Arly. I love you,' said Isobel.

''Bye.'

Isobel leant forward to kiss Arlene. Firstly, she kissed her gently on the cheek, then she kissed her on the lips, surprising Arlene with the ferocity of the kiss. Isobel kissed her harshly, sucking her in, locking her jaw on Arlene's like a pincer, drinking in what seemed to be her spirit. Isobel kissed her like a voracious lover.

Then she moved away, and skipped down the stairs. On the first turn she stopped and smiled, and mouthed, 'love you,' back to Arlene, and then she was gone.

Arlene went back into the flat, feeling weak. She looked at the dents in the sofa cushions, retaining the shape of the sleeping Isobel, this other shape-shifter.

It wasn't fair of her to kiss me. It would have been less

painful if she hadn't kissed me. Was the kiss a token of strong affection? Or was it oil to pour on Arlene's wheels, to smooth her in the event that Isobel might come back? You could never tell with this Isobel.

Arlene opened a bottle of whiskey, put on some music and started to drink. Time passed.

the beginning of the end

It was getting dark, and Arlene was sitting in her office, staring blankly at the wall. Occasionally she stretched out her hand to the glass and glugged back a mouthful of whiskey. Occasionally she gnawed at her fingernails, bitten to the quick. From time to time, she lit a cigarette and puffed on it as though her life depended on every gasp, tipping the ash onto the floor. But mostly her mind was empty, thoroughly empty, as blank as a sheet of typing paper. She didn't even feel the whiskey take hold of her. She felt a delicious nothing.

She hadn't been in her office in a week, and there were piles of everything everywhere. Post in a pile unopened and unanswered. The waste paper basket overflowing like a melting ice-cream – at least that was what it looked like when she wasn't bothering to focus her eyes. It was funny, that. One always thought that focussing was an instinctive thing to do, until one ceased to be interested in the wide world, and then one realised what a shagging effort it was.

She had spent the week in bed. Had eaten nothing. Had thought about nothing. In fact, she had been a non-person for a week. It was amazing, she had thought she was such a crucial cog in the machine of life, but now she discovered that she wasn't. She had been absent, and life went on, oblivious. There was no evidence that life missed her presence one little bit. There was no indication that life gave a shit about her.

She started to sniff. Not sniff as in whingeing; sniff as in reaction to bad smell. She got up and wandered round the room to the tea stand, and the bin, until finally she realised that it was herself who smelled. She sniffed her armpit. Yes, that confirmed it. A *major* whiff. She needed a shower.

She decided to go home and have a shower. Get clean. Cleanliness is next to ... eh, something. Yes, that was the solution. Stop this wallowing in dirt and self-pity. Get a grip. Get a *life*. She tried to put on her confident face, but it didn't really work. She looked like a loser wearing a sneer.

She stood up, and her legs went from under her.

'Oh fuck fuck fuck fuck fuck,' she half laughed, half mumbled.

Sitting in a heap on the floor, she considered herself. She was thirty-six, and had always felt young until now, when she suddenly felt ancient. She felt like Oisín, that she had for the first time put her feet on terra firma, after a lifetime spent in Tír na n-Óg, the land of the forever young, and the ageing process, which had been artificially stalled, now galloped through her system, rioted in her veins, partyed in her joints.

The phone rang. The machine answered it. Oh mighty machine. Is it any wonder that half the country is unemployed? Arlene summoned her ears and listened.

'Hi this is Shannon Mercier calling for Arlene Morrissey at 11 AM New-York time on Wednesday eight –'

It had that hollow faraway sound that long-distance calls have.

'–Yeah, well, I'm from the New York—Ireland Friendship Committee. Hi! Yeah, well, we're planning a festival, right, of Irish arts in New York for March, right, and we were wondering if you could supply us with seven performances of *Over the Moon*? The Isobel Coole play? We've booked the theatre from March seventeenth to twenty-third?'

Americans, so organised!

'Eh, maybe phone me back? My number is area code 212, then 78 40533. That you for your attention.'

That was a good one. Arlene started to laugh out loud. Great peals of uncontrollable laughter. Somebody wanted her to *supply* them with some performances of *Over the Moon*. And she didn't have to pitch for it? It had just dropped in her lap. Unbelievable! This would have really got her juices flowing a while back. Now? Well, now, she was in the mood for more whiskey. She struggled to her feet and poured herself another generous dollop. She clinked the glass against the bottle.

'Cheers, my friend,' she said.

'Clink,' returned the bottle.

Before she got the whiskey to her lips a blinding migraine struck.

Whoops! She panicked. Her migraines never came when she was away from home, far from her bed where she might lie down. Though the migraine had its own independent agenda, its agenda of pain, it normally observed that one single comforting and orderly rule.

Her heart started to race. She collected up her bag and coat and made her way down the stairs onto Baggot Street. She stood at the edge of the street and signalled the busy traffic for a taxi, closing her eyes as the neon lights acquired a zigzag splendour. If a car didn't come soon, she feared she would pass out there on the side of the street.

She slumped into the back of a taxi, and handed over a piece of paper with her address on it. The taxi-driver presumed her drunk because of the strong smell of whiskey which accompanied her into the cab.

'A hangover from Christmas!' he said and chuckled.

'Uck aw,' she said in an attempt at 'fuck off.'

The taxi drove very fast, dodging in and out of traffic and in no time at all, screeched to a halt.

'Here y'are, Missus,' he said. 'Two pound forty.'

Arlene pulled a note from her bag. She had no idea how much it was for, and cared less.

'This is far too much,' said the taxi driver, 'Yer a bit the worse for wear, but I'm not going ta fleece ya for a trip that's less than a mile.'

Arlene was keeping her eyes shut to stop the visual distortions. She ignored the taxi-driver and got out of the car. She peeped out through her closed eyes to see what direction to walk in, but it was hopeless. She could make no sense of the barrage of January's visual symptoms: wet shiny pavements, bare trees, lit-up buildings, completely lacking in perspective. An unreadable arrangement, a cryptic mosaic. She panicked again. How would she get herself inside?

'Missus, I'm not takin' the twenty off ya for driving just the length of Baggot Street,' said the taxi-driver, who had by now got out of his car and was at her side, 'just 'cos you've a few on, it wouldn't be fair.'

Arlene reached out and found the taxi-man's sleeve, and clutched it. 'Mee–ain,' she said, unable to quite formulate the word, but pointing in the direction of where she thought her head was.

'Migraine?' he said. 'Is that what's wrong with you, love? And me after thinking that you were jarred? Hang on there.'

He left her alone for a minute while he locked his car. He then took her by her arm and steered her to the front door.

'My wife gets them. Very bad. She always has to lie down.'

He rooted through her bag and found a key, and helped her up the flights of steps to her apartment.

'If you don't mind me saying, Miss, you shouldn't be drinkin' if you're prone to the migraines.' He supported her into the living room and the sight was appalling. There were lots of bottles lying around. Pizza boxes and chinese cartons congealed on the surfaces. One of the Cartwrights' cats had gained entrance and was helping itself to the remains of a prawn curry, animal and tinfoil carton balanced precariously on the mantlepiece.

The taxi-man helped her through to her bedroom and she lay on the bed. He took off her shoes, and opened the button at her neck and on her waist, and pulled the duvet up over her.

Terrible for the migraine to come when she was out, when she was vulnerable. That wasn't playing fair. She still daren't open her eyes, in case she started seeing things again. This taxi-man seemed kind but he could just as easily have been an axe-murderer.

'I'll leave a small light on in the lounge, Miss, and I'll call back later to see if you're OK,' he said, pulling the curtains to shut out the night.

'Ank oo,' she said in an attempt at thanks.

the weirdo

When Arlene came to, she had no idea how long she had been asleep. Her head was sore and she was terribly dehydrated. She made her way to the kitchen to get something to drink. Though in considerable pain, she was feeling better than she had for a while, clearer in her mind. There was no doubt about it, the migraines were great for head-hoovering. She opened the fridge to see what she had cool to drink. A bottle of chilled passion fruit juice. Appropriate, she thought, and poured it into a glass, taking long grateful gulps.

Then she remembered the taxi-driver. How kind. How lucky it had been that he came along, and not somebody else. A little unacknowledged act of kindness. He must have been sent by her fairy godmother or her guardian angel, depending on whether you had a Judaeo-Christian or a Hans Christian-Andersen view of the world. Just as well he came along, though.

She made her way into the living room, and surveyed the chaos. She'd have to tidy it up. Have a bath. As a preliminary gesture, she shooed the cat out the apartment door and down the stairs.

The piano phone rang: da-da-da-da, da-da, da-da, de-de ...
She left it to the machine to answer it. Probably Marcia on
one of her do-good missions, or somebody else wanting to
lard her with pity. The machine whirred and clicked, then:
'Beep. Hello, it's your well-wisher again. I haven't seen you
much lately and when I have seen you, I thought you looked
poorly, so I was just phoning to say –'

On impulse, Arlene grabbed the phone. 'Don't go. Please
don't hang up,' she said, and there was silence from the other
end of the phone.

'You phone here all the time, and you leave messages, and
I don't think it's fair of you to hang up on me. You're not the
only one who needs to send messages, and I've put up with
you for over a year now, and I think I'm entitled to blow a
gasket and you can jolly well just listen to me,' and there was
more silence.

'You seem to know all about everything, Mr Weirdo, so there
is some chance that you'll understand what I'm saying. I feel
terrible,' and once Arlene had started, she couldn't stop. '*He*
came over here, ostensibly because he wanted to make sure I
was all right. I bloody well had been all right, until *he* arrived
on the scene and did my head in rightly. And then *she* arrived,
I never asked her to move into my flat and get me tangled up
in all her problems. And between the two of them, I'm wrecked
and can't get out of the bed anymore.' She listened, and there
was more silence.

'Now, you might say why do I care, because they are gone
back to wherever they came from, and I'm back to the way
that I was before any of this shit, and you'd be right to an
extent, but that's not the way that I *feel*,' and she paused once

269

again and listened to the silence, that great engulfing silence of an unresponding line. The disembodied silence of telephonic space.

'So, I'm going to hang up now, and I'm not going to thank you for listening, because I've been listening to you for so long.' She gave him a second or two to speak, and then she hung up.

She felt odd after that. Alternatively a little better and a little worse. She went round the living room with a large plastic sack and half-heartedly picked up the debris. The phone rang again. She answered it immediately.

'Yes,' she said.

'Cunninghams, eight o'clock,' said the Weirdo.

'Nine-thirty,' she said, glancing at the wall clock. It was now a quarter to seven. Who did this Weirdo think he was? *She'd* make the schedule.

'Nine-thirty,' agreed the Weirdo.

'In the snug corner,' said Arlene and hung up.

She abandoned her attempt to tidy up the flat, and ran a bath, deciding that her person was urgently in need of maintenance. The bath was wonderful, luxurious, and she used up a full bar of apricot soap. She emerged from the bath smelling like jam, and went over to her wardrobe to find something to wear. Because she'd been slutting around in pyjamas and old leggings for the past few weeks, the wardrobe was full of cellophaned dry cleaning. She pulled out a velvet black and white suit, and felt for the first time in a long time, the ghost of the excitement of going on a date; whilst not being entirely sure was it a friendly ghost or a mocking one. She put on lots of make-up and when she finally inspected herself in the mirror, she looked normal, and expensive, and the heavy make-up rendered her just the slightest bit scary. Good, she thought. I'm going to meet a Weirdo who rings women who are alone in their apartment. I'd better look a little scary.

She opened her living room window and stuck her head out to test the air. The awful cold had abated, and it was now reasonably mild. It was substantially more pleasant. So much more fit for human existence. She'd walk to the pub.

She set off with a half-an-hour to spare, wanting to get there first, so she could watch this Weirdo's approach, and leg it out the back door should Atilla the Hun appear.

She was still feeling a little delicate, her legs a bit wobbly, as she made her way down the flights of stairs, picking her way around the cats at her heels. The Cartwrights' door was ajar, and when she passed it, Mister Cartwright appeared.

'Helen died yesterday,' he said.

'Oh,' said Arlene.

'Sorry, you *are* the person who lives upstairs, aren't you?'

'Indeed I am,' said Arlene.

'Helen died,' he said.

'I'm terribly sorry.'

'I knew when they took her into hospital, she wouldn't come out.'

'When did she go into hospital?' asked Arlene.

'Boxing Day,' he said. 'They said it was for a minor operation, but I knew she wouldn't come out.'

'I'm terribly sorry.'

'I just thought you should know, since you live upstairs, you might wonder where she is,' and he turned slowly and went back inside his apartment, shutting the door behind him.

Arlene shuddered. The slowness of him made her think he wouldn't be long after his sister.

That ghostly interlude took whatever spring she had in her step away, and she continued on down, less eagerly than before. It was the first time that either of the Cartwrights had spoken to her about anything other than the weather. Grief does open people up, she thought, not that he'd been exactly loquacious, but still.

She walked along Baggot Street, moving swiftly. Although the weather was milder than before, she persisted in feeling a slight chill.

Cunningham's was dotted with its regular folks, a Thursday-night scattering. Arlene waved over at Sheila behind the bar and gave her a huge smile, but Sheila just nodded back at her. Not Sheila's usual style.

Arlene went up to the bar. 'Hello, Sheila! I haven't been in for a while.'

'Yeah, we've missed your ugly mug. What do you want?'

'The usual.'

Sheila pulled Arlene a pint. As she stood there, Arlene could see a new stoop to her shoulder, the curvature of defeat. Arlene surveyed the bar. Some of the regulars were there, including Martin Campbell from the Deli. She waved at him, then turned back to the bar and sat up on a stool. She was half an hour early for the Weirdo.

'So, what's new?' asked Sheila. 'What exciting shows are you working on now?'

'Aw, nothing really,' said Arlene, 'that's why you haven't seen me for a while, 'cos I haven't been in the office,' and then Arlene noticed that Sheila's lip was trembling.

'What's wrong, Sheila?' she asked.

'I've terrible news,' whispered Sheila in a dead voice. 'You remember Linda, my sixteen-year-old, she's just got AIDS.'

Arlene stared at her.

'Apparently she's been positive for a year, but she kept that secret from me, but now it's full-blown, she's had to tell me.'

'God,' said Arlene.

'There is no God,' said Sheila.

'Oh Sheila,' said Arlene, tears welling up in her eyes.

'I'll tell you, Arlene, I'd give them all back. Because all the joy I've had from my children does not compensate for the pain of this.'

The tears started to fall down Arlene's face. She couldn't speak.

'Do you know, I haven't been able to cry,' said Sheila, 'because you need to have a bit of life in your body still to cry, and I don't have that.'

'Oh, Sheila,' sobbed Arlene.

'I'm sorry now, I'm after ruining your night, and you were probably out to forget about your own troubles. Your make-up is ruined, go on into the loo and wash your mug.'

'But Sheila –'

'C'mon now. Go in there and wash.'

Not entirely sure why, Arlene did as she was told. The Ladies' was chillier than the bar, and she shivered. She looked at herself in the mirror. Her eye make-up was running down her chin. She sniffled a little as she cleared up the mess with tissues. Her nose was bright red. There was something odd about her appearance, but she couldn't figure out what.

She went back out, and seeing as it was twenty-past nine, decided to go into the snug to await whoever was going to appear.

'Let's meet up for a coffee,' she said to Sheila.

'Sure, come in in the afternoon when it's not busy.'

'Okay, tomorrow,' said Arlene, and she turned and went into the snug.

The Twenties' ladies in the snug were haughtier than all the others in the bar, not having been softened by a fug of smoke. Arlene had brought today's paper with her to have something to do while she was waiting, but she couldn't read. She turned idly to the back page, the death notices. There it was. Helen Cartwright's notice. Funeral tomorrow at 10 AM. Sad, thought Arlene, but not as sad as Sheila's daughter, only sixteen. It was turning out to be a bad night. Disasters always happened in threes. She glanced at her watch. It was half-past-nine. Where was this Weirdo? And then she looked up and there he stood, framed by the door of the snug. Martin Campbell, the Deli-man.

'Hello,' he said shyly.

'Hello,' said Arlene carefully, not entirely sure if Martin was just being sociable, or if he was her rendez-vous.

'I thought you would hate me,' said Martin very gently, 'hate me for phoning you up like that, but I needed to connect with you somehow.'

'Martin. You're the Weirdo?' said Arlene. 'I don't believe it.'

'I needed to make contact.'

'But couldn't you just talk to me in the shop, or ask me out on a date or something?'

'I have asked you out several times, to this film or that

274

concert, and you've always said you were too busy.'

'I don't ever remember you asking me out.'

'Believe me, I *have* asked you out.'

'I don't remember.'

'I asked you to a Sinéad O'Connor concert in the Tivoli last year. And a Lyle Lovett concert a few months ago.'

'Well, I remember those, but you always said that you had a spare ticket because a customer had given you a freebie. Or to make up for me giving you tickets to the shows or something. I never thought you were asking me out.'

'I have loved you since I first met you. Six years ago, when you bounded into my shop and announced to me that you have "moved into the neighbourhood, and the neighbourhood had better beware".'

'Oh.'

'I see you pass by almost every day, and some days, of course, you come in.'

'And what brought on the telephone calls?'

'I saw you weeping in my shop one day. You excused yourself by saying that you got some dirt in your eye, but it was obvious you were upset. I thought: this magnificent woman needs a friend, needs a guardian angel, so I appointed myself.'

'I think I remember that. I *did* have something in my eye. An eyelash. I managed to get it out when I got home.'

'Can I sit down?'

'Sure.'

He sat beside her in the snug, and he looked as happy as could be.

'So what started you as a deli-man?' asked Arlene (deciding to change the subject).

'Well it was mainly the wine and cheese. I became an expert wine-taster at a youngish age, and then I worked for a while in a cheese factory, and finally, my Aunt Isa, whom you've met, sold her big house when she got on a bit and gave me some money to start a business. And I decided that this would be the thing for me. I had expertise in these areas, and in an affluent part of the city like this, there is a big demand.'

'Sure.'

'I'm particularly interested in the cheese side of it. My array of cheeses is the finest on the Southside. I've a new range of Gorgonzolas just in.'

'I have sampled many of your delicacies, as you well know.'

'Cheese has always held a romantic fascination for me. Did you know, that the dairy maid was always the most beautiful girl in her family, because she'd contracted the mild condition of cow-pox from the beasts and hence wouldn't catch the more virulent small-pox which left many of her peers so badly scarred.'

Arlene wondered why she had been surprised that Martin was the Weirdo. He was probably one of the weirdest people she had ever met. It was entirely appropriate.

'Also, she would have had access to a high dairy fat diet, which would give her the rounded figure that people used to find beautiful.'

She ordered another round of drinks. This was a turn-up for the books. Martin was very sweet and well meaning, and obviously totally devoted. Six years! she thought. He'd burned a candle for her for six years!

'Would you think you'd be able to come home with me?' he asked, 'to see my apartment?'

She agreed, and he led her out, past the other customers and the glass ladies, smoking their eternal cigarettes.

Martin's apartment was not unlike Arlene's own, but on the opposite side of the canal, further up, past the bridge. It was sparsely furnished, the modern furniture and fittings at odds with the high ceilings and ornate cornices. You could see Paddy from the front room window.

'Nice pad,' said Arlene, and smiled at him as he brought in a bottle of one of her favourite red wines and a couple of glasses. She needed this, somehow, she needed this at this moment.

'I would worship you, if you'd let me,' he said, gently. She glugged back the wine, feeling strange.

He lit a number of candles, and turned down the light. 'Come with me,' he said, stretching out his hand, 'I want to show you something.'

She took his hand and he led her into his bedroom. There, on the wall, were several blown-up photographs of her, sitting on the bench beside Paddy, walking along the canal, close-ups of her face.

'I hope you don't mind,' he said. 'I'd just bought myself a telephoto lens, and I couldn't resist snapping you.'

She stared at the giant pictures of herself. They looked ghostly, scary, parodic. She looked sad and serious in all of them.

'Do I *really* look like that?'

'When you're on your own. When you're in the shop, and chatting, you have a different face. A more animated one, a smile. But this is the face you have when you think no-one is looking at you. And I thought it was more ...'

'More what?'

'Just, more real.'

'Come with me,' he said and he led her out into the living room again. He switched on the television, and put a video into the machine. It crackled a little, and then the picture came clear. It was her, walking along the canal, eating chips, again wearing an expression of profound sorrow. The face animated momentarily to greet a passer-by and then sank again into sadness.

'I look terrible,' said Arlene. 'How come nobody has ever told me I look like such a moaning Mary?'

'Nobody sees it but me, and you're only seeing it now, because of my technology.'

'Turn her off,' said Arlene. 'She's terrible.'

'She's you,' said Martin, 'and she needs love.' He came up beside her and led her back into the bedroom. There, he started to caress her shoulder and kiss her neck. At first she felt nothing, neither repulsion nor attraction. She turned to him. He gently lowered the straps of her dress, very gently, and her body responded with nature, independent of her unfeeling will.

I am dead, she thought, as he kissed her. He stood back and smiled his huge broad smile. She smiled wryly back at him. You are the clown, she thought, and what does that make me?

'You are the most magnificent woman on earth,' he said, panting lightly.

I am the fool. That's it! I am the fool. I belong here, she said to herself, in this shadow-place. With the weirdos and the

278

perverts. She caught sight, over his shoulder of a huge picture of her sad and stony face. See what I have allowed myself to become?

the end

'You aren't used to seeing me so late,' said Arlene to Paddy, as she sat down, having bought her chips in the late-night kebab shop. 'The great thing about you, Paddy, is that you never disappoint me,' she said. 'You're always here when I come by, just sitting there thinking.'

'I've a cold arse,' he said.

'And you make me feel welcome.'

'And cold feet,' he said.

She laughed and sat up on his knee, and caressed his stiff, metal limbs. She leaned over him, and kissed his unresponsive lips. Poor old Paddy. Beyond help.

'Do you mind, Paddy, me kissing you without as much as a by your leave?' she asked him.

'No,' he said, 'it warms me. And it's always nice to get a bit. It's a pity I'm immobile, or we'd have a right bit of fun.'

'You're my pal,' she said, putting both hands around his neck, and resting her head on his shoulder.

'Doing business?' came a voice from behind her, which made her jump up. She looked at her interrogator, a middle-aged man in a suit. A bit fat, a bit bald, a bit drunk. Then it dawned on her what his question meant. This side of the canal backed onto Wilton Place which was a regular prostitution beat.

'I like the company of low-life,' said Paddy. 'It makes me feel superior.'

'I'm not a prostitute,' said Arlene to the man. 'When have you ever seen a prostitute in a black suit? This is nineteen ninety-seven. Day-glo jackets are standard issue for hookers now.'

'I beg your pardon, Ma'am,' said the man and went off to find a genuine one.

Nice manners, thought Arlene, especially for a trick, and she sat back down on Paddy's lap. 'I wonder how much they get for it?'

'In my day it was two bob and a toffee apple,' said Paddy.

Arlene peeled herself off him and wobbled her way home. She threw her chip carton on the ground, and then remembered that this was a terrible thing to do to her canal, but it blew away, and she didn't have the energy to run after it.

She made it home. Poor Sheila, she thought. Poor poor Sheila. I'll see her tomorrow. She has a *lot* to put up with. Arlene took off her coat and bag and went to inspect the machine.

It blinked a '1' at her. Who could *that* be? She pressed play. 'Hello! This is a message for Arlene Morrissey. My name is Shannon Mercier and I'm from the New York—Ireland Friendship Committee. I've tried to contact you at some other number, but directory enquiries gave me this one, well we're planning a festival . . .'

God! The American! Persistent. Arlene had completely forgotten about her. Well, great. They wanted *Over the Moon* and they could have *Over the Moon*. For a price, of course, Richard would naturally be unavailable, but never mind. There were plenty of actors who would play the part just as well. Better even. He wasn't well known in the USA anyway, so there would be no point in having him. Arlene scribbled down Shannon Mercier's number on a piece of paper. I'll phone her tomorrow, she thought, and she tumbled herself into bed, feeling neither bad nor good, but medium.